SEX

IN

THE

HALL

RICKY
CONLIN

Dream Oak Publishing LLC
3000 Village Run Road
Unit 103 #233
Wexford, PA 15090

EIN: 81-4936946

Dedicated to Dolly Mancari-

Your heart set a standard that I aspire to daily.

We miss you immensely Mom Mom.

A Note Before Reading

This book and the story told within it, are works of fiction. Names, characters, places, and incidents are the product of my imagination or are used fictitiously to build a believable representation of the Naval Academy in the late nineties.

A drug scandal did take place at the Naval Academy in the fall of 1995. I had neither involvement nor association with said drug scandal. All of the stories in this book relating to a drug scandal are fictitious.

Though this book is a work of fiction, I tried very hard to construct a story representative of the environment and culture of the mid-nineties Naval Academy. As a graduating member of the mighty class of 1999, I wouldn't have it any other way.

Lastly, to the current Brigade of Midshipman, know that some of your best future heroes are currently on restriction.

Enjoy,
-Ricky

Part I

Girls

Chapter 1

Pour Some Sugar on Me
Sunday, May 24th, 1998
Heather, 11:42 p.m.

I drove my car towards a small parking lot in front of a loading dock. I had circled through the area twice already, waiting for an open spot.

Bingo!

I tucked my hatchback into the open space. It was a little less inconspicuous than I would have liked. There was enough rust on my passenger door to give a Maco repair man a hard-on. I was told that parking might be tough to find but I decided to take my chances. Now I was in front of the building I needed to be in. Having a car close for a quick getaway wasn't a bad thing.

Fuck, the things I do for three hundred bucks.

I cranked back the parking brake and looked at the clock on the radio. I was fifteen minutes early. It was more crowded than I'd anticipated. That wasn't necessarily a bad thing. Maybe it would be easier to blend in.

I was scared just getting by the armed gate guard to enter the base moments earlier. My customers had told me exactly what to say to get in. They had done the same to get me up to their room.

My nervous sweat had me checking my makeup in the rearview mirror one last time before leaving the car. I gave my costume a final once over. The white blue rim t-shirt I was wearing as camouflage was practically see-through. Unfortunately, the purple sequenced bra I typically wore on stage wouldn't work tonight. I kept on the white lace bra I was originally wearing. My customers wouldn't notice the difference. They weren't paying to see the bra anyway.

My shorts were also three sizes too big. The stretched-out elastic band was held up by a less than dependable hairclip. If its spring decided to give way, I'd be showing my G-string before I had a chance to get paid for it.

Always a bad practice in my profession.

I reached into the back for my boom box then stopped. I remembered they told me they had a radio, but that I should bring my own music. They had insisted I carry as little with me as possible to maintain an unassuming appearance.

The military customers always loved giving orders.

I pressed down on the exterior of a small duffel bag. I could feel the clunkiness of my ten-inch platform heels without needing to see them. I had worn them earlier during my afternoon shift at the club. It was an especially profitable day, setting up the gig I was currently chasing. I grabbed the bag off the passenger seat and crawled out of the car, slamming the door behind me.

There was still a fair amount of pedestrian traffic around me in the parking lot. A few Navy people were around. Some were still in their white uniforms. A few more were dressed like me in blue shorts and white t-shirts.

I started to feel ridiculous in my oversized outfit. My heartbeat escalated. The last thing I needed tonight was to get arrested for sneaking into a military establishment.

Thankfully, the darkness of evening coupled with the uniformity of colors made my sloppy look blend in, at least that's what I told myself. Everyone was heading towards the same door. I assumed it was the primary entrance where the boys had told me to go. I ignored my nervous stomach and followed the herd.

I tried my best to blend in while keeping within close proximity of the group walking up the stairs. I could smell the strong state of drunkenness from the guys around me. One of the boys in the bunch was being carried up to his room by two of his loyal friends. He was flailing wildly and screaming outrageous profanities. It looked like he had pissed himself. The remaining group walking up the steps was drunk, or talking about how drunk they were, or all of the above. Unknowingly, they were giving me great cover.

As we made our way up each flight of stairs the crowd dispersed bit by bit. By the third floor, the last of the group stumbled into the hallway making their way to their rooms. I was finally alone.

"Ma'am, good evening, ma'am," I was greeted at the top of the stairwell by what looked like a twelve-year-old boy. He wore a black uniform, a white belt with large silver buckle, and his white hat was comically big atop his small frame. He looked like he was out for Halloween dressed-up as a midshipman.

"Hello," I said before taking the left I had been instructed. I did not make eye contact and picked up my pace.

5138, 5136, 5134

I paid close attention to the room numbers and names posted on each wooden door in the hallway. I'd almost made it without getting busted.

"Ma'am," I heard from behind me and paused. I squeezed my eyes shut trying to remember my recommended response.

What did they tell me to say if this guy asks for my ID?

My heart was pounding. I turned towards the voice behind me wondering if I had successfully washed away the body glitter from my afternoon shift.

"Ma'am, have you seen 2/C Harris around?" the miniature guard dog asked.

"No, don't know him," I hastily answered.

"You mean her, ma'am."

"See, like I said, don't know her."

The question caught me off guard. I turned and tried to blow him off as best I could. I imagined he got that a lot from girls.

"Oh, okay," he replied.

I didn't look back. I assumed he was already heading towards his initial guard position by the top of the steps. After another four paces I let out an enormous sigh of relief.

I feel like I'm in a James Bond movie.

My eyes shot towards those doors. No time to compliment myself just yet.

5132, Dawson, McGee, Okafor. This is the spot.

I made my way to the wooden door. I wanted to get out of the hallway. I knocked on the door with a sense of urgency.

No answer.

I looked to my right. There was a tall goofy-looking midshipman knocking on the door next to me.

"Come on, Haden! Open up," he said as he continued pounding on the door.

He looked angry. I knocked again on the door in front of me at a more rapid pace. That's when I noticed a light turn on under the crack of the door. I hadn't noticed that the room was previously dark. I heard rustling behind the door and a few seconds later it opened. A tall black man, fit and handsome, stood holding the door.

"I'm Star," I said. "I'm here for Ed's party," I cut right to the chase without speaking too loudly. I wanted to get out of the hallway as soon as possible. The guy next door stared my way. I could tell that he knew I was most certainly not a midshipman.

"Damn girl, you're early," I heard the African American adonis positioned at the doorway remark. "Quick, get in."

He waved me into the room. He could tell that I was scared.

"The party has arrived," I heard a second male voice from inside the room.

"Hey Joey," I said to the first familiar face I'd seen since driving onto the yard. He was sitting behind a desk in the room's interior. I smiled and offered a friendly wave. We had gone to the same high school a few years earlier out towards Baltimore. He was a football star and I was a cheerleader that graduated a few years ahead of him. We re-connected during my earlier shift at the club. A few friendly lap dances and he helped orchestrate this show.

"Man of the hour should be here soon," Joey said. "Ed bumped his head earlier and just finished getting stitched up at the hospital."

"I heard he got nineteen stitches, dawg!" the black guy that I heard referred to as "EZ" proclaimed.

Joey nodded. "Can I fix you a drink while you wait?" he asked as he poured rum into the cup he was sipping from.

"No thanks," I said. I was there to make money, not to make friends.

I reached in my bag and tossed my Def Leppard dance mix cd across the desk towards Joe. "See if you can que this up while I get ready."

Chapter 2

Just a Girl
Monday, May 25th, 1998
Summer, 1430 hrs.

It was mid-afternoon on the Monday of Commissioning Week. A mob of people surrounded the paved and unpaved area in front of the Naval Academy Chapel. Proud mothers, fathers, and friends circled a twenty-one-foot obelisk otherwise known as the Herndon Monument. It'd been roped off for the forthcoming festivities.

A thousand Naval Academy class of 2001 freshman were about to end their plebe year with one singular act of teamwork. Their shit sandwich was almost finished. This was the last bite. I knew the experience well. I was only two years removed from it.

Herndon and I were dressed for the occasion. The monument's dark grey granite appearance was coated top to bottom with an inch of white grease. My summer whites were glistening, freshly starched and spotless. The squared away uniform helped mask the dark circles under my eyes. It had to, I was never a girl that wore much makeup in uniform.

Atop Herndon's apex sat one last dragon to slay, a

plebe Dixie cover cap. Once the greased monument was scaled by the plebes, the Dixie cup cap would be replaced by a traditional midshipman cover. In an instant, plebe year would be no more for the "aught-oners."

There would be no more forced chopping in Bancroft, no more flame sessions at chow calls, and generally a lot less daily harassment. It was an instant life upgrade. The very moment that Dixie cover was replaced, life for the class of '01 would become easier. In a month another thousand new mids would be stuck being plebes for a year. Plebedom would finally be the Old Maid in someone else's hand.

Beyond the assembled crowd in front of Herndon, the entire plebe class awaited the festivities. They were wearing spirit-modified PT gear over their plebe issued bathing suits. Blue athletic shorts and blue rim t-shirts were torn, tattered, and inked up with motivational quotes. I could see their heads bobbing and bouncing in excitement. Hoots and hollers interrupted several ongoing chants and cheers.

The starting gun went off with a loud pop. Half of the unsuspecting parents jumped in fright. The plebes were un-phased. They sprinted the three hundred yards from Tecumseh Court through a human tunnel cleared for them amongst the mob. The tunnel opened up at the Herndon Monument. The crowd cheered wildly as the class arrived sprinting, full of piss and vinegar.

The first plebes to reach the monument climbed the base. They formed the first tier of a human climbing wall. That's as high as they'd get this early on. Before they could think about climbing higher, they needed to wipe off Herndon's grease. Shirts and shoes were thrown at the monument in an effort to knock off some of the grease as the class stripped down to their bathing suits. Every plebe within reach started wiping the monument down. Water hoses were provided by the fire department to keep the participants cool. Within five minutes, and for the next several hours, the entire monument and its immediate surrounding area would smell like hot, wet, greasy body funk.

I let out a yawn so big that I practically dislocated my jaw. I hadn't slept a wink the night before.

The crowd's early enthusiasm eventually faded. After about thirty minutes, even the first-time audience realized the task at hand was not as simple as it appeared. Most classes took at least two hours.

I remembered my own experience at Herndon. It felt like yesterday. The excitement of being inches away from something my class had waited for so long.

The crowd woke me from my day dreaming. Cheers encouraged new momentum in the climb. A second tier of plebes had solidified, expanding the base of the human wall. They were halfway home. More shirts were thrown upward. More grease was scrubbed away.

A girl amongst the plebes decided it was her turn to make a run for the third tier. She began her ascent, climbing over the sweaty and greasy heft of the massive football players solidifying the base of the human pyramid. A few parents spotted her momentum, and the crowd cheered in encouragement.

"Look at her go!" I heard another person from the crowd scream. Several other cheers amplified the encouragement.

Then, it happened, just like it always did. A random hand from the mass of humanity reached up anonymously. The heroic female was grabbed from behind and pulled down off the monument by one of her own classmates. She tumbled below into a pile of bodies, miraculously not getting seriously hurt.

That type of chauvinistic bullshit wasn't anything new. When I was a freshman in high school, a male academy grad visited our school to speak on career day. The Commander had finished skippering his first squadron and was in Monterey for shore tour at the Naval Post Graduate School.

I wasn't necessarily convinced that the Navy was my path back then, but I had an alumnus grandfather and I'd seen Top Gun no less than twenty times. I spoke to the Commander after the presentation. I wanted to know what I needed to do to fly F-14s. He laughed in my face.

"Sorry, that's only something they let the boys do, at least in combat when it counts," he said. "Maybe you can fly a helo."

Three years later I was assembling soccer recruit tapes, hell-bent on making my way to Annapolis. I was damn sure I would prove that fucker wrong.

My wandering mind had me seething in anger. Those dickhead male plebes would rather sit for four hours in ass grease than let a female show them up. If there were ever a more perfectly shitty way to sum up the life of a female midshipman, there it was.

WUBA.

Woman used by all.

Woob for short.

That's what the boys called us. Occasionally, I got called far worse.

Those nicknames were often thrown in jest. We played along, typically with a smile. Some of us even affectionately called each other woobs, myself included. Classic "if you can't beat 'em, join 'em" mentality.

Twenty years past female integration into the academy and we were still newbies to them. I never felt like a full member of their frat. It was still theirs. I was someone many of them would rather see in heels and a short skirt than in their grills competing with them.

Of course, not all of them felt that way. Still, some did, very emphatically so. Every thirty to forty minutes, I'd get another reminder that they did. Another girl would make her run at the Dixie cup and another asshole with an inferiority complex over his undersized genitalia decided to intervene. Down another heroine fell.

The same thing happened to me two years earlier. I was flipped into a head first position before colliding with a member of the lower base of the pyramid, and tumbling into the mosh pit at the base. Aside from a massive welt on my right hip and a slight bruise to my ego, I was okay.

Those male hands from behind, always fucking dragging us down.

Herndon wasn't the only place where those boys pulled me back. My midshipman ex-boyfriend had been nothing but trouble all year. Last night we got into yet another heated argument. I got carried away and all hell broke loose. I hadn't slept all night worrying about potential consequences. It's hard to keep secrets in a place where people are in my shit twenty-four/seven.

Junior soccer player singlehandedly cancels all commissioning week parades in Annapolis.

I'm sure the Naval Academy Athletic Association would love to see that headline on the front page of the Annapolis Capitol this week. The academy was already dealing with rumors swirling about the stripper caught in Bancroft last night, and in the room of the newly elected captain of the football team no less.

I let out another yawn. I needed to hit the rack for a few hours and get some sleep. It was hot and uncomfortably muggy out. Still, I remained where I was watching Herndon in full dress whites. The third human tier was finally formed. I saw another girl getting tumbled. Five minutes later I saw two corpsmen leading her out of the crowd of plebes. She was limping on her right ice-wrapped ankle. I kept watching.

I stayed put for the same reason the plebe girls kept climbing. Every year Herndon rolled around, every plebe dreamt of being the plebe that gets to the top of the monument. Why shouldn't the girls chase that same dream? Having the chance to be the first female made it all the more appealing.

Then, like every year, a male plebe finally reached the top. The cover was replaced and I was again stuck hoping for better luck next year. All because I was a girl. Just an annoying woob trying to break over a century of tradition.

All of this to top off a twenty-one foot greased fucking phallic symbol.

I hate this fucking place.

Part II

Welcome to the Jungle

Chapter 3

California Love
Monday, July 14th, 1997
Mick, 1645 hrs.

"Baltimore to Cleveland, Cleveland to Phoenix, Phoenix to fucking San Diego. Now we take the fifteen mile per hour scenic route from the airport to the base. Thirteen hours door to door, all in summer whites. Nothing like the Naval Academy Travel Agency!" complained Chris. His sarcasm was finally beginning to bleed through his generally laidback demeanor.

It had been a long day. My fellow midshipmen van mates and I had woken up in Annapolis at 4 a.m. to catch the bus to Baltimore Washington International Airport for the first flights out. That 4 a.m. wake up was 1 a.m. Pacific time.

"You know the Naval Academy, they're always trying to shove that two hundred and fifty-thousand-dollar education up your ass some way or another," I tried to ease the tension in the van. A few chuckles validated my effort to lighten the collective mood. Chris smirked, took a deep breath, and relaxed in his seat. We were almost done with the day's journey.

Of the four Naval Academy midshipmen joining me in the van, I vaguely knew three of them. All of them were male second class midshipmen from the Naval Academy Class of '99 like me. Two of them, Matt and Adam, were football teammates with my academic year roommate and good friend Ndbuze "N.D." Okafor. Matt and Adam had been in my room a few times over the years. Chris, the other familiar guy in the van, had been my lab partner in sophomore physics class. Anthony and I had met that day. I knew he was from New York and he liked the Wu-Tang Clan. We could hear his 36 Chambers CD blaring through his headphones most of the van ride.

I returned to unsuccessfully trying to fall asleep in the rear. The giant green canvas sea bags jammed in the back with me were bulky enough to make finding a comfortable sleeping position difficult. Doubling the discomfort, the van's air conditioner was on the fritz. The windows were rolled down in a futile attempt to cool the interior. When the vehicle's speed climbed above forty, the temperature was fine. However, being stuck in bumper to bumper traffic for the past forty-five minutes, the van was a sauna. All four of the midshipmen passengers' summer white uniforms were soaked through with sweat.

Third Class Petty Officer Melvin Watson was the poor bastard stuck as the ship's duty driver for the day. Picking us up from the airport was one of the many rides he'd be tasked with throughout the day. The air conditioning wouldn't run for any of those trips. Watson stared straight ahead from behind the wheel, every bit as hot as we were. I could see the beads of sweat dripping off his ear. The last thing he wanted to do was make conversation about it. He was dressed in his own enlisted whites and looked like a real-life version of the Cracker Jack boy. We were all miserable in the heat.

Not a damn thing anybody could do about it.

The inside of the van was beginning to smell like a gym sock. Watson kept both hands firmly on the wheel and tried not to make eye contact with anyone.

The smell of saltwater through the windows indicated we were getting close to the base. I grew up around the ocean so I knew the scent well. After what seemed like an eternity, Watson flashed his duty badge at the gate and zipped by the armed gate guard. We had finally arrived onto San Diego Naval Base.

"It's hot in here, Ace," Anthony said upon removing his headphones. Watson kept his thousand-yard stare, pretending not to hear the dialogue.

Guess the Naval Academy isn't the only place teaching that.

The view of the mammoth ships on the immediate horizon grabbed everyone's attention. The backdrop looked like the set of a multi-million dollar action movie. We all perked up trying to see the ship with #48 painted on the side, temporarily forgetting about the air conditioning.

While at the Naval Academy, a midshipman spends every summer in some form of military training. In the first two years this training was self-contained to Naval Academy staff, vehicles, and equipment. It meant that for the most part, we spent our first two years in the Navy entirely isolated from the actual fleet. Plebe year was mired in the muck of Plebe Summer. Youngster year was spent cruising smaller yard patrol crafts, manned almost entirely by midshipmen, up the Atlantic coast line.

For the vast majority of the Naval Academy's class of '99, this summer's fleet cruise was the first time any of us would actually get to experience the "real Navy." All oncoming junior midshipmen, otherwise known as "second class," were mandated a month-long fleet cruise in the summer before the start of the academic year.

Naval Academy mids were required to sign paperwork on their first day of junior year classes committing five years of active duty service upon graduation. Two more years of free school for a seven-year life commitment. We called it "two for seven."

That was the trade-off for going to school for free. We knew that going into it. If I had left that summer, I could have walked away from the academy without penalty or having to pay back my first two years of college. Leaving or getting kicked out once I signed my "two for seven" commitment cost at least sixty-five grand. This fleet cruise was the academy's way of giving us a small glimpse of what exactly we were signing ourselves up for in another few weeks.

There were well over one hundred Naval Academy midshipmen reporting for summer cruise duty this week around the San Diego Naval Base. In total eight Naval Academy midshipmen were reporting for three weeks of summer cruise duty aboard the FFG 48 USS Vandegrift. Two senior "firstie" midshipmen and six junior "second-class" midshipmen comprised our collective group.

We were five strong for class of '99 in the van. The two firsties and my last second-class shipmate had checked in about an hour before we did. That's what the duty driver had told us shortly after picking us up at the airport. My group was on the second wave of incoming flights and hence the last to arrive on the ship.

The duty driver finally made his way to our ship's parking spot by the pier. He shifted to park and turned the ignition off. Now safely parked, he finally broke character before exiting the car.

"Sirs, sorry for the hot ride today. I don't own the shit bus, I just drive it. You'll get to meet the owner of the shit bus soon enough." He stepped out of the van and closed the door behind him. I could see him smirk through the rear passenger window. He was on his way to help unload our sea bags currently accompanying me in the back bench of the van. He was impressed with his own obtuse sense of humor. So was I.

Can't wait to meet the owner of the shit bus.

We grabbed our bags off the curb and hustled behind a younger looking officer who was frantically waving us all together over to the base of the pier. The traffic had held us up longer than expected. I could tell by the LT's pace that we must have been late for something important.

"I'm L,La, La,Lu LUieutenant Johns. You guys can call me J,J, Ja,Ja, Oe, Joe, you can call me Joe. I'll try to give you the rest of the introduction on the way in. Gotta hustle, we're running la,la,la,late for the skipper."

Our stuttering guide hustled us past the pier guard. He had a chance to resume his introduction while we waited in line to request permission to board. I could see the water below us between the metal grates on the bridge that crossed from the pier to the ship.

"Welcome to the Vandegrift," Joe continued. "I'll be helping with your training c,c,c,ca,caru,cruise. Sorry for the stuttering, that happens when I'm ta,ta,ta,tired or stressed. I guess by now you can imagine how my day is going. Skipper gets a little crazy about rr,ra,ra,running late. One of those prompt types, ya kna,na,na,na,know?"

Before I knew it, I was next man up in line to board the ship. I had no idea what the protocol was for doing so. If they had taught that lesson back at the academy, I must have slept through it.

Thankfully Watson, the duty driver, was in front of me on the boarding ramp. I watched him with painstaking attention. I grabbed my ID and prepared to flash it. Other than that, I'd mimic whatever Watson did in front of me.

Try not to look stupid.

It worked.

Eventually, we were all hustled down to the cafeteria by Joe. He was a nice, though frantic person. We picked up the remaining mids that had boarded earlier and headed to meet the skipper in his private chambers. Past a few doorways and up a few ladders and we were where we needed to be, albeit a few minutes late.

The skipper was visibly frazzled when we arrived to his quarters late. LT Johns did little on our behalf to clearly explain our tardiness. Instead of a rational explanation, the captain was given a stuttering mess and he flippantly dismissed Joe mid-explanation. I was happy Joe had left the room. It was cramped with all of us in with the captain together.

Commander Michael Simpson, commanding officer of the USS Vandegrift, was more spit polished than your typical senior naval officer. Normally years of service and earned respect made an officer's uniform standard deservedly slip a little. Commanders, Captains, and Admirals usually had more important things to do than press Marine Corps creases into their shirts. Simpson was not that kind of senior officer.

The captain went around the room asking names and shaking hands. I could smell the starch on his shirt within three feet of shaking his hand for the first time. He had a firm grip. It was like he was trying to prove to us how surprisingly tough his five-foot-five frame really was. His skinny waist, long legs, and short v-shaped torso made him look like a strutting cartoon frog in his uniform.

He sat down and sipped from a steaming cup of coffee on his desk.

"CHRIST! The new pork chop must have spent too much of his time partying in Athens," the captain loudly complained about the new supply officer as he slammed the mug down on the table. "This tastes like friggin' shit."

He calmed down and after an "around the horn" session of introductions, his required two minutes of listening were done. He jumped immediately into his own introduction. We spent five minutes talking about the Vandegrift and the next twenty talking about how great the captain was personally. Then he went on to lecture us about what not to do. It felt like the Naval Academy had followed us out west.

We all nodded along waiting to get the fuck out of his stateroom. It was the biggest and nicest room on the ship. The entirety of the room was adorned with the skipper's own awards and copious pictures of himself. He had pictures of his Notre Dame ROTC unit and about ten different pictures praising Notre Dame football. He couldn't help but remind us about how long Notre Dame football's winning streak was against Navy. He took particular delight when he found out he could tell that directly to a few players from the team.

Simpson topped it off with a few more tales about how great Navy ROTC was in preparing him for the fleet. It was his passive aggressive way of shitting on the Naval Academy itself.

What a dick.

"Oh, and one last thing," he droned on. "Under no circumstance do any of you go to Tijuana, twenty-one or otherwise. Nothing good happens down there. Trust me on that, gents."

Here we go.

"No crew member is allowed down there, and especially no Naval Academy midshipmen. Those aren't Navy rules, those are my rules, gentlemen. Direct order. You heard them from me."

He paused and looked us each in the eye, then reemphasized his point, "Don't be the idiot drunken sailor that ends up ticking off a few crooked Federales over the border and screwing up my weekend. You won't like how that story ends."

None of us in the room said a word. I felt like a sixth grader getting a lecture in detention. He slowly nodded his head and looked each of us in the eye like a disapproving father one last time.

Sensing the awkwardness about two minutes after everyone else in the stateroom did, he broke the silence.

"Welcome aboard, we look forward to having you here on the mighty Vandegrift."

"Thank you, sir. We look forward to our time here. Permission to shove off, sir?" Trey, one of the two firsties on the Vandegrift, intervened in a direct attempt to get us all out of there.

"Dismissed," said the captain.

All of the mids exited the stateroom. Once I was confident I was beyond earshot of the skipper's room, I slapped two of my new buddies on the back and asked, "So we're going to Tijuana this weekend?"

Trey, whom I had not met before boarding the ship thirty minutes earlier, turned his head and looked me in the eye. "You fucking know it!"

Chapter 4

Not What You Want
Wednesday, July 16th, 1997
Summer, 2215 hrs.

"So are you getting tired of beating up the plebes yet?" Mick asked on the other end of the phone line.

"Yeah," I replied. "I guess so."

The plebes were the Naval Academy freshmen. The incoming class of 2001 were in the midst of their Plebe Summer, the Naval Academy's eight-week version of boot camp for incoming freshman. I had been assigned as a detailer, the Naval Academy's version of a drill instructor. For the past month, it had been my fulltime job to make their life miserable.

"Homestretch," he continued.

"Yup," I said in an intentionally cold tone from my Naval Academy phone booth. The phone room was entirely empty given that most upperclassmen were still out in fleet training and the plebes lacked phone privileges.

Mick was my boyfriend. He had been since spring semester of plebe year where we first met as '99 classmates and company mates. He was stuck on a ship for the next month in San Diego. Our schedules and bicoastal relationship meant we hadn't spoken much over the past week. Our military obligations and my grandfather's death had us apart for most of the summer, but that wasn't what had Mick in the doghouse.

A minute of awkward silence ensued. I knew damn well he was changing the topic of conversation deliberately. Even small talk with my boyfriend was becoming contentious.

"So have you thought about it?" I asked again.

"Thought about what?" he asked trying to play naïve. He knew exactly what I had been asking about.

"The chit," I continued poking.

Silence.

"So that's a no," I answered my own question. I already knew his answer, but even hearing it in my own voice felt deflating.

"Okay, you're right. NO, I haven't thought about it," he finally mustered a response.

"That's such BULLSHIT, Mick. You've thought plenty about it. In fact, you've already made up your damn mind six months ago and you're too chicken shit to tell me. Stop being such a pussy."

This wasn't a new argument. Back in Bancroft Hall, Mick and I were in the 6th company together, meaning our living quarters and chain of command were intricately shared. Dating amongst company-mates was a strict "no-no," potentially garnering punishment all the way up to expulsion depending on the scenario.

We did our best to keep our relationship on the down low. We even avoided spending too much time together in the hall so we wouldn't raise our company-mates' suspicions. Only our roommates and a handful of close friends officially knew about us.

After our plebe year, I begged Mick to submit a "love chit" to our chain of command and get transferred to another company. That would have ensured our relationship could finally be on the up and up and garner some level of normalcy. Mids of the same class could date as long as they weren't in the same company.

Unfortunately, Mick had zero desire to change companies. I didn't either. There was the rub. If a chit wasn't submitted within the next two weeks, Mick and I were all but guaranteed to start the academic year in the same company, something I wanted so badly to avoid. Mick was winning a battle of attrition.

"Summer, I still don't get it. If this love chit is so important to you, why don't YOU go submit one? You don't even really like your roommate, what's the problem with getting a new one?"

I bit my tongue to avoid a repetitively unresolved argument. He was partially right, my roommate Sarah and I were not the best of friends, but we still liked rooming together. Mick by contrast loved his roommates. His logic was always that the true sacrifice was on his end in having to leave his friends.

This was a flawed defense. Friendship was a "luxury" worry for me. So few females were in the academy to begin with, it was much more of a crap shoot with roommates when girls transferred to another company. More importantly, "love chitting" was far more detrimental to a female's reputation. It drew attention, and for all the wrong reasons. Mick couldn't get that through his thick skull.

"Look, it's getting late over here and I have to be upstairs for plebe "Blue and Gold" and bed check. Let's talk about this later," I said, quietly accepting defeat.

"Okay, sounds good. Get some rest. Let's talk in a few days. Say Friday when I knock off ship life for the weekend?"

"Sounds good, talk soon," I replied with as little enthusiasm as I could muster.

We both avoided hanging up the phone. Neither of us knew how to end the conversation. Neither of us wanted to end the call on a fight.

"I love you," he said breaking the temporary silence.

My heart and pride struggled in a moment of silence. "Love you too." I let my heart win yet again.

All of my piss and vinegar didn't matter. I had fallen hard for Mick, and it gave him all of the relationship upper hand in the world at a place like USNA. All of this made me feel weak. That feeling wore on me. It had been a tension that reared its ugly head more and more over time. I hated the way it made me feel, yet I loved Mick.

Chapter 5

Bustin' Loose
Friday, July 18th, 1997
Mick, 1545 hrs.

I stepped through a grey steel doorway, exiting the ship's helicopter hangar. I was one of four midshipmen quietly trying to sneak out of work a few minutes early for some well-earned liberty. Standing there alone in the sunshine, I was apparently the first to make it to our planned rendezvous point.

I didn't feel all that guilty about bolting early. At least a quarter of the ship's crew had already knocked off work for the day. Everyone back east in Annapolis had said that the San Diego ships were more chill than the more uptight ones in Norfolk. I had no point of comparison so I assumed it was true.

Since our first day onboard Vandegrift, we were assigned "running mates." These were glorified chaperones that we shadowed to learn what ship life was like. Firsties were assigned officer running mates. Juniors were assigned enlisted sailor running mates. The intent was to give future Naval Academy graduates a full ship's perspective.

Firsties spent their days eating with the skipper in the wardroom and doing the more "white collar" ship activities. This made sense. They would be doing the same type of shit in about a year.

A second class junior midshipman's summer, amongst the enlisted ranks, was a different animal. The enlisted sailors were sometimes called "blue shirts" for the light blue shirt worn with dungaree trousers. They were the Navy's blue-collar workforce.

I had spent the majority of my day in the electric darkness of the sonar room. The rays of sunlight greeting my escape burned my pupils. I felt like a vampire tourist.

It was hard for any of us second-class mids to blend in. Occasionally a mid would have prior enlisted experience, but my fellow classmates and I were clueless. All week long we generally tried to stay out of the way and not look like total dipshits in our khaki uniforms.

The blue shirt perception of our cluelessness was made infinitely worse by the fact that they all had to salute us and generally treat us as officers. This was a laughable notion considering our utter lack of qualification or experience. I tried my best to be quiet and stay out of the way of the real work.

Then there were the chiefs. They were the most senior of the enlisted ranks. They graduated from "blue shirts" to khakis through their competence, accomplishments, and about two thousand cartons of cigarettes. Nobody loved ship life more than a chief.

"Be on the lookout and listen to the chiefs," the academy pounded in our heads. "They run the ship and are the last people you want to piss off."

Yet there I stood waiting all by my lonesome, in the middle of the ship's only exit point to the pier, dip-shitting it up. It was the ship's most common path on a Friday afternoon. I was a big old bullseye sitting there already dressed in my weekend civilian clothes.

"You and the rest of the cub scouts catching the early train to TJ?" Senior Chief Johnson snarked my way the moment he hit daylight. He offered a smirk and a half-assed salute. Even though everyone on that ship knew who was really in charge, the chiefs were still required to salute us. We still technically outranked them. They were usually good sports about it.

"No, Senior Chief, I was," I began offering my best impromptu line of bullshit.

"Christ, cowlick, I'm fuckin' with ya," he chuckled. He lit the cigarette hanging out of his mouth as he continued his path towards the ship's outdoor smokers' pit.

"Why you call him cowlick, Senior?" a smart-assed blue shirt whose name I couldn't recall one week in asked trying to egg Johnson on.

"'Cause it looks like a daggun cow licked the side of his head, look at the back of his hair," Senior Chief explained to the petty officer's delight. "Don't know what you're laughing at, shipmate." he diverted his attention away from me and flipped it towards the petty officer. "You so country podunk you didn't see your first pair of shoes till boot camp."

The petty officer laid off. Chiefs knew how to control the ship without saying too much about it. Feeling comfortable that the extra undo attention had passed, Senior Chief looked my way with his lit cigarette still hanging out of his mouth.

"Hear this, cowlick," he instructed his wisdom, "whatever happens down in Tijuana or otherwise, remember this."

"What's that, Senior Chief?" I asked not really wanting to know the answer.

"FISHDO," he said.

"FISHDO?" I asked.

"FISHDO," he repeated. "Fuck it, shit happens, drive on."

"FISHDO," I replied nodding.

"You and your jamboree of green horns get into some shit south of the border, FISHDO, and get your asses back on the ship on time and ready to roll. In the interim, no late night calls from the Federales, no bullshit. Got it?"

"FISHDO," I said one last time verifying my mental note.

"Relax, cowlick," Johnson said with a smoky smile and outstretched arms basking in the warm sun. "You're in fuckin' San Diego, shipmate." He exhaled the remainder of his iron lung and continued his path to the ship's smoking pit at the rear of the ship where he'd surely continue his ball busting.

The sun wasn't the only thing making me sweat waiting for my slow-ass shipmates. I glanced down at my watch trying hard not to begin pacing. My new cruise homies said they'd all be here five minutes ago.

Fuck guys, come on!

At least my "civies" gave me a little visual cover while waiting to make my early escape. I glanced down at my watch a second time.

Frigates were among the smallest of the ships in the fleet. They still seemed enormous compared to the Yard Patrol crafts we had driven up the Atlantic the summer after plebe year.

The newness of being "out in the real Navy" still made me feel apprehensive and nervous. I could hear Johnson cracking jokes about me out at the smoker's pit.

Am I supposed to salute the flag in civvies? What do I say to the guy standing watch as I leave the ship? Did I remember to bring my military ID? What will I do if I lose my military ID tonight?

I looked at my watch a third time. I began nervously pacing. Then I saw my new USNA acquaintance Trey finally make his way through the door. Thirty seconds later and the missing dynamic duo, Chris and Anthony, showed up.

All four of us present and accounted for, now let's fucking bolt!

"Tijuana, here we come, boys!" Trey said as he slipped his shades on in the sunlight. He grew up in California and already had the sunglasses routine down. He was also in charge of hooking us up with a car situation.

"My old high school basketball teammate goes to San Diego State. He said he'd float us his car for the weekend," he had told us earlier in our mutual enlisted birthing bunk room. I gave it a fifty percent shot of actually happening.

Trey just wanted to fit in. He was in a unique situation. He had entered the academy at a young age. Even as a firstie he had yet to turn twenty-one. His other firstie shipmate was headed out to downtown San Diego bars on Friday night with a broader group of academy firsties also assigned San Diego for summer cruise. Two of my second class shipmates, football teammates Matt and Adam, were also headed there. They were a year older than their 2/C shipmates due to their extra year of prep school prior to plebe year. Trey was stuck slumming it with us "kids" down in Mexico. He didn't seem to mind too much.

Eventually, perhaps tonight, perhaps tomorrow morning, we'd return onboard the Vandegrift to sleep. In the meantime, we were looking to meet up with two other buddies from my company back at the academy. We were slated to meet right outside the gate closest to our mutual piers. Once we picked up Trey's loaner ride, we'd be rocketing down to Tijuana with a belly full of fire.

That was the plan anyway.

"Come on, fellas, let's get outta here," I grew impatient enough to prod the group along. It annoyed me to have to do it. Normally I'd relax and go along for the ride, but not this time. I knew that if we waited around long enough, we'd get caught sneaking out early. Then we'd be drawn into some ship crap. I had only known the skipper a week, but I was smart enough to know the type of ship he ran. Just ask Aunder, the poor asshole on the scaffolding on the side of the ship. I could hear him scrubbing away the paint on the hull.

First Class Petty Officer Aunder's story was the talk of the day back in the belly of the beast. Two nights earlier he got himself foolishly busted. Feeling deprived of beer, he drank a bottle of cough syrup and ended up crashing into the guard gate on his roller blades later that evening. This was after a few prior incidents with booze. There was even talk of busting him down a few rates. Luckily, he had otherwise been a stellar sailor. His immediate punishment was paint scrubbing duty alongside two other poor bastards a week out of boot camp doing the same. It was typical "Chief Justice."

Come ON! Seriously, let's fucking go!!!

I finally prodded the group off the ship and onto the pier. It was like pulling teeth.

"AUNDER!!!!!!!" I heard an explosive yell behind me. The bark was coming from our ship. It was surely one of the ship's chiefs getting after Aunder. "Get your ass up here, FUCKING NOW!"

Now even the laggards of my group could sense the urgency. We all instinctively picked up the pace. We needed to get as far away from that ship as possible. The Naval Academy hadn't made us as completely clueless as many of the chiefs jokingly insinuated all week.

We made our way to the end of the pier. Out of my peripheral I caught an older officer moving brusquely our way. His solid gold shoulder boards nearly jumped off his uniform shirt. For a split second I thought he might be approaching my group. It was an admiral in summer whites with scrambled eggs on his cover's visor, another name for the golden embellishment senior officers earn the right to wear. All four of us, in full civilian clothes, snapped to attention just seeing him walking our way. It was instinct. He was someone not to be fucked with.

"Good afternoon, sir," my '99 shipmate Chris offered a salutation.

The admiral completely ignored the greeting as he blew past us. He looked pissed, but thankfully not at us.

A few paces later, we heard two dings of Vandegrift's

bell over the ship's pier. "Carrier Group, arriving."

"Oh shit, I wonder what the Carrier Group Commanding Officer wants to do on the boat at 1600 on a Friday?" my other '99 shipmate Anthony asked.

"Shit, let's not hang around to find out," I said before we all instinctually picked up the pace yet again. We could feel the pressure change in our internal shit storm barometer.

Within twenty paces we found a group of sailors looking back. They must have been from another ship. I didn't recognize any of them. I could tell they were enlisted by their youthful look and the fact that half of them were currently smoking menthol cigarettes. They were pointing and laughing at the ship we had just departed. One was even snapping a picture.

"What's going on over there?" my new acquaintance Anthony asked the growing crowd. Luckily our civilian clothes hid our rank. At this point, only other midshipmen or sailors from our own ship could blow our anonymity. Our collective youth and bad haircuts likely had the sailors assuming we were fellow enlisted crew.

"Take a look for yourself," said one sailor pointing at our ship with a shit-eating grin.

We all turned together to look at our ship. There it was, right next to the Vandegrift's "48" hull number in giant six-foot letters. FUCK THIS was scraped into the side of the hull for all pier side onlookers to enjoy.

"Gotta admire Aunder's balls," I said with a laugh. "Now let's get the fuck out of here," I directed our group. There was no way I was hanging anywhere near that ship now.

Shit would surely roll down hill on this one. I'm sure the skipper was already getting an ear full from the admiral that had moments ago stormed past us. Soon that verbal thrashing would be extended to the XO, then to the officers and chiefs, then to the crew. As inexperienced as we all were, after being in the Navy for two years, we knew the drill. Nobody questioned my desire to get the fuck out of dodge.

In minutes grey paint cans would be cracking open. There was no way the skipper was going to let Aunder's artwork stay overnight, even if that meant painting it himself. I sure as shit wasn't hanging around long enough to get assigned paint duty on a Friday night.

Fuck me, just in time for the weekend.

Within an hour Trey, Anthony, Chris, and I were all dejectedly eating tacos and bacon cheese fries at the base's Del Taco. Though delicious, and under five bucks, the meal tasted like defeat. Thankfully we weren't back on the ship painting, but we were still a long way from cracking beers in Tijuana.

"Fuck it, Trey, let's take the trolley train outside the base down to the border. We weren't going to drive over the border anyway, let's get down there. I need to get off this fucking base. And there's no way we can return to the ship now," I stated aloud with growing impatience. The longer we hung around the base, the more likely we'd be pulled into something shitty.

He repeated that his friend was still on his way. I jammed another greasy fry down my throat to keep my tongue gainfully occupied. Twenty minutes later and we were on the public trolley to Mexico.

Chapter 6

Midnight Marauders
Saturday, July 19th, 1997
Mick, 0005 hrs.

"Please state your name, after the beep," the automated voice instructed. The beep soon followed behind it as promised.

"It's me, Mick."

I waited through six dial tones before looking impatiently down at my watch. Then I realized that not only was a collect call from Mexico something I'd never accept, I'd especially not take it at five past three in the morning East coast standard time. My girlfriend, Summer, was no exception.

I'll have to catch her tomorrow morning.

I was angry at myself. It was my Naval Academy midshipman girlfriend Summer's last weekend in Annapolis for first set Plebe Summer detail. She was a rare combination of a plebe's worst nightmare and wet dream all at once. I couldn't believe I had forgotten to call her.

With our conflicting schedules and lack of accessible email on the ship, Summer and I seldom had the chance to communicate. Today's distraction of Aunder's shipside artwork, the effort to make it down to Tijuana, and a few too many drinks had postponed our connection by another day.

Situated underneath the soft electric glow of an elevated sign that read Club A, I hung up the pay phone with a frustrated slam.

We heard a few of the enlisted dudes on the ship reference this place as "Clubba De Alpha." That's where we told the cab driver to take us after we crossed the Mexican border on foot.

I had no idea what the locals actually called the place. Aside from the people collecting a cover charge at the door and a few people handing out drinks on the dance floor, there were very few locals in sight. I don't think any of them cared as long as they were making money.

The twenty-buck cover at the door meant it was all you can drink underage heaven for the rest of the evening. They even took our American cash without batting an eye or asking for an ID. All of this serendipitous fun coupled with my heavy buzz, and I hadn't watched the time nearly as attentively as I should have.

Back at the academy Summer and I saw each other daily. We were not only '99 classmates, but we were also in the same company. Initially I had thought summer cruise would be a welcome break of freedom. It was making me feel like I was unwittingly abandoning our relationship.

Perhaps my neglect wasn't all unintended. Lately, Summer's patience with me seemed a good bit shorter than it had when we started formally dating almost a year and a half earlier as plebes.

Summer was heading to her fleet cruise in Norfolk

on Sunday. By Monday afternoon she'd be underway for a two-week Mediterranean cruise that eventually landed her a weekend in Naples on a port call. She had been talking about it all summer long.

The opportunity wasn't nearly as exciting to me. I was still bitter that she had chosen the east coast cruise with her soccer teammates vice trying to coordinate something in San Diego with me. It felt like punishment for all of our love chit arguments.

Between the bi-coastal cruises and Plebe Summer we had been apart almost two full months since commissioning week. It had already been the source of one major blowout and several arguments over the phone between the two of us.

"Hey brah, you done with that?" a bleach blond skate punk that looked to be no older than fifteen broke me out of my daze. We were all submerged in the glow of the club's pink neon exterior lighting.

Tijuana nightclubs weren't that big on checking IDs. It's why Club A in particular was such a favorite spot for mischievous high schoolers and underage Sailors and Marines. It was a more adventurous version of a fake license back north in the states.

"Yeah, sure man, here ya go." I stepped away from the pay phone without much fuss. The kid reminded me of many of the groms I knew in Ocean City, the ones still in high school at least.

I stepped away from the booth and out into the street for a breath. A cab obnoxiously beeped me onto the curb. The vehicle buzzed by, missing me by a few feet. I flipped the bird and almost stumbled over in the process.

I was already four beers and three shots into the night.

The grey hull of the Vandegrift seemed days removed from where I was. The dusty road beneath my feet was rocking. My land sickness from a week on the ship couldn't have been that bad.

Fuck, I'm shit-faced.

I looked around, feeling disoriented. I took a few more deep breaths fighting off the pangs of nausea and dizziness. I was alone. I had abandoned my friends inside the club once I remembered my forgotten call to Summer.

Half of the dilapidated buildings around me were abandoned or shut down for the night. I was no more than fifteen miles from the border but I might as well have been in downtown Beirut.

I turned around. The bright lights behind me guided me back in the right direction. I stumbled towards the bouncers and into the club, flashing the wristband I had traded a twenty for earlier. The bouncers waved me though despite nearly falling face first as I staggered up the stairs to the second-floor nightclub.

Aside from the plethora of underage San Diego suburbanites searching for trouble, Club A basically looked like a military base. It seemed like every enlisted Sailor and Marine under the age of twenty had found this place. The club was a total sausage fest.

In the center of all of the action was the dance floor. A DJ alternated between rap and techno dance beats. The sound was deafening and the dancing was terrible. Three quarters of the dance floor was filled elbow to elbow with enlisted Marines. You could tell by their cowboy boots, high and tight haircuts, and the wads of dip packed under their lips. This scared off most of the females that had been formerly brave enough to venture out onto the dance floor. A few bold females remained, enjoying the attention that the male to female ratio ensured.

I searched for my crew. A few more scans of the dance floor reaffirmed that they were not the dancing types, at least not the type that wanted to dance with a bunch of drunken, horny Marines.

I finally saw my Vandegrift shipmates outside on the veranda overlooking the street. It was the only remotely quiet spot in the whole joint. My crew was there the same way I had left them, getting drunk and desperately chasing whatever pretty girls would give them the time of day.

"MIIIICK!!!!! What's up, my man?" I heard my new friend Anthony call out above the deafening music coming from inside the club. Trey and Anthony had secured a cluster of stools. Miraculously, they had also found a pack of girls to sit around them.

There were four girls sitting in our cluster. They were without a doubt the hottest women in the club, which wasn't saying much. However, the brunette pushing off Anthony's drunken advances for the past hour was a standout, in any crowd. The belly button ring exposed by her mid-drift tank top highlighted her tight stomach. Her well-tanned cleavage pleasantly glistened with sweat above her shirt's low neckline. I couldn't get a good look at the blonde Trey was currently making out with. His tongue was tickling her tonsils while his hand firmly grasped her right breast. From the looks of things, she didn't seem to mind.

As a general rule of thumb, most of the hot girls in

the place looked younger than the typical bar crowd. As southern Californians aged, and better alternatives for the twenty-one and over crowd opened up, people generally stopped going down to TJ. If you were over thirty and in Tijuana you were either Mexican, poor, or a serial killer. We were some of the older, more experience people in the club that night.

"Who's your friend, Anthony? Did I hear you call him Mick?" The attractive brunette asked. I couldn't tell if she was into me or she was simply trying to further fend off Anthony's unwanted advances.

"Yup, the one and only," Anthony replied. He caught the hint and tapered off his advances. He was at least three beers ahead of my tally, but still sober enough to know better.

Cock block, averted!

Anthony was a true shipmate. I offered him a smoke and I helped him light it once he had it in his mouth. I followed suit.

"Yeah, Micky is one of the few mids out here that actually fits well in California. He's been bitching all night about not surfing yet," Anthony did his best to spur on a conversation.

"Surfer huh? Well you are in the right place," the cute brunette said. "Or maybe the wrong place," she pondered after surveying the dusty dry landscape of an urban Tijuana night. "I'm Julia," she said as she flipped her short hair out of her face. She rubbed her finger against her full lips before offering her hand.

I shook her hand gently and took a seat on the empty stool next to her.

"This seat taken?" I asked after I had already sat down. It was a polite formality that followed suit with her offered handshake. I already knew what her answer was.

"Maybe," she said with a giggle.

As I sat next to her, I could smell the alcohol in her sweat.

"So Anthony, give me the scoop on these fine young ladies," I looked away from Julia and tried to include Anthony in the conversation. The two other girls sitting at our group's table stood up once they knew Anthony was newly unoccupied with Julia. Trey continued his grope session with his new blonde friend.

"Naughty sorority girls from UCLA," he said. Julia portrayed a shocked face and playfully slapped Anthony on the arm as she looked dead into my eyes.

"Sounds like the title of a porn film," I returned her stare and replied exhaling the last puff of my cigarette. I had already burned through an entire pack since leaving the ship.

"You only know the half of it, big boy," Julia joked as she patted my left leg gently. She leaned in towards me to deliver a private message. "I'm not a porn star, but I do think you're cute," she whispered seductively. Her warm breath tickled my ear and goosebumps made their way down my neck.

"Yo man, you'll never believe what I saw in the bathroom!" my long-lost friend, Chris, loudly announced to the group upon his return.

Cock block, RE-engaged!

Chris's return was a sudden cold shower to the entire group. Even Trey pulled up for air upon Chris's prodding.

His volume conveyed the gravitas of his announcement.

Chris returned to our outdoor seating for the first time since I had returned from my earlier phone call attempt. His arms were filled with as many Dos Equis as he could carry. He was swaying like he had taken an upper cut from Mike Tyson. It was an especially comical posture considering our current drinking situation. At least ten workers behind the bar were handing that shit out for free all night long. The beer wasn't going anywhere.

"Hey man, the cover was for all you can drink. You know I'm not passing up free beers. Who wants some?" Chris could sense my gawking stare and felt the need to pre-emptively explain the need to carry ten bottles of beer at a time.

Then a group of about five short Mexican men swarmed in. They raucously circled our group. The lively men held sparklers and blew whistles in a loud celebratory commotion. Then they pulled out bottles of tequila from double sided belt holsters. Our new best friends began pouring the tequila bottles directly into everyone's mouth in our group. I tilted my head and kindly took a swallow. I didn't want to turn down the free gift nor did I want to keep my mouth closed and have tequila spill down the front of me.

"Slipped those little fuckers a twenty and they've been bringing that shit over here every fifteen minutes. FUCK, I love TJ!" Chris obnoxiously continued his happy stupor. When we were lab partners in physics, I don't think I heard more than twenty words from him all semester. Now he was practically howling at the moon like some sort of wolf man.

"So, what did you see my friend?" I brought Chris back on course, curious about what he had seen in the bathroom.

I grabbed another beer. I gave up counting my drinks and emphatically swigged. I was attempting to wipe the taste of shitty tequila out of my mouth. Unsuccessful, I turned my attention to Chris. I hiccupped and struggled not to vomit.

This ought to be good.

"Some older chick in there was showing off her newly pierced clit in the men's bathroom to about half of Camp Pendleton. She even let a few of those jarheads touch it. It looked like she could have been their grandma!"

Fuck me, you're killing my buzz, man.

Rolling my eyes at Chris I turned towards my better-looking companion. "So you're not a porn star," I resumed my conversation with Julia.

"Well," Julia picked up the conversation without the faintest hint of former clit piercing talk. "I'm actually at the UCLA School of Theater."

"Home girl is going to be in an upcoming AIDS commercial," Anthony inserted himself in our conversation after quietly returning to our group with five beer bottles of his own.

Fuck man, AIDS!?

"It's a health awareness commercial. Don't worry, I don't have AIDS," she jumped in over Anthony once she could sense my trepidation. "I'm in the first ten seconds of the commercial. I'm the hot chick with short hair in the tight spandex on the gym's Stairmaster."

"So you live in LA and study film. You want to be an actress?"

She looked at me with a flirtatious sneer. Annoyed that I was spending so much time trying to converse. She scooted her chair closer to mine. Her skin felt warm as her thigh touched mine.

"Well, hello there," she said as she completely changed the conversation. She had long passed the point of wanting to talk. She leaned in. I had an even better vantage point of her ample breasts. My eyes had snuck a not so obvious peek about ten times already. This was the best vantage yet. Animal instincts took over. I leaned in as well.

Our lips locked in a fervent kiss. I rubbed my hand up and down her body. It felt new and different. I felt like I was on fire. Every sound and sensation external to Julia temporarily disappeared.

Mick, what the fuck are you doing, man?

Then a commotion interrupted something that I already should have.

Chris pulled me away from Julia. "Sorry dude, Pistol Pete won't stop acting crazy. We gotta bolt. NOW." Chris had been simultaneously scared and sobered up.

As I pulled up for air I could feel the mob around us getting antagonistic. Pistol Pete was one of Chris's company mates from the academy. He had been in the club with a group of his summer cruise friends all night. That same group was currently in the midst of a building cluster of charged up jarheads.

I had met Pistol Pete briefly a few hours earlier. He was a scrawny, goofy looking caricature of a midshipman.

I could only imagine how he earned his nickname back in Annapolis. I couldn't remember his actual name.

After a full night of jack-assery, there Pete was squaring up to two strong jawed Marines. Both looked like they might fight each other to see which one gets the privilege of knocking Pete out. Both hard chargers individually outweighed Pete by fifty pounds. Their cowboy boots and hats only exacerbated the height discrepancy.

I watched things unfold. It was clear that the other mids situated in the middle of the building crowd weren't there to join Pete in the fray. They were there to get him out of it. The situation was heading to one of a handful of places. Most of them would not end well for anyone involved, most especially Naval Academy midshipmen.

"Julia, sorry, I have to take care of this," I hesitantly said. I briefly considered asking for her number, but I was already feeling guilty about hooking up with her. The drinking hadn't totally dissolved my moral compass. My boner subsided and I used the pending commotion as an excuse to eject myself from the temptation.

Julia took the hint. In an instant she had already joined her friends in another group at the other end of the veranda. She had enough confidence to recognize that the love of her life would likely not be found in Tijuana.

I turned my attention back to the dance floor. Two of my classmates were sweeping the floor with Pistol Pete in a path directed towards the club's exit. Pete's skinny arms spastically flailed. He continued his sharp verbal barrage of insults. Cursing continued down the stairs and into the pink neon glow of the Tijuana street below.

Chris shepherded Anthony, Trey, and me into the

exiting group. As a company mate, Chris felt partially responsible for Pete's safety. We all understood the situation. It was part of an unwritten code we had already been learning.

We hailed two cabs to nab our pack of impromptu gang of seven. Anthony, Trey, and one of Pete's friends I hadn't formally been introduced to yet hustled into one cab. I joined Chris, Pete, and another one of Pete's friends. We expeditiously hopped into the second cab. We didn't want to give any of the trouble upstairs time enough to find its way downstairs on the street. In a matter of minutes we were speeding behind a cloud of Tijuana street dust.

******

Mick, 0145

"No señor, NO señor, NO SEÑOR!" the cab driver yelled to the backseat. A flurry of loud Spanish dialogue frantically continued in the front seat. I couldn't understand any of it.

Chris and I surrounded Pete on both sides. On the seat bench in front of us we could see multiple stickers advertising Club A. The rest of the seat was littered with taped up pictures and phone numbers of a variety of Mexican prostitutes. Pistol convulsed like the recipient of an exorcist. He alternated between nearly throwing up to trying to escape the moving cab about every two minutes.

Lorenzo Ortiz, Pete's friend from back on another ship pier side in San Diego, sat in the front seat next to the cab driver. Thankfully, he spoke fluent Spanish. Chris and I had really only known Ortiz for five minutes, but we already liked the guy.

Ortiz worked hard to further stall the driver. He engaged the driver in what I assumed was attempted small talk in Spanish. He was trying to buy us enough time to make it to the border. If it weren't for him we'd have already be kicked to the curb and dodging Federales by now.

From the looks of our outdoor surroundings and the distance of the lights on the night's horizon, we were at least two miles from civilization and about three miles from the border.

Chris and I were desperately trying to do anything we could to keep Pete from barfing all over the taxi's interior. We had already rolled down both windows. All we could do now was keep his head upright and hold his mouth shut. Eventually when it looked like the kettle was about to burst, we stuck Pete's head out of the window.

The brakes screeched as soon as Pete let his innards loose. Vomit covered the outside of the driver's side rear door, enough for the driver to see it. That was the last straw. We had stalled enough to make it to civilization, but not enough to make it fully to the border.

Ortiz immediately began pleading with the driver in Spanish again from the front passenger seat. As he did so, he simultaneously reached his left to the backseat rubbing his fingers together, frantically signaling the need for immediate cash donations. It was our only hope. Chris was empty. I reluctantly grabbed my wallet. We didn't even bother trying to get cash from Pete.

Ortiz added his own funds to a wad of sweaty cash in his left hand. He continued his pleading and offered our wad of cash penance.

"Por favor. Por favor," Ortiz worked his charm.

The cabby pondered for a second. "Eh, eh-eh," the cabby shook his head. Our offer was rejected.

"Veinte mas," he countered.

Ortiz looked my way. "Hey man, that's all the cash I got. You got a twenty? We can settle up on base."

I reached in my pocket one more time. My cheapness still made me reluctant. I was already twenty in on the transaction. Another twenty and I'd be riding my credit card balance for the rest of July. I grabbed the twenty and held it over the front seat. The cabby snatched the money out of my hand.

Holy shit, did we pull that off?

"Cleaning fees, PUNETAS! Now get the FUCK out of here before I get the Federales!" The cabby officially killed our hope for a drop off point closer to the border.

NOW the guy fucking speaks English.

Ortiz and I took the hint. My prior lecture from the skipper made me fully aware of how much Federales and cab drivers liked fucking with U.S. military types on their way home from bars. We were easy money. Worse yet, we stuck out like a sore thumb.

I refocused. We couldn't get arrested tonight, especially knowing the skipper was already pissed off by the graffiti scrubbed into his beloved hull today.

"Come on, let's get out of here and hoof it," Ortiz compelled us into action. "It's only a few more blocks. Not ideal, but we can make it from here."

We crawled out of the cab and simultaneously slammed our doors before the cabby sped off. He was likely headed back to Club A to scam a few more drunk military types while he still had the opportunity. I doubt he'd even have to clean the puke splatter off the car door.

We returned our attention to the curb and getting over the border. Chris was pissing on the sidewalk. The puddle of urine beside him glistened in the electric glow of the street light above. His shirt was splattered with Pete's vomit and he leaned against a telephone pole to keep himself upright. We all looked like we had enough action for one night.

Almost all of us.

"Shit. Where the fuck is Pistol?" Ortiz suddenly became aware of the absence in our group. We all took in our surroundings.

"Where the fuck did he go?" I asked Chris. He mumbled a few unintelligible phrases as drool dripped from his lower lip to the sidewalk below. The last round of tequila shots twenty minutes earlier finally did their damage. We'd be dragging two bodies across the border tonight. We had to act fast.

Ortiz and I grabbed Chris and threw his arms around each of our shoulders. He was at least able to keep the pace under our guidance. We figured Pete would be drawn toward the lights at the border which could be seen on the horizon. We made it a block and a half without much trouble. There was still no sign of Pete.

Each block ahead looked progressively more happening. Directly across the street, a few bars and street stands serving food were still packed with activity. There was no sign of closing time anywhere in sight. We waited on the street corner for the light to stop traffic.

The light changed and my trio made our way across the street and towards the action. The oncoming block's festivities spilled towards us. Two vocal gentlemen were carrying on and handing out pamphlets to anyone that crossed their proximity. We finally made our way past them in the middle of the street.

"Señor, señor, donkey show!" One member of the persuasive duo passed me a pamphlet. We made it safely to the next street corner. I stopped to read the pamphlet. Ortiz and Chris were not ready for the abrupt halt and all three of us almost bit it on the sidewalk.

The donkey show pamphlet was all in Spanish, but the gist was self-evident. It's not every day you're given a baseball card sized picture of a young woman giving head to a barnyard animal. I didn't even need Ortiz to translate the address. I could see that the letters on the card matched the neon marquis above the most crowded store front on the block.

"At least now we know where to find the fourth stooge."

Part III

How Do U Want It?

Chapter 7

All Eyez on Me
Friday, July 18th, 1997
Summer, 1645 hrs.

"Three! Two! One!" I counted down. I stared down at my wristwatch to make it look like I was keeping accurate time. I wasn't. It was all for show. "You're DONE!"

I adjusted my hair and pulled it in a tighter ponytail. All of my previous yelling had loosened it into a mess.

The empty hall way suddenly filled with a sea of Naval Academy plebes dressed in camouflage uniforms. They poured out of their rooms like a flooded ant hill.

"Good afternoon, Miss Harris! Good afternoon, Miss Harris! Good afternoon, Miss Harris! Good afternoon, Miss Harris!" A room full of scrambling plebes passed me in the hall. I was greeted with proper salutations as mandated by their plebedom. Two more roomfuls of plebes passed me. They followed their classmates' lead with the same loud succession of required formalities. I'm sure every plebe in 6th company hated my guts right now. That was how Naval Academy freshmen were supposed to feel about their upper-class detailers.

"You're LAAAAATE! You're LaaaaAAAAAATE!

You're LaaaaAAAAAATE!" I summoned the bitchiest voice I could muster.

Half of the plebes that hadn't yet made it into the hallway needed some extra prodding. They were likely still scrambling through the last-minute adornment of their freshly requested CAMMO uniforms. They were given the order to finish dressing in two minutes. I was creating a sense of urgency without actually timing them. I simply waited until the first few rooms made it back to the hall and screamed at the rest left behind. It was textbook Plebe Summer mind games.

It was their third such uniform change in less than ten minutes. Uniform races were one of the favorite ways upper-class detailers tormented plebes when they had thirty minutes to blow.

Our original professional training at nearby Chauvenet was rescheduled for the following week. Our afternoon was serendipitously made less occupied. Now there was enough opportunity to fuck with the plebes one last time.

It was much more difficult to yell so late in the summer. I had been screaming daily for the past three weeks. The detailers were essentially "wannabe" drill sergeants. We all spent months watching films like Full Metal Jacket prior to the plebes' I-day arrival learning the finer points of how to be a loud-yelling asshole. It would take the rest of the summer for my vocal chords to heal.

"MOOOOOOOOOVE!" a booming voice erupted from around the corner. The echoes bounced across the walls like an air hockey puck. My tall, skinny partner in crime outpaced the jogging plebes. He walked with long frantic strides. He looked like an angry grasshopper.

"I'm friggin' WALKING faster than YOU!!!!" the angry man turned up the heat right on cue. "LET'S GO!"

Midshipman Second Class Dallas Bickley was one of the three junior detailers selected for 6th company's first set Plebe Summer detail. We were all squad leaders in our company's platoon of new plebes. Tomorrow, there'd be another set of three company mates taking on the second half of Plebe Summer.

The first set of Plebe Summer detailers were supposed to be the harsher of the two sets. We were expected to break the plebers down. Second set would build them back up. All in all, I think we did our job in first set. Bickley was particularly evil to the plebes. He earned his nickname "Dickley" quite genuinely.

This afternoon was first set detailers' last hurrah. At 1700 we'd have our last meal, do a turnover formation with second set, and I'd be out on liberty in no time. I could smell the finish line but I reminded myself to keep my energy up. Dickley was a blender full of water.

Not done yet.

The scattered plebes increased their desperate pace. The timelier plebes funneled into formation as commanded three minutes earlier.

"Let's go! Let's GO! LET'S GOoooooOOOOOOOOO!" Bickley was so natural at being a mean prick. Any plebe not already in the hallway was scrambling not to be the last person out of the room. Only about half of the plebe rooms had made it safely on time in the hallway.

Two more plebes late for Uniform Race Muster made their way out of their main hallway room. Their third roommate remained inside. The first two plebes made it to the middle of the hallway before they realized they were missing their third amigo.

"Oh my FRIGGIN' GOD!" Dickley screamed as he aggressively approached the recently arrived duo. The veins in his neck pulsated in anger. "I guess you two are A-okay with leaving your roommate Lance Corporal Rother out in the desert to die, huh? UN! FRIGGING! SAT!"

The plebes' roommate was not actually a Lance Corporal, nor was his name Rother. The real Lance Corporal Jason Rother was a deceased teenage Marine that unfortunately lost his life when left behind by his fellow Marines in the Mojave Desert on a training exercise. Rother's sad story was a week one lesson of Plebe Summer.

"Alright gang, assume the position!" I followed Dickley's yelling with an immediate order to the plebes waiting in the hallway for the remainder of their classmates. Shipmates were never left behind. It didn't matter whether the mistake had been intentional or not. There would be hell to pay for this oversight.

The plebes immediately hit the deck. Almost four weeks in and orders required much less explanation. The plebes fast enough to make it out to the hall's formation were rewarded by holding the top pushup position. The rest of the laggards that didn't make it out yet extended their classmates' pain.

"SPEAK UP!" I continued my harassment.

The crowd of angry plebes dutifully began their mantra. "We're waiting on our classmates, ma'am, we're waiting on our classmates, ma'am, we're waiting on our classmates, ma'am." The sweat from their faces dripped and pooled between the hands holding them in upright push up position. Their palms slipped on the floor.

It was a forced charade. I was over the harassment of plebes days ago. I knew I would barely mess with the plebes during the academic year. I had my fill during the past month. My last bit of intensity was really meant as a favor. If we got too soft on them in our last days as detailers, they would be slaughtered by the oncoming set. That "building up" mission of second set was partially bullshit. Second set was chomping at the bit to lay into the class of 2001 every bit as much as we were four weeks earlier. They watched Full Metal Jacket endlessly too.

One of the two remaining rooms made their way out to the hall while their more prompt shipmates suffered on the ground below.

"Ma'am good morning, Miss Harris, ma'am," the first female plebe in a straight line chopping towards the hall formation offered a formal greeting.

"Come on, ROBERTS! Do you even know what time of day it is?" I called her out before the two roomies behind her had a chance to either make the same mistake or make their other roommate look bad.

Roberts was in for a long year ahead. She was pretty. That meant just about every male midshipman in the academy would be ruthlessly hitting on her. Already half of the male detailers couldn't stop blatantly gawking at her. Worse yet, she had a resting bitch face. That certainly wasn't going to do her any favors.

Roberts kept on chopping towards her classmates in the P-way as though she hadn't even heard me. I had to step in and remind her that I was there.

"ROBERTS!" I yelled loudly enough to grab her full

attention. She stopped as I sped forward to intersect her path.

"WHAT do you think?" I started an angry scolding before I noticed the alligator tears running down her flushed and puffy face. "Come on, go to the ladies' head," I ordered her quietly to get herself together.

Vanessa Roberts was a borderline shitty plebe that had given me plenty of evidence for weeks that this Navy stuff might not be for her. My yelling at her wasn't me piling onto a weak link. Rather, it was for all of the women here.

Every time a detailer broke down a woman to tears, it built on the narrative that we were too weak to be there in the first place. Roberts bawling in the hallway was giving some asshole another story to tell over beers about why girls don't belong at USNA.

Bear the strain, sister!

I avoided the temptation to go into the ladies' room and coach Roberts. With all of the eyes and attention in the hallway, we'd be doing neither of ourselves a favor if we fed into the stereotype of "soft" females. I made a mental note to say something to her in private before I headed out on leave later in the evening.

A loud bang diverted everyone's attention. It was the last door being kicked open by Dickley. Every other plebe in the company was stuck in an upright pushup position sweating their asses off in cammies. One room remained stuck in the drill. Dickley went in to remind them of it.

Before anyone made their way out of the room, articles of clothing started flying through the open doorway. Next came a few pillows. Then the bed blankets. Then a mattress.

"UH OOOOOOOOH!" Dickley's yell worn voice crackled loudly through the open door. "Looks like a HURRICAAAAAAAAAANE!"

Dickley threw another mattress into the P-way for good measure. He had tortured Jones, Smith, and Watson all Plebe Summer, and I was sure he'd be doing it for the remainder of the year.

"Well, what are you waiting for?" I queried the group sweating on the floor. "Get up and help your classmates!"

The plebes collectively stood up to help clean up their classmates' suddenly ransacked room. They gathered the mess scattered across the hallway. "Hurricane Dickley" moved on to the room next door. Another set of clothes and linens made their way to the hallway. He repeated this cycle three more times until half of the plebes' rooms had been appropriately fucked with. It would take them until dinner to clean up the mess.

Bickley returned into his own room ahead of the grand finale. He tossed a ball of watches into the hall. They were all closed upon each other forming a giant ball of plebe-issued watches. He had taken them from the company plebes last week when they showed up late for platoon drill formation. Not having access to a watch, given the importance of plebe timeliness, was a major inconvenience for them.

"Alright, you have ten minutes to clean up your stinky plebe trash outta my P-WAY! Any time you have leftover you can dedicate to un-hosing your watch pile. I sure bet they'd come in handy before second set gets their paws on you!"

The plebes would be lucky if they could wrangle two

or three more watches from the pile. Dickley wouldn't make it easy. If they cleaned up their stuff in the hallway too effectively, he'd just throw more out there. Then whatever little amount of time he'd give them, he'd scream in their faces to distract progress.

Dickley was profusely sweating from the exerted effort. He loved every minute of it. I was left there standing by myself once the hurricane cleanup got underway.

"Man," Dickley made his way next to me with a shit-eating grin. He was trying to catch his breath. "I'm going to miss this."

I politely smiled and nodded. It was certainly not a surprise that Dickley loved fucking with plebes. Even as a Sophomore Youngster he made flaming on plebes a daily habit. Youngsters were one year removed from plebedom and typically ignored plebes altogether. Not Dickley, he was a fulltime asshole to plebes the moment he wasn't one.

Thankfully, I saw one of my other fellow detailers make his way out of the wardroom down the hall. It was our fearless platoon commander, Midshipman First Class Matt Hackett. The wardroom was the one common television room for every company. It was the only place on the floor that was air conditioned. Matt had been napping there since lunch.

"Geez, don't you guys ever let up?" Matt entered the conversation. It was a welcome distraction from hearing Dickley brag about how much he loved yelling at plebes. "You fuckers woke me up an hour early," he continued in a joking tone.

I figured he might be sleeping. I knew he had hopped the wall with a few buddies to booze up in town last night.

Many of them were football players living on the other end of Bancroft while attending mandatory summer school. I only knew about the bar hopping the night before because my boyfriend's roommate N.D. was on the football team. Similarly, N.D. was in summer school to lighten his academic course load to the minimum fifteen credits for the upcoming season.

A knee injury had ended Matt's football playing days his freshman year. He remained friends with many of his old teammates. He also roomed with the starting quarterback. They were both in my company and I considered them friends.

"Are you up to anything tonight?" he asked.

"Not me," Dickley answered. I knew the question wasn't intended for him.

"What about you?" he asked me with a smile. The tone was innocent enough. I knew he liked me, or at least found me attractive, but it seemed like he was just being friendly.

"Me? I'm boring. I'm hanging at my sponsor's doing some laundry. Mick is supposed to give me a buzz at eight. After that, who knows?"

"Cool. How's my man Micky?"

Mick and Matt had been friends largely through N.D. They genuinely liked each other and hung out often.

"You know Mick, I'm sure he's having fun out in San Dawg," I replied. We both continued completely ignoring Dickley. We had both had enough of listening to him.

"You want to catch up for a late dinner at McGarvey's? An end of Plebe Summer celebration before we all take off," Matt offered. "My dad has his boat docked up in Ego

Alley and is planning to grab some beers with a few old classmates."

Hackett's dad was a ring knocker too. He was a whole lot older and higher ranking than any of us. I never met him but heard he was a Navy Captain. He didn't live in D.C. but a bunch of his classmates worked there.

"Super, that sounds great," Dickley chimed in. I don't think Matt had intended for the invitation to include Dickley.

"Yeah, cool," Matt replied with a tinge of dread. He was too nice of a guy to un-invite Dickley.

"How about you, Summer?" he transferred the invite my way. "After you talk to Mick of course," he smiled acknowledging my girlfriend duty.

"Sure, that sounds cool," I accepted. I wasn't necessarily planning to go out. I could have just as easily gone to sleep at 9 p.m., but a celebration the last night of first set seemed appropriate. We had worked hard and had plenty of funny stories to relive. It was also cool hanging with older alumni. They always had a few entertaining sea stories to tell, especially when they had a few beers in them.

"Done deal," Matt replied. "Meet me at McGarvey's around nine."

He headed back to his room to shower for our last dinner with the plebes. He could have hung longer, we still had over thirty minutes till chow. I think he was bolting before he had to spend any more time with Dickley. Most of the football players and guys like Mick and Matt hated mids like Dallas Bickley.

There's good reason everybody called him Dickley.

Chapter 8

You Learn
Friday, July 18th, 1997
Summer, 2230 hrs.

"So who REALLY had the last real Plebe Summer?" the tall handsome man sitting at the filled circular table asked the group gathered. His hair was cut short like the rest of the table. The top was grown out a little longer than most mids would keep it. It helped cover his receding hairline. There was also a little salt shining through his pepper, typical for a man of his age. Matt Hackett's dad looked like an older, more put together version of his son.

"Ninety-EIGHT no doubt," Matt replied. He was met with strong opposition from the other side of the table. His dad and three of his own Naval Academy classmates immediately booed and followed with a "Seventy-twooooooooo!"

"Yeah right. Four hours and five minutes?" I replied as an antagonistic taunt to Matt. The class of ninety-eight still held the dubious honor of having the longest time to climb the Herndon monument. The peanut gallery across the table went nuts. I knew how to work my charm with this type of crowd.

McGarvey's Saloon and Oyster Bar was packing up in a hurry. Its location directly in the middle of Annapolis' historic waterfront was a prime one. In the summer, tourists and yachtsmen helped perpetuate the nautical side of the city's atmosphere. If we were in this place at 10:30 p.m. three months from now, it'd be a USNA meat market. I had heard all about it from my older soccer teammates.

McGarvey's catered to two distinctly different seasonal crowds. During the school year, it was packed with mids. Its walking distance location from the Naval Academy made it a safe way to avoid DUIs. By 10:30 p.m. in the fall, McGarvey's would be knee deep in alcohol induced pissing contests amongst a disproportionate population of young, mostly handsome, and all sexually frustrated males.

I wasn't twenty-one yet, I didn't turn until the upcoming fall. In my first two years I only viewed this sausage fest from the sidewalk looking in. Places like that had their own dangers for someone that looked like me.

The summer tourist season made McGarvey's seem different. It had more charm and ambiance. Its decor wasn't fancy. The brick walled pub theme was replicated at bars and restaurants all over the historic downtown. Its distinction was that it was the town's only aviator bar. That meant something considering almost a third of every graduating Naval Academy class was associated with Naval aviation.

The mix of jet jocks and yacht skippers gave the place an heir of genuine machismo. Shared amongst twenty-two year old boys, this atmosphere fueled braggadocios tales and other penis measuring contests. The summer brought a flavor of this too, it just came from an older more genuine place.

On the wall hung at least ten different pilot helmets. All of them were likely hot shit jet jock ring knockers. Each helmet had its own unique artistic pattern and color scheme. The wall was laced with the lids of pilots named "Yoda, Wildman, Smokey, and Hacksaw." Each painted script represented either a clever "one off" of their actual name or a titillating story about its origin. At least the people telling said stories thought so. I was sitting with two such gentlemen. The "Hacksaw" helmet belonged to Matt's dad.

"Good to see somebody around this place keeping Matty in line," the elder Hackett replied. He was in his element hanging with his classmates, cold draft beer in hand. They were telling loud sea stories. At six foot three he towered above his classmates and caught plenty of female attention. The only ring on his finger was his large Naval Academy class ring. I knew Matt well enough to know his dad was already divorced.

"Oh don't let her civvies fool you. She was every plebe's worst nightmare," Matt chimed in. "A total hard ass."

"I'll bet she is," chimed in Smokey, a newly retired Marine Corps full bird Colonel cobra pilot and elder Hacksaw's former academy roommate.

I smiled and laughed along, reaching for another nacho. The pitcher of beer on the table was tempting, especially during my last night in town. However, a fake ID three blocks from the academy with three senior officers would have been a very poor decision. I happily drank my Coke.

Matt had been drinking since he finished with his plebe duties in the afternoon. He said his goodbyes to the plebes at the early evening after-dinner formation. Four hours later and Matt's boozy smell had long since overpowered his Drakkar Noir.

Dickley was in hog heaven hunkered down next to his new best friend, Colonel "Smokey" Lawrence, USMC. It was Dickley's wet dream to become a Marine Cobra pilot. Accordingly, he was doing everything and anything to kiss Smokey's ass and look smart.

"Sir, it must be something to fire off those sidewinders with the newly upgraded fire control system," Dickley droned on.

"Yeah," replied Smokey, his gruff voice fit his nickname well.

"Does the Hellfire target differently than the sidewinders?" Dickley continued his grilling like a curious toddler. For a second, I thought Matt's dad may hop over the table and give Dickley a wedgie.

"Huh?" Smokey asked, he had already long since pressed the mute button on Dickley's never-ending line of questioning.

"Does the Hel-"

"Look, making a great helicopter pilot is a hell of a lot more than memorizing weapons forward to aft," Smokey more deliberately tried to halt Dickley's interrogation.

Dickely dutifully shut his pie trap and refocused his attention as though staring directly into a burning bush.

"The best pilots are competitors," Smokey continued. "Yeah, you gotta be smart, but there's also that X-factor.

You have to want to compete. You have to hate to lose. That's why some of the best pilots I ever met were great athletes in their academy days."

Smokey affectionately slapped Matt's dad on the shoulder. I had already known from Matt that his dad had been a football star. I learned that evening that Smokey had been a varsity wrestler in his academy days.

"Summer, you strike me as an athlete, someone with loads of X-factor," Smokey complimented.

I tried not to blush. Compliments from such a senior officer were flattering.

"Pretty damn good soccer player, Smokey," Matt interrupted to chime in on my behalf.

I knew Matt really would have preferred a more private night out. It had been two years since we hooked up in the fall of my freshman year. We were both in the same company, which meant romantic relationships were forbidden. We also both had had a few beers that night and I was underage. It was an epic culmination of plebe no nos. Matt was even more in the red considering he was a sophomore, and therefore senior to me at the time. Luckily we never got caught.

The thing was, I liked Matt. He was a tall, handsome jock, the type of guy I dated in high school. Sure, he was an immature boy with the manners of a twelve-year-old, but he was a sweet guy. I hadn't planned on hooking up with him, it just happened. I certainly didn't mind kissing him.

Once we got past the hook-up however, reality sunk in. There was no way I could keep a relationship with Matt quiet. He was far too big of a character, far too visible. He had no desire to lay low, nor did he have a desire to date me exclusively. We flirted a few times, but beyond that it was a short-lived romance. We never took it too seriously and neither of us seemed too broken up about it. We remained friendly.

Sure, there were rumors, a snickering joke or two, but miraculously we kept the cat in the bag. I was actually relieved it didn't go anywhere. As much as I thought Matt was cute, I had a reputation to protect. It was the same double standard that existed outside of the Naval Academy, made worse inside by the skewed male to female ratio.

I was lucky that my upper-class soccer teammates taught me that stuff early. If Matt got caught hooking up with me, he would have served a few days restriction but simultaneously been deemed legendary for hooking up with the "hot plebe." I would have been known as another weak girl using her looks to skate the system, regardless of whether or not it was true. Worse yet, many would call me slutty for hooking up with anyone in the first place.

Then along came Mick. He made me forget about any relationship rules I had ever made for myself while at USNA.

Mick never did call me like he promised. In a way, I was relieved. Most of our recent calls had been less than fun. Mick resented that I didn't blindly go join him in San Diego. The argument was far from resolved. It wasn't going to be resolved in a long-distance phone call either.

I fidgeted in my seat with anxious energy thinking about it. One minute it made me angry, the next minute it made me sad. It was the helpless feeling that I hated the most. I was gladly distracted by mostly good company around the table.

"I gotta go use the head," Dickley announced.

"Thanks for letting us know," I sarcastically replied. Everyone chuckled. Dickley shot a peeved look my way. I couldn't have cared less.

"Permission to shove off, sirs?" he asked the senior officers at the table. It was ridiculous protocol. Most senior officers in uniform wouldn't ask for that level of courtesy much less ones out of uniform drinking amongst friends. It was almost like Dickley was showing off his subservience.

Matt's dad and friends looked at Dickley and nodded without humoring him. There was no doubt by now they thought he was as big a tool as the rest of us thought he was.

As soon as Dickley left the table, Matt turned to his dad. "Alright, that's our cue. I'm bolting while we have the chance."

Matt gently grabbed my arm to pull me away from the table. It caught me off guard. I was still in a daze, fretting over Mick.

"Come on, let's get outta here before we're stuck with Dickley all night," Matt said.

Matt's dad interjected our discussion, "You two should go while you can. We can drive Dickley off no problem."

"NO problemo," emphasized Smokey with a Marlboro hanging out of his mouth.

"It was an absolute pleasure meeting you," Matt's dad offered with a smile. "Have a great night and hope to see you again."

As I was getting up, Smokey tapped my arm and

waved me closer into his proximity. "If you want to talk more about flying, stop by my room over at the Marriott Waterfront later tonight, say midnight. I have plenty more stories to tell."

I grabbed a folded napkin in his hand. I saw that it had ink penned on it. I assumed it was the room number.

Thanks, I think.

"Where to now?" I finally questioned as we hit the street outside of the restaurant. Though lively, it was quieter than usual out in the brick paved streets of downtown.

"Wanna check out my dad's boat?" Matt asked pointing towards the inland waterway fifty yards away. As it was peak summer and boating season, Ego Alley was packed full of docked boats. Some of the boats were more modest, some deserved an intro from Robin Leach.

I hesitated, not because it didn't sound fun. I didn't like the optics of the situation.

What if someone saw us? It wouldn't matter what actually happened, I'd be labeled "that girl."

"Come OOOOOON!" Matt chided me along. "One drink, I'll give you a quick tour, and then you can be on your way." He let out a drunken hiccup.

It sounded innocent enough. Matt could sense my consideration of the proposition.

"C'mon, C'mon, COME OOON! It's the end of Plebe Summer! You've earned yourself a party," he continued to argue his case with a devilish grin. "Don't worry, my dad will be crashing at his other roommate's place. No senior officers around. I swear."

"Oh alright, I'm game." I did feel like celebrating something tonight. Matt was right, Plebe Summer deserved at least one celebratory drink.

******

Summer, 2345

The pier-side water of Ego Alley reflected the wide array of street lights and restaurant signs illuminating the otherwise authentic brick edifice of colonial downtown Annapolis.

"Down here is the cabin area," Matt continued giving me a guided tour. He mistook my willing participation as interest in his dad's boat. Truth was I hated the yacht scene. More than anything I was looking for a convenient escape from Dickley and his steady state of obnoxiousness. The past month had filled me well past my limit.

I humored Matt and continued my way to the innards of the cabin. At the base of the stairs leading downward was a small kitchenette area. There were three bottles of hard liquor opened alongside several dirty glasses. Matt grabbed the Jack Daniels.

"Dad drinks this high-end scotch, tastes like rocket fuel to me. I prefer the classics," Matt justified his liquor of choice before he placed it on the kitchenette's counter. He reached into the mini fridge and grabbed a can of Coke. He grabbed two cups from the cabinet next to the microwave and dropped a few cubes from the ice bucket into each. He continued his impromptu bartending by pouring a hearty amount of whiskey over the ice then topping off each glass with Coke.

"Jack and Coke?" he asked holding a glass out to me.

"I don't know, it's getting late and I thought it might be

cool to catch up with your dad's friend later. Didn't he say for us to drop by the Marriott at midnight? That's only a few blocks away."

"Who? Smokey?" Matt asked and then started chuckling.

"What's so funny?" I asked.

"He asked you to drop by at midnight?" he queried shaking his head with a smile and a sip of his booze. "I think that was a private invite."

"Get outta here," I said. "No way. You were standing right there with me."

"You fit the perfect Smokey profile," Matt explained. "Hot, fit, under twenty-two. Fifteen minutes before you showed up at McGarvey's, he was talking about how nice it would be to find something new to play with tonight."

I felt like I was going to vomit. How dare that creepy old colonel hit on me? As if I would even consider getting involved with a senior officer much less someone almost old enough to be my father. I felt so validated by all of his compliments an hour earlier and it was all a ploy to get in my pants later. It made me feel so small.

How could I be so damn naïve?

I sat at the kitchenette table fuming. I was scrambling for another excuse to get off the boat. It was time for this night to end. I knew the moment I saw Matt pour the liquor that I didn't want it.

I should have bolted right then.

But then he'd think I was a stuck up bitch.

It was precisely these types of situations that made being a female midshipman so tough. While the assertive woman in me wanted to express my desires on the spot, perception was always a consideration, even amongst friends. I hated that it was.

There was no laying low as a female midshipman. Everyone watched your every step. Every action I took was noted and analyzed by most of the boys around me.

Want to hook up with a cute guy that likes you? Then you're a slut. Don't want to go on a date with someone you're not attracted to? Then you're an icy bitch. Many of my classmates would have said that any military accomplishment I achieved was primarily due to my looks. A few thought that I should be glad I wasn't hand cuffed to a urinal like they did to one a few years ago. I could only imagine what the brigade would be saying if word wrongly spread that I was sleeping with a colonel.

Every action had a disproportionate opposing reaction. My awareness of this paralyzed my ability to make timely decisions. It also really pissed me off.

Matt could sense I was beyond having fun. He dumped the Jack and Coke in the sink. He repeated the exact routine he did for my last drink, skipping the whiskey.

"Here ya go," he offered with attrition.

"Sorry to be the party pooper tonight," I explained. "I'm just really taken aback by the Smokey thing."

"I understand," Matt replied. "Nobody has to know about that shit but the two of us. Smokey was a drunken ass tonight. He's much more appropriate sober."

Eventually tales of Plebe Summer and all of the many stories garnered in the experience took over the night and helped me forget about Smokey. If there was one thing I admired about Matt it was his ability to tell a funny tale.

We laughed about the absurdity of certain plebes and various Plebe Summer traditions.

After an hour, the tales eventually petered out. I yawned unintentionally which prompted me to look down at my watch. It was already a half hour past midnight.

"Holy shit, I have to get back to my sponsor's house," I reacted aloud. "I wasn't expecting to stay out this late and they're probably wondering where I am." It wasn't an excuse.

I reached for my purse on the table. Matt gently grabbed my hand in protest.

"Summer, wait," he asked softly. "There's something I've been meaning to say for a while now." His serious tone was interrupted by a drunken hiccup. Knowing Matt, I wasn't sure if he was being serious or silly.

I stayed put and smiled politely. "What's up?"

He took a deep breath either to muster courage or ward off nausea.

"Seriously, what's up?" I continued beginning to get annoyed with the extended hand touching.

"Look Summer, I know you and Mick are still a thing," Matt began.

Oh god, here we go.

"But for a small period of time before you and Mick had a thing, I thought you and I had a thing."

"You mean when the two of us drunkenly hooked up my plebe year?" I reframed the context appropriately.

"That wasn't a drunk hook-up for me," he continued.

"Sure could have fooled me," I countered.

"Look Summer, I really did like you then," he explained. "and I still like you now."

I looked into his eyes. I could see the pain in them when I didn't reply. I tried to find the right way to bow out gracefully. Meanwhile Matt mistook my silence for something else. He leaned in for a kiss.

"Woah!" was the only word I could muster. Our lips touched for a brief moment. "I can't do this, Matt."

Matt backed off right away. Even though his affections were misguided and likely alcohol fueled, he was still a gentleman enough to know better. I was seeing red. I stood abruptly and made my way to the cabin door.

"Summer, shit, I'm sorry." Matt sensed the awkwardness immediately. "Look I'm really drunk and I have a feeling I'm going to feel like an ass tomorrow."

"Probably right about that one," I verified. "This," I continued, "never happened." I expressed my immediate desire to keep this quiet. Thankfully everything went down in the cabin well outside of public sight. My seething anger made a few nastier words spring to mind. I kept my mouth shut and decided I'd said enough.

"I'll see you later, Matt," was all the nicety I could muster. I wanted to punch him in the face.

Why can't I have a normal friendship with a male? Why is it that every guy I'm remotely nice to wants to hook up with me?

I left the boat as quickly as I could find my way out. My mind was racing as I stormed up Main Street. I dodged drunken pedestrians scrambling for a handful of cabs. Looking back, I could still see Matt's family yacht tied up in Ego Alley. I squeezed my eyes shut for a few seconds fighting angry tears.

Mick's dad had passed away several years ago. Even

if he hadn't, he definitely would not be motoring a yacht into Ego Alley. Lack of yachts were only the beginning of Mick's beautiful imperfections. Like me, he didn't come from a traditional family. He spent a good chunk of his childhood fatherless. His mom battled addiction. He came from meager means.

I had some random male midshipman proposition me for a date at least once a week since the moment I started plebe year classes. Occasionally I'd indulge my imagination and daydream about being with someone other than Mick.

I'd play out the full imaginary courtship. What dates I'd go on, what the relationship with my new suitor would be like. Then I'd imagine explaining why my father left my mom and think about introducing my mother and lesbian stepmom. Then I'd think about the awkward reactions and the silent judgment from the yacht club crowd and the daydream would turn to shit.

I was never embarrassed about who I was or where I came from when I was with Mick. We bonded over our non-traditional upbringings. We loved each other in spite of them and because of them. We loved each other. In a place where I was always forced to consider perception, it was good to have someone I could still be myself around.

Had an advance been a part of Matt's plan all along? It was probably just a few too many drinks around a pretty girl. Still, I hated how someone like Matt or Smokey could be my friendly professional colleague one minute and the next some hot piece of ass they met at a bar. I'm sure I wasn't the first girl Matt brought down to Ego Alley to hook up with on his dad's yacht.

I wanted to talk to Mick. I needed to speak with someone in my own voice, without the shame of being vulnerable. I wanted to tell him that I loved him. I know things between us had been fucked up this summer. I wanted to fix them. I wanted to tell him what happened with Matt and Smokey. Instead I was stuck trying to remember where I parked my car. I walked two more blocks without seeing my ride. It was getting late. It was near dawn out west. Mick was on the opposite end of the country doing god knows what on a Friday night.

And I was a total bitch the last time we spoke.

My angry tears became sad tears. They were too heavy to hold back.

Chapter 9

Love Me Two Times
Saturday, August 2nd, 1997
Summer, 1445 hrs.

A sliver of orange sunshine met my waking face. The door to my first-floor room opened directly into the parking lot. It was safely secured with a dead bolt. The curtains I thought I had closed last night were apparently not fully shut. My mind wandered to the evening before. After more closely examining the curtains, I still felt confident in my room's privacy from passing pedestrians. Then my eyes caught the trail of clothes from the door to the bed and I smiled, blushing.

I shut my eyes and stretched. Sleeping in was a rare treat in my life. I listened to the hum of the cranked-up air conditioning and cocooned my naked body more tightly under the blankets.

The Norfolk Naval Shipyard Bachelor Officer's Quarters were a temporary housing option on base for visiting officers. Whenever it had enough rooms unoccupied, the base would extend nightly rentals to midshipmen. The first thing I did when my ship returned to port was check the availability. Fifty bucks on the credit card and I had my very own room for the night.

The BOQ was no Ritz Carlton. It also wasn't quite the Motel 6, at least not the older ones. My room had a relatively new bed mattress and a private shower. It had cable television and a partially working microwave. Before last night, I had slept in a ship's berthing that felt more tuna can than bedroom. I was in heaven.

The intruding slice of sunshine reached my face once again. I deftly moved my head and body back into the shade. With my face still turned toward the curtained window, I shifted five inches towards the center of the bed. My naked body nuzzled into the warm spoon of my bedmate's. I was close enough to feel the warmth of his breath on my neck. Then I felt a hand firmly grab my hip as he pulled me in closer. I loved it when he was assertive.

He began stroking my side. His hand was warm. The breath on my neck became warmer as he drew closer. The wetness of his mouth and tongue tickled my neck in the best possible way. I soon felt warmth spread to other places.

I arched my neck and brushed away my hair. His lips hovered their way to my ear.

"Hi," he whispered.

"Hi," I replied as I turned my head towards him. Our lips connected in a deep kiss.

I reached down behind me. He was ready. He was always ready.

He flipped my body towards him and took his time. He found new places to kiss. I wrapped my arms around him. I could hear myself breathing harder.

God damn, he's sexy.

His face returned to my lips. Our hands continued

to feast on each other. I was covered by his warm body. Touches moved southward. I could feel my body craving him.

He grabbed my breast and pinned my shoulders to the mattress. It felt good to let go. I had an itch that needed to be scratched. The only problem was that the more he scratched it, the more I wanted him to. I reached downward and guided him inside of me.

"Mmm."

"Damn, I love the way that feels," he said.

I loved the way he felt on top of me. I submitted control to the moment. Our naked bodies found our instinctive rhythm.

"Oh, Mick," I purred.

******

Summer, 1630

I lay in bed while Mick showered. It was the third shower he'd taken in the last twelve hours. He told me earlier that he had gone a full week underway on the Vandegrift without a shower after a "phantom shitter" had been delivering daily gifts in the shower room. I understood his gluttony for simple luxuries.

I heard the water shut off and the shower curtain pull open. I could see Mick's naked reflection in the partially steamed bathroom mirror. I loved watching him when he didn't notice I was watching. He certainly wasn't hard on the eyes.

Despite our other relationship issues, the sex was great. Neither of us were virgins before we met, nor were either of us exactly sexually experienced. Once we figured out what we were doing together, we were able to relax and enjoy it. And enjoy it we did, lots of it, any chance we could get.

He moved left to throw his towel over the drying rack. I took in his silhouette reflected in the glass. His strong back, that ass that looked great in clothes and even better naked, I wish he wasn't leaving so soon.

Mick would be heading out in another half hour. I was meeting up with a few of my soccer teammates for dinner and a movie shortly thereafter. It was a girls' night activity. Mick understood. We'd see each other in a few weeks once the brigade reformed for the fall semester.

Pre-season soccer camp for my junior season was days away. My teammates and I were super excited about it. We took immense pride in what we were trying to build as a team. We weren't yet satisfied with what we had accomplished and I was focused on the season ahead. This could finally be the year we won the Patriot League Championship. We'd talked about it since Plebe Summer. Tonight was our last night to have a little fun before the seriousness of the season started.

I wanted my blissful feelings to last. They didn't. Seeing Mick pull on his boxers made me realize I'd soon miss my opportunity to come clean about the Hackett situation. I hated that I couldn't force myself to tell him.

I had debated telling Mick about the Hackett incident since the moment I secured my impromptu BOQ room. It infuriated me that I had to deal with the issue in the first place. Hackett had made the move on me and I rejected him. I hadn't heard from him since that night on his dad's boat. I was hardly over being steaming mad at him but that was a different fish to fry. Sitting up in bed I cringed at how awkward reform of brigade would be.

I had thought the situation through too many times to count. Telling Mick about Hackett now would only ruin the rest of our time together. He'd definitely overreact, then I'd be in soccer camp while he stewed back home on vacation. People would hear about it and somehow I'd be the one viewed as the slut. It was so fucking unfair. I'd done nothing wrong. I kicked the can down the road a little farther and promised myself I'd follow through in a few weeks.

One way or another, he's going to hear about it.

I didn't want to face the drama at the moment. Mick and I had our problems before this Hackett situation and I had a soccer season to focus on.

Besides, why look a gift horse in the mouth? Mick and I finally were able to make our schedules work. My cruise came into Norfolk a few days early and Mick was already home on the east coast for summer leave. We were physically together, temporarily a normal college couple. It was a rarity this summer. I didn't want to fuck that up.

Last night was a chance to not think about our issues. We had a nice dinner by the water in Virginia Beach and then we spent the next twenty hours rotating between sleeping and fucking each other's brains out. It was a much needed, though short-lived, escape. My vagina was pleasantly sore.

"You staying here tonight?" Mick interrupted thoughts as he threw on a shirt. He was trying to gage exactly how messy he could leave the bathroom.

"Yeah, I think so," I replied. My mind returned to the present. His messiness drove me nuts. I had no idea how he had survived two years of class alpha room inspections.

"Cool," he replied. He hopped in bed next to my naked body, still warm from the shower. He gave me a long, deep kiss. For another moment, we felt like a normal couple. We did not get that feeling nearly enough.

Mick hopped out of bed and grabbed his bag. "I'll see you in a few weeks."

"Sounds good, Micky," I said with a sweet smile. We weren't perfect, but I loved him anyway.

He leaned in for a final kiss. I was still naked. His wandering hands didn't seem to mind.

"Love you," he whispered in my ear.

"Love you too," I whispered back.

Moments later, the door closed with a thud. I had officially chickened out.

Chapter 10

Backseat
Saturday, August 9th, 1997
Mick, 8:13 p.m.

The last visible tip of sun disappeared over the Rehoboth Bay. Night was descending rapidly in Dewey Beach, Delaware. I felt the wood floor beneath my feet rock back and forth. I wasn't on a boat, I was hammered.

I sat at a lively table of four in the outdoor seating area of the Rusty Rudder. The solid stained wood exterior made the seafood restaurant and bar seem much more like a seaside shanty.

It was the early part of an August Saturday night in the middle of primo tourist season. The place was already nuts. Well over half of the fully occupied tables in our section had been drinking there since before 3 p.m. Every one of the several bars within eyesight was already two deep. A live reggae cover band playing at the Rudder was thumping the bass in their second set. It was another big August weekend in Dewey, a staple of Mid-Atlantic twenty-somethings. It seemed like everyone from D.C. to Delaware was out to have a good time.

"Here you handsome gentleman go," interjected Melanie, the cute waitress serving our table for the last several hours. She was a junior communications major at University of Delaware. She began redistributing the latest round of drinks.

"Thank you, ma'am," my friend Ed politely said with his charming smile.

My Naval Academy roommate, Samuel "Ed" Dawson, had come all the way down from upstate New York to the Delmarva shore for a few days of fun and a last hurrah ahead of brigade reform. Ed's older brother, Joe, lived in D.C. but was down at the shore visiting his boyfriend, Gary, at his beach place in Rehoboth. All four of us huddled around a table covered in empty glasses and plates. We were gulping down anything they put in front of us.

"Oh, I guess we don't need this anymore," Joe said as he began rolling down the table's umbrella.

"Will you stop?" Gary said to Joe. "I'm sure they have a process for all of that. You'll make Melanie look like she's flaking on her job."

Joe gave Gary a playful slap on the arm. "But I wanted to be able to see the stars come out. Melanie, what do you think?"

"Gary's right, there's a process, and I appreciate his sensitivities. There is however a great view out there, and I'd hate for you to miss it." Melanie kindly joked as she finished taking the umbrella down. Then I saw her slip a folded piece of paper into Ed's hand. I assumed it was her number. He often had that effect on women. He was a master swordsman.

"Atta boy, Ed!" I complimented my roomie's seemingly endless ability to score with chicks once Melanie got far away enough from the table.

"Wait a minute," Joe said. "Why do you keep calling Sam, Ed?"

It hadn't dawned on me that neither Joe nor Gary had been told about Ed's nickname back in Annapolis.

There was an awkward moment of silence.

"Oh!" Joe exclaimed. "I get it. Ed. Like Mr. Ed. Hung like a horse. How VERY clever those Navy boys are."

Ed rolled his eyes. Another awkward silence ensued.

"And they say we're the ones that are penis obsessed," joked Gary. Everyone broke into a good laugh.

Ed relaxed in his chair with the same grin he had since Melanie slipped him a note five minutes earlier. Like Melanie, most girls naturally flocked to Ed. He was the tall, dark, and handsome type. Ed was a magnetic guy. Fun followed him everywhere he went. His brother, Joe, threw off a very similar, though much gayer, vibe. By 5 p.m. our table at the Rudder felt like the center of everything going on at the Delmarva shore.

Joe was in his late twenties. He was a recent Georgetown Law grad and had stayed in D.C. as a legal associate at a big firm. Joe's boyfriend, Gary, appeared to be in his forties. From what I heard he was a hot shit heart surgeon up in D.C. His Rehoboth place alone must have been worth over a million. Both he and Joe were fun to hang out with, especially considering that neither of them would let anyone else pay for anything.

Ed had spent the last year as my roommate listening to my stories about the Delmarva shore and Dewey Beach. We had planned to catch up together out here since before the summer had even begun. Ed was doubly excited when he discovered his brother in D.C. suddenly had a much nicer place for him to crash down here.

Ed drove into town Thursday night and hung out with Joe and Gary most of Friday. He caught up with me Friday night and we crashed on the Maryland side of the Delmarva shore at my aunt's place in West Ocean City. I had his ass up at 0530 to drive over to Assateague for the only surf-able break that day.

Earlier in the day, my local buddies and I had Ed on a 12-foot single fin for his first surf session. Nobody in the water that day was more stoked to catch a knee-high mediocre ripple. We showered up around lunch and moved north. By two, we were hunkered down bayside in Dewey at the Rudder crushing rum runners with Gary and Joe.

Ed may have looked like a barney all morning long boarding down in Assateague, but the Rudder was a different story. It was much more Ed's environment.

Ed was a little older than your average college student. He had spent a few years between high school and college enlisted in the fleet followed by a stint at the Naval Academy's Prep School. He played lacrosse his first two years at the academy but quit once he knew he had no shot starting with a new underclassman taking over the coveted starting goalie position.

Ed was a junior like me yet almost twenty-four years old. Ed's lacrosse career may have been over, but he was a veteran bar-hopper. His boozing career was in its prime.

Ten drinks in to the early evening and even Ed was drinking frozen strawberry daiquiris like it was his job. If we had been partaking in such behavior two hours inland, Ed would have been the first to bust our balls. Somehow day drinking in Dewey existed under a different set of rules.

Unlike Ed I was still underage, a few months shy of my twenty-first birthday. Luckily, I didn't really need my ID in the Rudder. We had been ordering food all day, so nobody minded me sitting at the table. Joe and Ed kept on feeding me alcohol every time anyone at the restaurant wasn't looking. They'd slip a shot in my drink, or switch my non-alcoholic slushy drink with an alcoholic one. Even if our waitress Melanie had caught on by now, which based on my level of visible drunkenness was highly probable, she still looked the other way. By sundown, I was blasted. I was content to stay put for a few more hours or until they had to wheel me out, whichever came first.

"So tell me more about this Dickley character," Gary refocused the conversation we had started five minutes earlier.

"Ah man, that guy is a fucking joke," Ed replied as he described a hated member of our Naval Academy company.

"Word," I chimed in.

"Dude was our neighbor all last year. Must have turned our room in for one violation or another no less than four times," Ed continued. "The dude even got the janitors in trouble for carrying on too much during their day time shift because they were disrupting his study time."

"And don't forget spring break," I said.

"What happened over spring break?" Gary asked.

"I was stuck in the hall for lacrosse practice last season. I got the flu two days in and spent the rest of my time sick, all alone stuck in Bancroft. Being sick, I couldn't drive home on vacation like everyone else. None of my teammates wanted anything to do with the flu, so they only visited me periodically. Meanwhile Dickley, unbeknownst to me, intentionally stayed back at the Hall in his room while everyone else he thought was out of town. He even volunteered for company watch so he could hang at the academy and bone his plebe midshipman girlfriend who was home with her Commander daddy in Northern Virginia."

"Didn't you say he was some kind of bible thumper?" Gary asked.

"Yeah, so is his girlfriend. Didn't matter. His room was like Sodom and Gomorrah that whole week. They had me up all night, every night. You should hear the colorful ways that girl uses the Lord's name in vain."

"Dude, you should have just gone in there and snapped a picture really quick. That would so come in handy," I pontificated. "If you got something like that, we could bribe him to do anything we wanted."

Everyone chuckled at the suggestion. It might have sounded ridiculous if it weren't such a genius idea.

Thankfully none of this really mattered. We had already picked our rooms for the start of our junior academic year. My room from last year, Ed, N.D., and me had made a point to live as far away from Dickley as humanly possible. We picked a room on the exact opposite end of company area.

"Then there's the captain," Ed continued.

"To the captain," I raised my glass in toast.

"Wait, who the hell is the captain?" Gary asked. Joe

immediately started laughing.

"None other than Haden 'Captain America' Bilcher," Ed answered with air quotes. "I actually stole that name from a guy our dad went to school with up at West Point in the sixties."

Ed and Joe's dad was a ring knocker from that other academy up north.

"Captain America is Dickley's roommate and our other neighbor," I explained. "He's even worse than Dickley if you can imagine it."

"How so?" Gary asked.

"Well, for starters he's even more of a bible nut than Dickley. He's also much more of a dick about it," Ed replied.

"He's constantly saying inappropriate things at the table. You know, preachy, holier than thou type shit," I added. "He especially loves to do that with the plebes."

"And then, of course, he's also saying weird shit to the plebes," Ed continued.

"Like what?" asked Gary.

"Oh I don't know," I pondered. "A few weeks before graduation I overheard him tell a couple of plebe football players in the company that they were looking much more vascular these days."

"That's only half of it," Joe finally broke his silence. He couldn't resist not joining in on the fun. "These guys told me stories that would blow your mind, Gary. No doubt this guy is secretly hanging out at Remington's on the weekends."

"What's Remington's?" I asked.

Joe laughed. "Just an extremely gay honkytonk line

dancing joint in South Capital, D.C. The type of place where people dress up to play a little cowboys and Indians."

"Sounds about right," I laughed.

******

Mick, 0450

"Who got that pussy?"

"Mmmmm, I got that pussy right here."

"Who got that pussy?"

"Oh, I got it, I got that pussy."

"Who got THAT PUSSAYYYYYY?"

"Oh, oooooh, oh yeah!" echoed from a female silhouette bouncing up and down in the backseat. I could see her ponytail bobbing up and down in the rearview.

I sat motionless in the front seat. My head was resting atop the steering wheel *Club* anti-theft device. My eyes were facing the rearview mirror. I had been passed out in the same exact position when I was woken up by the commotion moments earlier.

I continued watching from my front-leaning position in the driver's seat. I would occasionally see Ed's forehead as his partner bounced all over his naked lap.

Ed must have rolled down the side and rear covers of the Jeep's soft top while I was passed out in the front. Each plastic window of the soft top was steamed with body heat. It was a feeble attempt at privacy. Anyone within a half a block could tell what was going on in the backseat.

Ed and I had split up a few hours earlier. By 3 a.m. everyone walking the streets of Dewey was looking to fight or fuck. Given my reconciliation with Summer, I decided to not push my luck. Ed understood. I drunkenly crashed in the Jeep Ed had stashed on Van Dyke St. while he chased ass a few blocks away at an afterhours house party.

I maintained my silence in the Jeep as any good wingman would, pretending I was still passed out. The smelly mixture of sweat, pussy, alcohol, and pine tree air freshener permeated the Jeep's interior. Ed needed a few more of those fresheners, the two already there weren't doing much.

My eyes clenched shut as I hoped they'd finish up soon, and that his sword was adequately sheathed. I tried my best not to laugh at the dirty talk happening. I wasn't about to ignore it. Instead I took careful mental note of every word for future ball busting. I was getting golden material.

"Mmmmm, oh yeah, fuck me, fuck me, fuck my ass, fuck my ass, FUCK MY ASS!" she continued coaching Ed along.

"You want me to fuck you in the ass?" Ed countered in drunken confusion. He sounded like a tax accountant asking for W2 information.

"What, WAIT, just fuck my ass," she said panting in drunken sexual ecstasy. "Wait, no. I mean, just fuck me. Fuck ME! Oh yeah. OH, YEEAAAAAAAHHHHHH!!!!"

The Jeep continued to rock. I prayed to God that no cops were willing to patrol this far south in Dewey this late at night. I had no idea what time it was. If I checked my watch, the two love birds would know that I was up. It was still early enough in the new day to be completely dark.

Ten more bounces, two more moans, and finally the

loud conclusion. I made mental note to never sit in the backseat of this Jeep ever again. Three minutes of wrestling clothes on and I could hear fake phone numbers being exchanged. She hopped out of the door-less passenger side over top the pulled down front passenger seat.

Typical Dewey, typical fucking Ed.

I waited a few more minutes. Eventually the sound of my previous Jeep mate's flip flops faded off in the distance.

"Looks like you found what you were looking for," I whispered once I was convinced that Ed's latest conquest was far enough away from the Jeep.

"Fuck that chick throws back leg like a La-Z-Boy recliner," he replied. "She was an older divorcée that knew what she wanted. We were in the shrubs for a bit before eventually making our way to the Jeep."

"This type of shit only happens to you, dude," I said with a level of amazement.

"If it's got four wheels, I'll drive it. If it has two legs, I'll ride it."

"You're a filthy dude," I said with a chuckle.

"How much of that did you hear?" he asked in piqued curiosity.

"Don't worry," I assured him. "Only the best parts."

"Fuck!" he replied. Then we both burst out laughing hysterically.

"Dude, I almost lost it when you guys started talking asses," I said.

I looked down at my watch. It was a quarter passed 5 a.m. I smiled as I grabbed my backpack stashed in the front seat. There was a sweatshirt and a towel stuffed in there. It was finally late enough in the morning where

I could safely grab some shut eye on the beach without getting arrested by the cops or nipped by a ghost crab. I stumbled as I exited the Jeep, catching my balance and taking a deep breath. Neither helped my building nausea. I was definitely still drunk and felt like hell.

"I'm gonna go crash on the beach," I yelled towards the Jeep. "You cool here?"

"Yeah dawg, I'm cool," he assured me his current backseat position suited him fine. Once his date left the Jeep he curled up under a blanket. Ed could sleep just about anywhere with just about anyone.

"Alright man, come grab me in a few hours," I said to Ed. "Once we sober up enough to drive we can shoot up to my aunt's place in Ocean City and grab a quick nap before heading to Annapolis."

Our summer break was officially over later today when all midshipmen were to report to Bancroft by 6 p.m. to start the new school year.

"Mick!" Ed yelled from the Jeep. I had already turned to make my way to the beach.

"Yo!" I yelled in return, trying hard not to barf my late-night pancake snack rumbling in my unsettled stomach.

"Dewey is fucking A'IGHT, dawg!"

I smiled and made my way to a sandy bed. It was almost comical that we'd be back for evening meal formation in about twelve hours.

Part IV

Welcome Home (Sanitarium)

Chapter 11

Juicy
Monday, September 1st, 1997
Summer, 1802 hrs.

"At EASE!" ordered the 6th company's new Company Commander, Midshipman 1/C Jeremy Dolby. The order echoed down the dead silent hallway.

Relaxed, I itched the scratch that had been bothering me throughout our previous minutes affixed at attention. I didn't have the luxury of being hidden in formation like my first two years of evening formation. I was now front and center as the new company Platoon Sergeant, the highest ranking 2/C midshipman in the company. I stood front and center, a few feet away from Dolby at the head of our three platoon formation.

"Alright company, listen UP!" Dolby continued as everyone eased out of their stance of attention. Three platoons of three squads with about a dozen mids per squad relaxed but stayed within their designated squad area.

Dolby ran through a few announcements to a fully assembled version of our 6th company. He kept it brief and spared us the typical ra-ra shit. I was gracious for the brevity. My legs were still aching from another brutally hard soccer preseason camp. I couldn't wait to get out of uniform and relax in the privacy of my own room.

The full brigade had only been reformed in Annapolis for a few weeks but we were already back into the full swing of things. By now my '99 classmates and I were well past signing our two for seven commitment. Uncle Sam officially owned our asses into the next millennium.

I felt a puppy dog stare from my left, Matt Hackett had a habit of doing that lately. I caught him with a disapproving glare. He looked away and played it off. I had been avoiding him like the plague since reform a few weeks earlier.

I still couldn't look at Matt without being angry about the boat fiasco. I hated that I had to share simultaneous space with Hackett and Mick so often in daily military obligations. It reminded me of the uncomfortable story I had yet to tell Mick.

"Hey, BUCKLE IT UP!" Dickley scowled down the line of plebes in his squad. He had spent all of August lighting up plebes at every opportunity. It seemed he decided that his Plebe Summer detailer role would simply extend through the rest of the year.

Dickley wasn't helping my cause. Mick was already in enough of a foul mood. Not only were he and Dickley squad mates this semester, they were once again neighbors. Mick's room found out at reform that Dickley and his toolshed roommate Captain America would be their neighbors for the second year in a row.

When we all checked in from summer break, Dickley's original room had a pipe leak. One of the two youngsters that was supposed to live next to Mick had gotten kicked out of the academy for some trouble he got into over summer cruise. They bunked the solo man left behind into an existing two-man room. They gave Dickley and his roommate Haden "Captain America" Bilcher their room.

Mick sported an utter look of disgust every time Dickley opened his big fat mouth. There was no way I'd be telling Mick my "boat kissing" stories tonight. I resolved to yet again chicken out.

Despite his Dickley angst, Mick and I had finally found a partial hiatus in arguing over our love chit issues. The newness of returned physical proximity, and the blushing joy it created, happily didn't give us much time to talk. With soccer and school in full gear, I welcomed the oasis of a temporarily drama-free relationship. I didn't care what potential false pretenses it stood upon.

I actively looked for a distraction from my boy ponderings. I returned my attention to Dolby's announcements. I knew that Mick would retain at best ten percent of evening formation's announcements. He'd be asking me about them twenty minutes from now back in my room. It drove me nuts.

But damn is he cute.

Announcements transitioned from the Company Commander to out into the platoons.

"Welcome back from the weekend, shipmates," said 1/C Holmes, the company wardroom officer. "I wanted to remind everyone that I'll be collecting wardroom dues all week. I listed what everyone owes per class. ATM is down the stairs. No excuses."

The announcements shifted from first platoon to second platoon.

*

"Hey guys," 1/C Foster, the company training officer chimed in. "Wanted to let everyone know that the week's military training schedule was emailed out at 1530 yesterday. If you've already deleted it, I did everyone a favor and printed it out. It's posted on the company bulletin board. All sessions will have recorded attendance, including the Thursday night Forrestal Lecture. Be there or be fried."

Everyone in the company winced. We knew damn well that attendance was always recorded for required training and lectures. We all hated being reminded of it, especially from a dick like Foster.

The announcements shifted to third squad. A few more firsties pestered us about a myriad of required military obligations filling our abbreviated work week ahead.

"Hey, I've got a couple of announcements," blurted out Captain America. "First of all, whichever plebes painted that transom at the end of the P-way, it looks like friggin' trash. I can't tell if the picture painted up there is Wolverine or Tweety Bird. You can just report to my room after formation for extra instruction."

Everyone in the company collectively groaned. That evil elf loved complaining about plebes publicly. It was his official hobby.

"Second announcement, if anyone out there is the person that stole my Big Mac out of the fridge last night, I hope you enjoyed it." He continued, "And oh yeah, that special sauce, it wasn't special sauce if you catch my drift."

The company all let out a groan in disgust. Mick and Ed routinely stole leftover fast food out of the shared wardroom fridge, especially if they knew it was Captain's.

Luckily for Mick he had been home surfing over the

long weekend while I was tied up at practice. Mick had no opportunity for a weekend fridge raid. I shifted my eyes a platoon over to Ed. He looked green.

Poor fucker.

Chapter 12

Fight Fire with Fire
Monday, September 1st, 1997
Mick, 2130 hrs.

"Fuck man, no way Hamerlick scores that goal in real life," I steamed in anger. "This game is total fucking BULLSHIT!"

I pounded the wall with my fist three times as a way to vent my frustration. I had blown a four-goal lead in the third period as Team Canada was relinquished by Team Czech Republic in a PlayStation hockey game.

My roommates and I lacked any particular urgency in our unpacking process. We'd almost been moved into Bancroft an entire month and we were still only about halfway unpacked. We did however make sure that our video game system was set up on the first day. Since midshipmen were not permitted to have televisions in their room, much less video game systems, our entire set up was illegally stored in my con-locker. We chose my con-locker because it was hidden from our room's entrance behind the corner. That was particularly important now that we were neighbors with Dickley and Captain again.

As soon as the game finished my company mate Jimmy Jarvis went into my con-locker. Beneath the illegally stashed television and PlayStation was my guitar. I had tried learning a few chords over vacation and wanted to continue the pursuit in Bancroft. Jarvis had no such interest. Instead, he grabbed the axe and started strumming out an impromptu song.

"You're my biiiiiiiiiiiiiiiiiiiiiiiiiiiiitch!" he sang with gusto while violently strumming the chords. "You're my biiii iiiiiiiiiiiiiiiiiiiiiiiiitch!"

"Unheard of, man, unheard of," N.D. interrupted the guitar solo with a smirk.

"What's that supposed to mean?" I asked my roommate as my blood pressure slowly returned to normal.

"Yo man, I thought people that PLAYED hockey were crazy," N.D. said.

"Dawg, not nearly as crazy as people playing hockey video games," N.D.'s football teammate Ezekiel "EZ" James said.

We all had a good laugh at that notion. I knew EZ from high school. He had played football at Decatur with a few of my surfing buddies. EZ also lived a floor below us in seventh company with a few other Navy football teammates. EZ and N.D. were particularly tight. EZ was our unofficial fourth roommate. I didn't mind, everyone in the room loved him.

"Later man," Jarvis lifted his hand walking out of the room.

"Rematch tomorrow, fucker," I said as he left. "That win was pure fucking luck!"

He flipped me the bird before the door closed behind him.

"Yo man, can EZ and I get a game of NCAA football?" N.D. asked as he pulled the game disk out of his personal desk cabinet.

"Sure, man," I replied handing over the controllers.

"I got Florida State this game, dawg," N.D. called dibs as he flipped disc one of Tupac's All Eyez on Me into our stereo system. It had become our room's official sound track, we'd heard the double CD at least thirty times in the last week alone.

"No sweat," replied EZ bobbing his head to Pac's menacing rhymes. "I'll whoop your ass with Navy."

"Shit, I'll be burning #9 up and down the field all game," N.D. countered. He was referring to EZ, who as a new starter at safety for Navy's football team, had finally had his digital image rendered into that year's version of the PlayStation game. The game used numeric proximities of the slated starters for the season.

"That six speed rating is some buuuuullshit, man," EZ complained about the digital athleticism programmed into the video game version of himself.

"Prove that shit on Friday, dawg. You still got next year's game," N.D. looked over at EZ with a smile.

Navy's actual football season kicked off a few days later on Friday on the road against San Diego State. They were flying out on Thursday morning.

"Come on then, let's ball," EZ said as he focused his intensity into the forthcoming digital tilt.

"Man, I'm clownin', dawg," N.D. said, feeling bad about trash-talking his own teammate.

"Easy for you to say," EZ laughed it off. "Digital version of number ninety-nine is a damn BEAST!"

"So is the real one though," N.D. said.

"You guys playing or you gonna talk about the game for the next hour?" I coaxed them along. I wanted to get one more practice game of hockey in before bed. I'd be damned if I was going to lose to Jarvis again this week.

The sink started running again as Ed obsessively brushed his teeth for the third time. Though he never admitted it to us, N.D. and I knew he was still scrubbing out the notion of Captain America's special sauce. We avoided asking about or even mentioning the topic. I even held off complaining about him borrowing my newly procured boxers without asking because as usual he forgot to send his weekly laundry out on time. Clean laundry tended to disappear without a trace in our room.

That was our room's dynamic. We were all friends. We all looked out for each other and tried not to complain too much about one another. N.D. and I had lived together since Plebe Summer. Ed moved in last year.

Ed was part of the 9th company shotgun. After the class of '99's plebe year, the academy decided to consolidate its thirty-six companies down to thirty. The midshipmen in the lowest ranking company within each of USNA's six battalions were dispersed evenly amongst the five remaining companies within said battalion. At the start of last year, Ed and three of his classmates joined our 6th company.

N.D. and I lost our initial third room member, Gonzo, mid-way through plebe year. Gonzo left voluntarily after getting me entangled in a major disciplinary infraction. He took off and I was left behind with sixty days of restriction, one hundred demerits, and a famed Black N letter sweater. The Black N was awarded to any mid receiving maximum disciplinary punishment without getting thrown out. N.D. had earned one on his own in a separate incident a few months before mine. As for Gonzo, I hadn't seen or spoken to him since the day he left the academy unannounced. I'd be happy if that trend continued forever.

Ed stepped in youngster year. I had never met Ed before he joined the company, but N.D. knew him from some of his Naval Academy Prep School alumni on the football team. He fit in immediately.

Ed was the wild one of the room, but he was great at not getting caught. He was practically bullet proof. N.D. and I were relatively well-behaved mids, but we had also both earned Black Ns plebe year. Company leadership thought that putting an older prior enlisted in with us might be a good influence. That notion was laughable to anyone that actually knew Ed.

Ed was a disaster academically, barely passing the 2.0 GPA standard required to graduate. It wasn't that Ed was stupid, he basically never studied and skipped class often. N.D. and I did well academically and generally tried to lay low and out of trouble. We were by no means "dig-its" but hardly anarchist "dirt bags." I spent most of my non-Navy time with Summer. We all had a really good situation in terms of Naval Academy existence, but we still bitched and moaned about it every opportunity we could.

Ed spit his mouthful of toothpaste into the sink. He sulked over to his computer desk without saying a word. The typically gregarious and laid-back personality was replaced with a rare look of stewing vengeance.

Suddenly, the door swung open again. Instead of Jarvis it was our good friend Dickley. As soon as I saw his goofy looking head, I immediately swung my con-locker door shut. In hiding our room's makeshift arcade, I completely screwed EZ and N.D.'s game. The last thing I needed was Dickley ratting out my room for our contraband. He was the type of guy that would snitch on his own mother if it scored him brownie points with the higher-ups. N.D. was already down two touchdowns. He wasn't complaining.

"What's up, gang?" he entered the room like he owned the place. He was acting as though we were excited that he was our neighbor again, like we suddenly forgot all of the shit he pulled on us last year. He was every bit as socially inept with his classmates as he was with the plebes. We hated Dickley every bit as much as the plebes did.

"Hey Bickley, what's up?" N.D. replied in his typical calm manner, again trying to keep the peace. I ignored Dickley while Ed continued to stew in front of his computer.

"Hey Mick, I heard you mention a big party this weekend. Mind if Haden and I come along?" he asked.

Where the fuck does he get the balls asking about that?

I looked over silently while my mind rifled through a whole list of excuses to select from. "Not my party, man. Can't really give away invites," I said. It was the best excuse I could come up with.

"Dawg, you didn't hear?" Ed interrupted before I had a chance to expand the rationale of my made-up excuse. "That house party got postponed but there is a big party going down in a D.C. dance club to replace it."

"What big party?" Dickley asked with genuine intrigue.

Ed scribbled something on a post-it note and handed it to Dickley.

"The Cowboys and Indians throw down," he said as he handed off the note.

"Cowboys and Indians party?" Dickley replied in curiosity reading the note. "What's that all about?"

"You know, a cool party at a cowboy bar in D.C. Costumes, booze, hot chicks. It's going down 10 p.m. this Saturday night at that club," Ed replied, pointing to the post-it stuck to Dickley's right thumb.

"Hmm, sounds cool," Dickley said with surprise in his voice. N.D. and I tried to be civil to Dickley most of the time, but Ed was never this nice.

"639 Pennsylvania Avenue, South East," he verbally instructed what I assumed was scribbled on the post it note. "Place called Remington's. It's a few blocks from the Capitol Building in D.C."

That was the first I had heard that the upcoming Saturday off campus house party had been cancelled. Ed was full of surprises today. N.D. and I continued staring silently in disbelief. It was as though we had entered the Twilight Zone. Maybe Captain America's sperm sauce had infected his brain.

Dickley took the note and was on his way. "Thanks guys, we're looking forward to it. This year is going to be so kick ass!"

"Don't forget the costumes," Ed reminded Dickley. "They won't let you in without them."

I waited a few seconds after the door closed. Then I walked to the door and opened it immediately to ensure

Dickley wasn't eavesdropping outside.

"Dude, what the FUCK was that all about?" I asked once I reassured myself I could safely interrogate Ed about what happened. I stopped short of reminding Ed about the Big Mac situation.

"Don't get your panties in a ruffle, Micky," Ed smiled softly and chuckled. He broke out a tin of wintergreen Kodiak dip and stuffed a large pinch into his mouth. Then he reached into the garbage and found an empty plastic Coke bottle to spit in. He walked back to his desk and continued tooling on the internet.

"The house party is still going down," he assured us before spitting into the bottle.

"And where are Dickley and Captain America heading to?" N.D. asked with the same level of curiosity of my own.

Ed spit again and revealed a shit-eating grin. "Let's just say I sent our friends on a little weekend field trip."

Chapter 13

Say It Ain't So
Monday, September 8th, 1997
Mick, 0630 hrs.

"Reveille, reveille, all hands heave out and trice up. It is now reveille," I heard the muffled intercom system announce through my closed room door. I pulled my pillow over my head to muffle the sound and rolled over.

I had exactly twenty minutes before I had to scramble into a uniform and make it to formation. Upperclassmen weren't permitted to stay in their bed past reveille but thankfully non-compliance was rarely enforced. The poor plebes were not so lucky.

"Sir, Midshipmen fourth class Speneti, Walker, and Smith reporting for come around, sir." I heard a few plebes in my squad announce after they knocked on my neighbors' door. They were all showing up for what I assumed was a Dickley-mandated Monday morning flame session. I could hear them lining up around our door.

Most of my classmates would at least wait until Monday morning formation to mess with plebes. No such luck when dealing with Dickley and Captain America.

Poor fucking bastards.

I could hear the door next door aggressively open.

"Good FRICKING morning, plebers! How are ya'll doing this fine Navy morning?" Captain announced his entrance into the passageway.

"Sir outstanding, sir," they mumbled their expected response to the completely disingenuous question in unison. I could barely hear their side of the muffled dialogue through our shut door.

"Bull crap, NOT MOTIVATED ENOUGH!" Captain America replied. I could hear him loud and clear through my closed door. He was spun up like a windup toy.

"SIR OUTSTANDING, SIR!" they replied in a more motivated manner.

Ed's retaliation for the Big Mac had gone even better than expected. A few youngsters that had been eyewitness to the duos' Saturday night return gave us blow by blow details in the wardroom last night. Captain, with Dickley in chase, came storming up the stairs in before midnight bed check. He was overheard wildly flailing his arms and loudly yelling about society, the devil, and overcoming the sexual advances of a three-hundred-pound African American man dressed like Tonto.

"How about one more time to wake up my neighbors," Dickley said loudly. This time he cracked open our door to let the volume in. The academy required that all doors remain unlocked.

"SIR OUTSTANDING, SIR!" they replied again.

"Fuck dude," Ed mumbled from the top-bunk, half-asleep. He rolled over and put a pillow over his head. Even his anger toward Captain America's secret sauce prank couldn't drag his ass out of bed on Monday morning. He was hungover from his weekend of drinking a tub full of yucca, a lemonade vodka concoction literally mixed in a bath tub. It always amazed me how he could roll in a drunken, tattered-clothed disaster before Sunday evening meal formation then somehow survive formation and find a way to be functional by Monday morning.

N.D.'s bunk was vacant and already made. He was up and out at the football facilities receiving treatment on the ankle he had sprained during the previous weekend's varsity football game.

A few more intentionally loud narrations and I had had enough. I stormed off my mattress and scrambled to find a shirt and shorts so I wouldn't be screaming at Dickley in my underwear. By the time I reached my door's threshold I could already hear him laying into his plebes.

"So you're telling me the primary mission of an F-14 Tomcat is for submarine hunting?" I could hear his pious rambling. "Mav and Goose, flying around hunting for Red October, huh Speneti?"

"Sir, no sir," Speneti replied in a sheepish manner. He was getting his morning serving of shit sandwich before breakfast.

Hearing their condescendence made my blood pressure rise. It only compounded the rage of being out of bed before 0645.

I opened the door aggressively and gave Dickley my best "what the fuck" face.

"Oh, Mr. McGee, how kind of you to join our come around. Funny seeing you out of bed at this hour."

"Don't touch our door again," I confronted my unpleasant wakeup call in a low, dark tone. I turned on my heel and made my way over to my rack. I made three steps' progress before hearing a response through the closing door.

"Oh, you mean you now plan to get up on time without being told. Good for you, Mr. McGee," Captain America responded with the exact same tone he gave his plebes.

I stopped in my tracks. I was tempted to respond. I stood there in silence, debating the notion of being the bigger man. I had done so for most of last year, but it was wearing on me. Ever since being fried plebe year with a Black N, I pretty much had to act on my best behavior in fear of ultimately getting kicked out for another offense. The douchebags outside the door weren't worth it.

In my contemplation I eavesdropped on the training session outside my door.

"Oh my FRICKING GOD, Speneti!" Dickley continued laying into the unfortunate plebe. "You're now telling me that the F-14 Tomcat launches Trident Missiles?"

Admittedly Speneti was a clueless plebe, but the F-14 wasn't even a required topic of study this week. Dickley was pressing Speneti's lack of knowledge for public shaming. It was the same type of shit I saw our upper-class do to him when he was a plebe.

Can't stop the cycle of abuse.

"Alright Speneti, I'm sick of you," Dickley continued his tirade. "You're all hosed up. Go over there and bring back that loving feeling to the gedunk machine."

I continued my silent observation. I couldn't help but listen in. I could hear Speneti sounding off and squaring his corners. He must have been heading to the snack machine directly across the hall.

"You never close your eyes," I could hear Speneti rattling off the first verse of the Isley Brother's You Lost That Loving Feeling.

I had officially heard enough. I opened the door and made my way out into the hallway.

"Mr. Bickley, can I talk to you for a second?" I asked sternly. I tried hard to maintain a level of military professionalism in front of the plebes. It was difficult.

"That's okay, Mr. McGee," Dickley responded. "Anything you have to say you can share with this group."

"Seriosuly, man?" I replied in disgust. I could hear Speneti continuing his serenade to bags of potato chips. He began the second verse.

"We're all friends here, please share," Dickely prodded my outrage.

"Fine," I said with a huff. "For starters, why are you grilling plebes about Naval Aviation when that's not even the professional topic of the week?"

"This is the NAVAL ACADEMY. I'm asking NAVY questions to prepare future NAVAL OFFICERS," Dickley defended his off-curriculum grilling of plebes.

"How exactly is Speneti learning to be a Naval Officer then?" I gestured toward the snack machine, acknowledging the ridiculousness of the ordered vocal performance.

"I don't know, McGee, maybe it will help him pick up chicks," Captain America replied.

"Oh yeah, like you two are the authority on that!" I couldn't help myself from escalating this into something personal. "How was that cowboy bar this weekend? I bet you picked up a ton of chicks there."

I could see Captain America's face turn beet red.

"You know what?" Dickley asked. "You're right, McGee. We could all use a little help picking up chicks these days."

Dickley stepped away from the door and assumed a more confrontational position in front of me. I could tell that I had gotten under his skin.

Mission accomplished.

"Speaking of picking up chicks, you should really talk to Hackett. He had all sort of success during Plebe Summer. I mean with Summer. I mean with Summer during Plebe Summer. Oh heck, you know what I mean!"

I didn't know what he meant. My mind was scrambling to figure it out.

"No Dickley, what the FUCK does that mean?" I replied throwing military decorum out of the window. The plebes' eyes widened as they could sense they were going to get more than they paid for in this morning training session.

I felt a hand firmly grab my arm and pull me back in the room. It was Ed. I guess he had finally risen from bed when he heard me go out in the hall.

"Dude, so not worth it, man," he tried to keep me calm and out of the hall. He knew I was inches away from clocking one my neighbors with my fist.

"What the fuck is that motherfucker talking about?" I replied. I attempted to wrestle out of Ed's grip. He pulled me further into our room and away from the hallway confrontation.

"Who cares? It's Dickley we're talking about. Everybody knows he's a fucking joke," he continued talking down my attempts to free myself from his grasp behind our closed door. He wasn't quite as strong as N.D., but he was no pushover.

"I know he's a joke, but what's with that Summer shit?" I asked. I ceased trying to get free. "What the fuck is he talking about?"

"Who knows? He's probably talking out of his ass. Why don't you just ask Summer. It's likely some made up bullshit to begin with," he continued.

"Yeah, we'll find out, won't we," I said as I calmed myself. I was still breathing heavily in anger.

"Come on, dawg, we have formation in ten minutes. Fuck those two dicks out there. They're still all torqued up from their gay line dancing escapades this weekend."

My chuckle overcame my menacing scowl. The thought of Dickley and Captain America square dancing in costume was too damn funny not to cheer me up a little. Ed felt confident enough to let go of my arm. He gave me a friendly tap on the shoulder.

I'll figure out this Summer shit soon enough.

******

Mick, 2100 hrs.

"Did you hook up with him?" I asked. I had been in Summer's room for precisely eight seconds. I spent all day waiting for her to get back to Bancroft. She recently returned from getting treatment on her left hamstring that she strained at a soccer game a few days before. She had spent the rest of the day in class and over at the soccer facilities breaking down game film. In the meantime, I stewed over what I had heard from Dickley earlier in the morning.

"Hook up with who? What are you talking about?" Summer replied. She was her normal low-key self. I guess the rumor mill hadn't swirled its way to her from Dickley's come around. If she did know, she was doing a good job playing dumb about it.

"Hackett, this summer," I responded with additional detail. I tried hard to control the tone of voice.

I could tell that I struck a chord. She broke eye contact before re-engaging as soon as I mentioned Hackett.

"Hackett?" she replied. "No, I most certainly did NOT hook up with Matt Hackett this summer."

"No?" I asked.

"No," she countered.

"You seem pretty sensitive about it," I countered.

"Mick, I got in a fight at practice with some bitch plebe trying to be a practice all-American. Tried to slide tackle me in a half field scrimmage. We have a big game coming up. I'm way behind on my homework. I'm a little spun up right now," she explained.

"So you're saying nothing happened with you and Hackett?" I continued pressing. I had to know the truth.

"Mick, I don't understand. What would give you the idea that I hooked up with Matt Hackett?"

"DICKLEY would give me that fucking idea. He told me and all of his plebes at his come around this morning about how we should learn how to pick up chicks from Hackett given what a great job he did with you this summer."

Summer's face turned red. I'd seen the hue before. She was angry. She stared at me with a scowl. I couldn't tell if she was going to start crying or punch me.

"Fucking ASSHOLE!" she broke an awkward silence. "That prick Dickley has no business talking shit in front of plebes, or ANYONE for that matter. My personal life should be none of their business."

"But it is MY business," I interjected. "So what's with his story?"

She looked away again. It wasn't like her to back off. She was initially going to say something along the lines of "It IS NOT your business." She bit her tongue. I could tell despite her anger she did not want to fight. "It's nothing," she said. "I promise."

"What the FUCK does that mean?" I asked. Veering away from a good fight was not typically Summer's style.

"It means it's nothing," Summer replied less patiently.

Summer walked over to her bed without saying a word. She sat down and stared across the room refusing to look my way.

"Well if it's anything more than a no, then it's not nothing," I verbally jabbed. "It sounds a lot like something."

I walked over to her. I wasn't ready to let this go. I drew closer. I could now see tears filling her eyes. My heart rate escalated.

"Shut the door, sit down," she said in a crackling voice. "We need to talk."

"No thanks," I said coldly. "I'll stand."

She stood up in a huff and closed the door.

I knew Summer's roommate would be tied up in her boyfriend's room in the fourth wing "studying" for weapon's engineering class the rest of the night. Dating midshipmen were keenly aware of their roommates' various routines. Hooking up in each other's rooms was so much more convenient than sneaking around the yard. I knew for a fact that Sarah wouldn't be back until at least 10:30. Summer and I were most certainly not going to hook up tonight. There was no reason for getting the closed-door treatment other than my worst suspicions.

"Look, Mick," she started and then buried her face into her hands. It was a very uncharacteristic posture for her considering her normal overflowing perky confidence. She lifted her face after composing herself.

"I'm all ears," I replied impatiently.

Summer took another deep breath, wiped her new tears, and continued. "On the last night of Plebe Summer a few of the company detailers went out for drinks. I joined but didn't drink. There were a bunch of us out. Even Matt's dad and a bunch of old alumni were out with us. One of them was a creepy old colonel that hit on me, but that's an entirely different story. Hackett and I took off together, partially to get away from the Colonel, and partially to lose Dickley. We ended up on Matt's boat trying to ditch them both."

"So that's where Dickley got his story?" I said. I could feel my heart beat lowering to normal levels.

"I don't know. I guess. I never saw Dickley otherwise the rest of the summer. He took a piss at McGarvey's and Hackett and I bolted. I didn't see either of them again until reform."

I went over and sat next to Summer. I felt bad that I doubted her integrity. She was one of the prettiest girls on the yard. It wasn't the first time someone had made up some bullshit story about her social life. Each subsequent instance only compounded her anger.

She rubbed more tears from her face. They hadn't stopped falling. Summer was still upset.

"Fuck Dickley," I said. "I'll make sure Karma pays him a visit."

It didn't seem to help Summer's mood. Her face returned to her hands as she continued to cry.

"That's not the whole story," she said from between her hands with a sniffle.

I sat more upright and pulled my arm from behind her.

"What?" I asked.

"Hackett, he was drunk. When we got on the boat, he kept drinking. Mick, he was wasted. He tried to hook up with me and I said no. That was it," she explained. "He backed off right away. He hasn't even spoken to me to this day because I think he's still embarrassed. There was no way anybody saw it. Hackett was so loaded, he was just being a drunk ass as usual."

I sat in silence.

"Did you kiss him?" I asked.

"No," she replied.

"You're telling me your lips didn't touch his?" I stood, looking down at her.

"He tried to kiss me and caught me off guard. He was drunk. Yes our lips touched. No, I did not kiss him," she stared straight ahead and explained rapidly without making eye contact. She stopped her teary explanation midsentence. She looked up at me. "Who the FUCK are you? The kiss police?" she asked. Her sad tone switched to angry.

"Who the fuck am I?" I replied while standing up aggressively. "I'm your fucking boyfriend!" I said as I made my way towards the door, my own anger building.

She stood up with equal urgency and moved toward me. She was as emotionally confused as I was.

I did an about face back towards her, sensing her chase. "You know, you could have fucking told me," I said.

"I DID want to tell you. This summer, when were together in Norfolk," she explained herself as she grabbed my arm.

I pulled out of Summer's grasp and continued to move toward her door. "Instead I have to find out about it from fucking Dickley!"

She was probably telling the truth about everything. I trusted Summer. She was fair, even in our most heated arguments, but at the moment I didn't care. She had hooked up with Hackett plebe year and that knowledge still stung. Maybe he still had feelings for her. Perhaps she still had feelings for him. I certainly didn't want to deal with such a debate, especially not company-mates.

"Dickley doesn't know what the hell he's talking about. He's making shit up because he's a dick that woke up on the wrong side of the bed," she rationalized, "like every other fucking morning."

Her argument didn't hinder my heated exit. I opened the door. She grabbed my arm again. Our argument was veering into the hallway.

"He must know something, because his bullshit isn't all BULLSHIT," I explained. I refused to lower my voice. The whole company would eventually know about this shit from my argument with Dickley. Summer must have been completely immersed in her soccer season, because she was probably the only person in the company that hadn't heard the rumors about her yet.

Summer remained at the threshold. Even in anger she was smart enough to maintain discretion. "This is EXACTLY why I wanted you to get a love chit," she explained. Her voice struggled to remain quiet as I continued walking. She reluctantly left her door's threshold as I kept walking the hundred yards back to my room down the middle of the P-way.

"Whatever," I said dismissing her counterarguments.

"Whatever?" She quickened her walk to catch my hurried pace. She moved from behind me in chase to directly blocking my path. "WHATEVER!?" her voice tone escalated but remained appropriately hushed. The hallway wasn't crowded, but she knew that plenty would pay attention if the argument became too public.

"Mick, you see everyone around here? They don't give a shit about you. You could go be like Ed and fuck every female mid in Bancroft and they'd treat you like a king."

"So why don't YOU go get that love chit?" I asked.

I knew the topic of a love chit was an unresolved argument that continued endlessly on repeat. We'd had this argument at least fifty times over the past year. The question was rhetorical. We both knew our own answers. Summer gave hers again anyway.

"Yeah, that's the way to get a more anonymous life. Move to a new company where over a hundred horny guys know the reason I moved there in the first place was because I decided to fuck a mid in my old company," she replied. I had heard the argument before.

I rolled my eyes and side stepped right to get Summer out of my path. I didn't need to continue this argument any further, it never ended anywhere good. I didn't want to leave the company either. "We're done here," I coldly answered.

"Yeah, I guess so," she said.

I wasn't sure if she meant the argument or our relationship.

"Yeah, I guess so too." I wasn't sure which one I meant either.

Part V

C.R.E.A.M.

Chapter 14

Wherever I May Roam
Wednesday, October 15th, 1997
Bird, 1:55 p.m.

The building ocean power pushed each new set of waves forward with greater power than the last. I felt the wind die down a little. Things could still clean up, I could feel it. I was completely alone, not a Bunkie in sight.

Come on, I know you got something left.

It had been a light hurricane season for the Outer Banks. In September, Erika's category 3 force missed the Carolinas entirely. October brought an early Tropical Storm Fabian and we were within hours of Tropical Storm Grace hitting land.

I had been living out of my car for nine days between October's two storm fronts. I was hanging in town one last day for likely the season's last decent swell.

Two years earlier I had taken on a drug deal that forced me to leave my home break and my family. It also estranged me from my cousin Mick, who was more like a brother than cousin to me. That was a few hours north, up in Ocean City, Maryland. I'd been bouncing around the coast living like a gypsy ever since. I hadn't seen Ocean

City or Mick since the winter of '95.

A low profile was an entire lifestyle unto itself. Sometimes that meant renting a basement room twenty miles inland. Sometimes I lived out of my car. I never lived in the same place more than a few months. I spent as many summer and fall months in the Outer Banks as I could, trying my best to stay around the ocean while the waves were still good. When the ocean was too cold for my balls' standards, I'd find my way to snow-covered mountains for a minimum wage job and free lift tickets. I lived to ride, and hide.

In moments my quiet surfing life would be over for another season of snow duty. I hoped the ocean would reward my patience one more time this surf season. I kept my eyes fixed on the horizon.

One more good wave.

A big set of three waves came screaming in. I pulled up late on the last wave of the set and barely made it safely to the other side. I tasted the saltiness in my nose and could hear the thunderous rumble of the large crashing wave behind me. I let out a deep breath. I didn't get pulled over the falls. I was lucky.

Or maybe a little fucking stupid.

If I had been out surfing with other people they probably would have called off my paddle before I even started it. It was one last safety net that I did not have out there by myself.

I reached my cupped hands into the ocean and splashed the water over my shaved scalp. My head and hands were the only unprotected areas of skin on my body. My spring wetsuit maintained my warmth outside the water. The cold air against my wet face helped me regain focus. I scanned around my surroundings and saw that I was still alone. I needed to stay sharp.

If it had been a tamer storm on the horizon, I might still have more company in the lineup. Even avid surfers had limits to what they were willing to stay out in.

My limits were different. They always had been. Somehow the promise of one more wave seemed to keep me in the shit longer than most everyone else. This was true in the waves and it was true in life. It got me in to trouble often.

Three more minutes, then I'll call it quits.

I could feel the wind calm down on my wet face. The next set of waves were too small and I was too deep in the break. I remained far out in the lineup where the last big set had forced me to go. It was the only place to safely catch the big ones. My window for a clean wave was fading.

Come on, motherfucker, what you got left for me?

My heart skipped a beat. I could see what looked like a monster swell building in the horizon. This was what I had been waiting for. I could see the first wave of the set advancing towards me. The break in the wind had cleaned it up.

I made my move. Instead of waiting around for the third wave I took my chances on the one that I could see. I wasn't going to come up short on the third like I had the last time. I turned my board and paddled with every bit of energy I had left in my tank. My arms burned with exhaustion.

My board got out in front of the wave and I could feel

its power sucking me in. I stayed focused and paddled through. The board accelerated like a magic carpet.

Here we go.

I popped up strong. The cold wind tingled my scalp as I dropped deeper into the wave with building speed. I could feel the turbulence in my legs. The wave was clean, but not perfect. Its size and power jolted my board at each point of imperfection. My thighs shook at the downward force of the bottom of my front side turn. My line carried me farther away from the barrel. I climbed slowly up the face. I felt the mist of the barrel catching up behind me. Eventually it swallowed me. I repositioned and was spit back out of the barrel, escaping the green room. When I felt the barrel was safely enough behind me, I hit my backside turn. The universe stood still.

I let the white wash carry me towards the shore. I coasted until I lost momentum then fell backwards from the board into the water. My patience had paid off.

I popped my head out of the water. If my ride had been the best of the day, there was nobody there to see it. That type of shit never mattered much to me. Local authorities had been encouraging island evacuation since early this morning. I was happy to see the town cleared out.

I paddled hard into the shore. I could hear another large set of waves breaking safely behind me. Every inch of my exposed skin was numb. I smiled as I hit dry land. I was happy my stubbornness had eked out one more ride of the season.

I wrapped my leash up and dried my face with a towel I had left behind on the shore hours before. I was surprised the wind hadn't already blown it away.

I knew my adrenaline wouldn't keep me warm much longer. I vigorously rubbed my head hoping that the warmth would thaw my frozen brain. I shook my head to get the water from my ears and stared out the ocean.

Take the good times when you can get 'em.

Most Carolina locals viewed hurricanes and tropical storms as bad things. I didn't. Surfers thought differently about storm fronts, for a few hours of the experience at least. Big storms made big waves.

Waves weren't the only reason I liked big storms. Storm fronts were an opportunity. They facilitated my lifestyle. In a matter of hours Grace would make landfall. Mother Nature would selectively annihilate any number of high-priced vacation properties. In the months following, as they were being rebuilt, I'd be riding freshies.

Over the coming months the unfortunate homeowners would be getting insurance checks to fix all of the previous season's storm damage. Their cribs were mostly summer vacation homes. They'd spend the winter haggling with insurers. Maybe they'd get lucky and trick the insurers into upgrading their damaged kitchens.

While the previous fall had been a light storm season, there was still plenty of damage done. By the spring, there would be no shortage of drywall to be hung, rooms to be painted, or brooms to be pushed. I'd pick up any of that shit for the right price. I had picked up actual shit for the right price.

I felt bad, rooting and cheering for disaster. I got over the guilt by thinking about people that could actually afford two to three homes at a time. Then I thought about how I spent a week sleeping in a car. The guilt went away.

******

Bird, 4:15 p.m.

I drove almost an hour inland before stopping. The city of Creswell was a place I stopped regularly while staying in the Outer Banks. Beginning when I arrived in the Carolinas in the spring, I'd come here to the post office about every other week until I finally stopped in one last time on my way out of town. It was my one life line back to my former life, plus their cartons of smokes were dirt cheap.

Only a handful of people knew I kept a PO Box there. It was the one way to surely reach me. I picked its location strategically. I knew anyone hunting for me, cops or otherwise, would scour every post office on the island and within fifteen miles inland if they were desperate enough. I had enough enemies in my past who might be that desperate. I picked a post office fifty miles inland, feeling safe that no one would be that obsessed with finding me.

Another fifteen miles eastward and there would be no shortage of shitty hotels in the outskirts of Plymouth, NC. Free HBO and a hot shower were especially appreciated after living in my vehicle for the past week and a half. I had two more quick stops before I headed in that direction.

The hotel stay would buy me a few days' rest for less than a Benjamin. I needed the time to figure out which mountain to drive to for the winter. It would take a couple of days and a few phone calls before I determined my next landing spot. If I planned any more proactively, it would be that much easier for people to find me. I was trying to lay low and keep my path unpredictable.

Late October was the perfect time to plan a quick escape to the mountains. Getting in ahead of Thanksgiving was key. That was when the mountains started getting particularly aggressive in hiring ahead of the season. I could use that timing to negotiate better pay, or at least more discrete pay.

I drove up to the parking lot of my destination. Two small rectangular buildings shared a paved space that hadn't seen new sealant in years. I pulled into the lot. The blacktop was severely cracked and faded. My tires sounded like they were driving over gravel.

The lot was empty save the one maroon Oldsmobile double parked in the lot's two lone handicapped spaces. Most of the beach evacuation traffic had long since got the fuck out of dodge and made their way west of Creswell already. I parked in the first non-handicapped spot closest to the entrance to Walt's Minimart and Bait.

I climbed out, slammed the car door shut, and made my way past the fridge with "bait" spray painted in black across its front door. It was white but a third of it was covered in rust. I had yet to see it filled with anything but six packs of beer. I stopped in the store and bought a carton of well-priced smokes from an idiot named Hal.

Some bait shop.

The post office beside Walt's Bait shop was the home of the one and only Walter H. Jackson, the owner of his namesake's mini-mart and twenty-years-retired post master of the county.

Legend had it that Walt bought the bait and tackle storefront after it burned down a week after he retired as postmaster. He bought the scorched remains cheap, bulldozed them, and built Walt's Bait and Tackle with his own hands and a few hundred cinderblocks.

Walter handed over the store to his only son, Hal, a short time before I originally landed out here about a year and a half earlier. I heard the entire history ten times over. Walter would yap on about it every time I ran into him at the post office. The poor bastard had reached a level of senility where he could not remember me from one visit to the next, even though I found myself there every few weeks.

"Hey Bunkie, how's it going, old timer?" I said as soon as I opened the door to the post office. I didn't even need to see Walter H. Jackson sitting in his favorite corner rocking chair to know he was already there. He was always there. He sat there rocking in his chair with a big wad of chewing tobacco occupying his mouth. His dentures were stained brown with tobacco spit.

Walter held the paper's crossword puzzle in his lap. He tapped a sharpened No. 2 pencil on his rocker. It was all for show. He was waiting for the next stranger to stop in so he could tell one of three fucking stories he'd already told a thousand times before.

"This old timer still got some time left, don't ya'll fo'get it," Walter said with a smile. He dropped the pencil and paper on the floor in favor of fiddling with his red suspenders. His face lit up at the prospect of someone new to listen to his endless babbling. His bony knees made sharp angles in his well-worn khaki trousers. He was rifling through his shallow catalogue of long-winded, profani-ty-laden stories. I hoped he'd pick one of the three stories that didn't include multiple iterations of the N word.

"Good grief, ya old hoot, it takes ya'll ten minutes to think of the story to tell and then anotha forty for ya'll to tell it," a voice came from behind the mail counter. It was Walter's replacement as postmaster, Mrs. Dollie June Jackson. She was also Walter's third and current wife.

Walter found himself fornicating with his replacement postmaster shortly after retiring. Miss Dollie June and Walter H. Jackson started dating two weeks after she took over his post as postmaster. They were married two months after that. They've hated each other ever since. At least that's the story they'd each told over and over between bickering every time I came in for a visit.

"Oh, who needs to hear from you, DEVIL woman?" Walter boomed in response to Dollie June's criticism.

"Walter H. Jackson, did yo mamma not love you enough when you was a youngin'?" Dollie continued her verbal poking. It was standard fare in the Creswell Post Office. They'd be bickering with each other until one gets fed up enough to die. My money was on Walter.

"Watch it there, Dollie June. You know Mamma was a GOD-LY woman!" he shot back scornfully. His head shook in exasperation.

"Yeah, yeah, and yeah, Papa preached on the cross," Dollie June dismissed the dramatics. "They also been dead since about the Civil War."

She pulled out a Virginia Slim and lit it, drawing her attention from her husband. "How can I help ya, darling?" she asked in an attempt to save me from another one of

Walter's long-winded stories. Walter kept on yapping. We both did our best to ignore him. I tried to be polite. Dollie June couldn't have given a flying fuck.

"I built that damn bait shop with my BARE hands, a stack of cinder blocks, and a FUCKIN' level. I told old man Elliot that I'd shove that LEVEL up his ASS when he came up here tellin' me my roof line's crooked. He got me hotter than a fuckin' four balled tom cat."

"Walter, can you get that dirt bag, lazy ass son of yours to get off his ass and sweep the floor over there. It looks like the grapes of wrath on that floor, y'all. Mmmm, that boy is a bee in my bonnet." She redirected her attention my way a second time, confident that she had distracted Walter from trapping me in another story.

Walter rolled his eyes in disgust. He rocked his chair more fervently, as though to rev up his yelling engine. He leaned back into the chair and bellowed through the open but screened window beside his chair, "Hey HAL! HAL! Dollie June said to SWEEP UP THAT GOD DAMNED FLOOR!" He looked forward again, took a deep breath. He sat silent, avoiding the temptation to rock.

A few seconds of silence and then an answer. "Tell that bitch she can suck my ass. She ain't my FUCKIN' MAMMA!" I heard Hal loudly retort.

"What price pussy?" Walter snarled to no one. It was one of his favorite sayings. A mantra to explain his condition. He spat a wad of tobacco juice on the floor then picked up his pencil and crossword puzzle and returned to the land of make believe.

Dollie June rolled her eyes with a smile, as a way to non-verbally excuse the shit show going on around her.

"Now what can I do you for?"

I shrugged off the crazy. Who was I to judge? I'd seen plenty worse.

"I'm headin' out of town for the next few months. Gotta run some errands up north. Family stuff," I replied. "I wanted to stop in here one last time to see if anything had turned up.

"As a matter of fact, I know you gotta couple of things," Dollie replied. "I got your PO Box but I also got a local drop that I wanted to give you."

What fuckin' local drop?

She waddled her way to where my official mail was stashed. I was suddenly much more interested in what she was gathering. She returned and dropped three weeks' worth of junk mail on the counter. The bulk of the unchecked mail must have exceeded the space in my PO Box. Dollie June already knew this. She had grabbed my bulk mail before I even checked my #207 PO Box. Then she went back to the coat room. I could see her reach up onto the top shelf of the closet. She waddled towards the counter with a manila envelope. She dropped the envelope on top of the pile of junk mail. Scribbled in black marker on the front of the envelope was the word "Bunkie."

"Some smart-assed twenty-something came in here a few weeks ago and told me to give this to you. Actually, he didn't necessarily say you," she began as my heart raced.

"What do you mean by that?" I questioned. I was done being a passive participant.

"This guy, Hispanic lookin' fella, he was a real pushy asshole, even for a Yankee. He kept goin' on and on describing a surfer fella."

I kept a calm face while I internally scrambled for my explanations.

"He said he's lookin' for this surfer fella that called everyone Bunkie," she said as we locked eyes. "Y'all are the only two people I EVA heard call ANYONE Bunkie."

Gulp.

"He left this for you. He insisted you have it. He paid me a hundred bucks to get it to you. If you don't want it, I'm throwin' it in the garbage."

I knew she wasn't bluffing. I didn't want to hang around any longer to answer potential questions. I grabbed my bundle of mail, inclusive of the manila envelope atop the stack. I didn't say a word as I turned for the door. My feet moved me as quickly as possible without looking suspicious.

I hopped into my truck and tossed the mail into the passenger side of the bench. I couldn't take my eyes off the black marker "Bunkie" labeling my locally dropped package. I turned the ignition and immediately shifted into reverse. I took in my surroundings.

No visible traffic, that's good.

I pulled out in the road and drove slowly for the first ten yards paying particular attention to any tails in my rearview. When I was confident the coast was clear, I gunned the gas pedal.

******

Bird, 5:25 p.m.

Forty miles from the post office, I pulled into a crowded Piggly Wiggly parking lot. I was almost twenty miles east of where I had originally intended to stay. I decided to drive somewhere farther away from the post office. Anywhere within twenty miles of there was far too risky.

I hadn't seen any cars tailing me after thirty minutes of single lane country roads. I wasn't a newbie to ditching tails. I was confident that even the best bounty hunters wouldn't have been able to sniff their way to my current spot. I hit park and took a deep breath. The air smelled of pork rinds and garbage. A three-hundred-pound white woman with purple hoop earrings adjusted her sweatshirt. It was black and read "Degeneration X" in fluorescent green letters. It was stretched beyond capacity. Her gut peeked out from under it. A toddler walked diligently behind her, left on his own to watch for traffic. I looked elsewhere. A young mother smoked half a cigarette hands free while carrying a thirty-pound bag of Alpo over her burly shoulders.

How the fuck did I end up here?

I rubbed my tired eyes. I could still feel the stickiness of saltwater in my eye lashes. I thought I'd be in a hotel by now. That plan needed to change.

I grabbed the envelope I'd been mentally obsessing over for an hour. I had to take the appropriate steps. Anybody trailing me needed to be ditched. Anyone anticipating my next landing spot needed to be disappointed. I had to break any trend remotely predictable. Snowboarding season was officially cancelled. I had already started thinking about what off season lake community I'd squat in this winter.

I lamented that I would never return to Walt's Bait and Tackle. I avoided asking myself how the fuck Gonzo found me. It was a question mentally repeated for the thousandth time in the past hour. I suspected my answers were in the envelope.

I noticed the glued portion of the envelope had yet to be opened. Dollie June was a simple sort of folk. She wasn't the nosey type. She was too busy being angry at Walter and Hal. She hadn't even asked me anything after I took the envelope. I think she was happy to make an extra hundred bucks. Wherever Gonzo was, he had gotten close to finding me. I needed to change that.

I ripped the envelope open with the ferocity of dangerous curiosity. I reached in and pulled out the contents. A handwritten letter on a smaller piece of paper spilled onto my lap along with a stack of pictures. I held off reading the paper note, skipping the vegetables and going right for the steak.

I rifled through the stack of photos in my hand, taking my thumb off the front facing picture. I didn't want my sweat to damage the images. My eyes refused to blink. I frantically flipped through one picture to the next.

A car trunk filled with drugs, my cousin's car, my cousin's license plate below the trunk filled with drugs, a picture of me and my cousin driving said car's fully loaded trunk.

I threw the stack of pictures down and grabbed the handwritten letter from my lap. There was a number. I immediately scanned the parking lot for a secluded phone booth. My heart was racing. All of my running couldn't hide me forever.

My breathing quickened into a huffing. I broke into a cold sweat and opened the car door. The cabin felt suffocating. I was having difficulty breathing, like someone was sitting on my chest. I leaned forward on the steering wheel and did my best to compose myself. I sped to the phone booth at the gas station on the other side of the highway.

Come on, man, get your shit together.

Chapter 15

Bad to the Bone
Tuesday, October 21st, 1997
Jennie, noon

"I'll be there in a fuckin' minute," I yelled down the stairs towards whoever was pounding on my bolted front door. "Give me a minute to get dressed, GOD DAMMIT!" I screamed over the banging. My slippers barely stayed on my running feet. My robe flapped open exposing my naked legs running down the stairs.

The door was hammered another four times, this time more violently. My boyfriend, Tom, scrambled to get dressed upstairs. I had handed him my loaded revolver before running for the door, so at least I had back-up.

I still smelled like sex. I tied up my robe as tightly as possible and took a deep breath to compose myself. I wiped the tears of fear from my eyes, unlocked the dead-bolt, and swung open the front door.

Two large bearded men with shaved heads stood on the other side of the threshold.

I hope Tommy knows how to use that revolver.

It wasn't the first time I opened my door to find these guys standing on the other side. They looked annoyed about the three minutes they had to wait for me to answer the door. They were lucky it hadn't taken me longer. I was in the middle of a good nooner when they interrupted me.

"You seen Gonzo?" the slightly smaller of the two asked. He was at least twice my size. The muscle of the duo stayed quiet. His looks alone were intimidating.

I heard a sniffle come from behind me and looked to find my daughter staring wide-eyed from the kitchen. She has dried chocolate smudged over a third of her face.

"Marisol!" I yelled her way. I thought she was still upstairs playing in her bedroom. She must have snuck down to the kitchen for some candy. I looked frantically at the floor around Marisol trying to find her favorite stuffed animal on the floor. I picked up the brown stuffed bear with a red bandana.

"Marisol, Marisol, here, HERE! Take Teddy up to his room. He needs a nap on Mommy's bed. HURRY, he looks awfully tired."

"You seen Gonzo? I ain't askin' a third time, Jennie. Sixty-five grand don't care if you got a good baby sittin' situation."

I knew these guys from before they wanted to kill my soon to be ex-husband Gonzo. They were bar friends, guys he used to party and gamble with. Freddie, the smaller of the two, was a long-time local thug. His retired Senior Chief dad ran the biggest local book in Norfolk. Freddie's much larger partner in crime, Trey, was a high school football teammate. He played college ball but got cut by the Redskins before he ever made any real money. Two years later he was shaking down poor white trash like me. The behemoth certainly looked the part.

Gonzo was my husband only by legal title. The divorce process couldn't happen fast enough. He mixed with Freddie and Trey the most when his gambling was heaviest. One minute they're buying him shots at the bar, the next minute they're ready to break his hand with a meat tenderizer.

"Look, like I told you three months ago, I ain't seen that scumbag in months. He's equally bad at paying things like his kid's groceries and clothes too. I got plenty of bills to chase him with too if your lookin' for extra business."

I think I had sold Trey. Freddie looked skeptical.

"Look, Freddie, do you think you'd be interrupting a nooner with my boyfriend if Gonzo was hangin' around here?"

The dramatics didn't really sway their disappointment of not getting in touch with Gonzo. Their bosses wanted cash on their return, not stories.

"Look, the moment I see him, I'll let you know," I pleaded to Freddie as he entered the door.

He walked me back into the wall beside the door. He cleared a path for Trey who made his way towards the stairs. My heart pounded with fear.

Please don't go upstairs. PLEASE don't go upstairs!

"Give me a number to call, as soon as I know something, you'll get a location. Should only take a few days tops. PLEASE!" I said before Trey made it to the first step.

Trey stopped his march towards the second floor and settled in front of my brand new thirty-inch television. It was the most reliable babysitter we had in the house. It was currently playing a Barney VHS tape my daughter had grown bored of an hour earlier.

"I know he's been around here, sweetheart. Whether you want him here or not, I don't fuckin' care," Freddie explained.

He looked over to Trey and gave a nod.

A lead pipe dropped from Trey's long sleeve. It was the size of a baseball bat. He twirled the pipe to adjust his grip. It looked like a toothpick against his massive frame. He swung the pipe with one arm into the television. The image of the giant purple dinosaur exploded into a display of lights and glass. Debris cascaded to the floor. My neighbor's two German Shepherds began frantically barking in the yard next door.

Freddie and Trey had made their point. They began their exit before the commotion drew undue attention. Trey stepped over the glass and the assortment of toys and dirty laundry strewn about the floor.

I was lucky. They already knew that I hated Gonzo's guts and that they didn't need to work too hard to get me to give up his location. The broken TV was an exclamation point.

My fear was trading blows with my anger. My brand-new television had been smashed. I'd be stuck watching a shitty black and white with rabbit ears and tin foil for at least another two months before I could afford a replacement. I bit my tongue and barely avoided saying something stupid to my houseguests.

I shut the door closed as soon as Trey passed over the threshold and immediately locked the deadbolt. I pounded the door with my fist and shook as I sobbed angry tears.

I had seen Gonzo earlier in the morning. I'd be seeing

him again in a few hours. He was a gambler, with zero financial responsibility. He was a shitty husband, but he was still my daughter's father. Her face lit up every time he came to visit. Every few months he'd feel guilty enough as a father to string a few visits in a row. This happened to be one of those times.

I stared again at the smashed glass shards of television screen. My slippers crunched as I walked towards the stairs. The television was a pit stop on Trey's path upstairs. He knew my daughter was up there, he saw her go. What would have happened if I hadn't stopped him?

Gonzo had made this my new normal. That fucking bastard.

Chapter 16

Boomin' System
Tuesday, October 21st, 1997
Gonzo, noon

"GONZO!" I heard a voice startle me from the open door ten yards behind me.

I was alone on the loading dock. The delivery guys were taking their lunchbreak. I was on my second smoke break less than an hour into my afternoon shift at Tony's Performance Audio. Tony was the guy yelling at me. He owned the joint.

Tony's was a decent-sized car audio place. It was one of many that sustained itself almost exclusively from enlisted sailors stationed out of Norfolk. Tony sold me a half-priced kicker box six months into my first enlisted ship assignment. That shit broke two days after it was installed.

Tony had insisted that I had to return the broken speaker to the manufacturer myself. Half of the shit he sold in his store was like that. The other half was either stolen or damaged in some phony insurance write off.

I took a deep drag of my mid-smoked menthol cigarette. I was taking in what I could knowing my smoke break was officially over.

"GONZO! Get your ass back inside! There's a customer inside says he's been waitin' ten minutes on you. N'you're here fuckin' off on a smoke break!?"

I still don't think Tony recognized me as a former customer from four years earlier. Tony had scammed so many fucking e-dawgs over the years that we all ended up looking the same to him. I was hardly upset that I was pissing him off.

Tony slammed the door before I made it there. I heard a few more muffled curse words continuing behind the door while I stood waiting outside. I assumed they were intended for me. I didn't care. I had only been working here a month and I certainly wouldn't be in another month.

I got to the shut door, took one last drag, and flicked the half-smoked cigarette toward the end of the loading dock. I watched the orange tinder spin over ten feet clearing the edge of the loading dock. It reminded me of my days smoking on a ship.

I saw my impatient customer at the register. I trotted my way to the front counter where he'd been waiting for his car keys for over ten minutes. I had pretended to have trouble finding them. It was an excuse to grab a smoke, but it was part of the hustle too.

"Fred, I'm SO sorry, man. The install guys are lunk heads. One of 'em left these on the garage floor. We had to scour the place to find them." Meanwhile I smelled like a walking menthol cigarette.

Fred was too much of a pushover to sniff through my obvious bullshit. He wasn't enlisted. He was local civilian white trash. Black, white, Hispanic, civilian, or sailor, it didn't matter. Our customers were almost exclusively poor. They were usually so excited to be buying half-priced stereo equipment that they didn't notice my own criminal intentions.

Fred owned a used Nissan Maxima. He must have bought it from an enlisted sailor because it had about five grand in rims and silver accessories already installed. We were replacing an existing post-factory installation that we had originally done about a year earlier. We bought that shit back for pennies on the dollar. We'd be installing them into somebody else's ride before the end of the week. Then a week later we'd be telling him to return the broken speakers to the manufacturer for new ones. It was all part of the routine.

"Fred, tell ya what," I continued my attempt to get past his annoyance over waiting. "Let me take another ten percent off the price. I'll give you my employee discount. Give ya another hundred bucks. How does that sound?" I was going off script. This was also part of my hustle.

"Tight," Fred replied. He tried hard to conceal a smile.

"Cool, man." I offered my hand and gave him a soulful hand slap. Fred was a cupcake. "Let me run to the office and I'll get some paper work. I PROMISE this will only take two minutes."

I held up two fingers as I hurriedly headed to the office in the store room. It was all show. I could have done this shit at the register.

I grabbed a few maintenance forms from Tony's office desk and put them on an empty clipboard I found on his seat. I knew he'd be gone by now. He'd never be late for his daily quarter past noon date with Taco Bell across the road. That fat fuck ate three Mexican pizzas and two large diet cokes for lunch every day.

I hurried my way back toward to the register in less than two minutes as promised. "Alright man, I got your keys, now I got the paperwork."

Fred already had his credit card ready to charge. I dropped his keys on the counter. He happily picked them up. I flipped through the papers I had recently attached to my clipboard, filling in a few scribbles here and there. I was faking like I was reviewing some official employee discount form.

"Oh shit, I forgot to ask," I continued the hustle. "We have a bunch of mutual discount deals with the local businesses. I remember you said you worked at the Bennigan's up the road. The one in Neptune plaza?"

"Yeah, that's right," Fred replied. "That's where I work."

"Awesome man, well, that means I can get you an extra 5% off," I said.

Fred couldn't contain his smile. The extra fifty bucks had broken his barrier for self-control. "That's awesome, man. Thanks. I can't wait to show everyone at work the new system."

"Yeah, that bass was thumpin' when the guys were testing it earlier," I buttered Fred up. "You said you're workin' tonight at Bennigan's?"

"Yeah, I close tonight," Fred answered.

"That's tight. You get that closing shift often? I heard that's where you make the best money at places like that," I interrogated. Fred was too euphoric to notice.

"Yeah, money is good. I get Tuesday and Friday happy hour to close every week. I also get Sunday brunch. My cousin is the manager there."

Bingo, that's the last bit of information I needed to know.

I scribbled some more nonsense on the clipboard paper. I pulled the top sheet out of the clip, signed it, and placed it under the register, lulling Fred into thinking I was processing his discounts.

"That's tight," I said.

I entered the typical 15% employee discount into the register. It automatically adjusted the price without any required manager's approval. I had lied to Fred, the employee discount was 15% all along. I quoted him the 10% so I could fake the five percent extra Bennigan's discount that doesn't actually exist.

I processed Fred's card and handed him his receipt. "Alright, sign here and it's all yours, homie."

Fred signed and joyfully made his way out of the shop to his car. I waved goodbye and made my way back to Tony's office. He was at least a half of a Mexican pizza away from returning. I shut the office door after taking one more precautionary look ensuring nobody saw me enter.

Tony's office was like a converted broom closet and it smelled like an animal's den. Among the crushed cans of soda, the empty packs of smokes, and the random scattering of receipts and business documents, I found what I was looking for. I picked up the black rotary phone underneath the half-eaten bag of Doritos. Putting the receiver between my shoulder and ear, I dialed watching as the wheel spun back after each number.

The phone rang once, then twice. There was no answer. I kept my eyes fixed on the giant glass window in

Tony's office overlooking the stock room. The last thing I wanted was to have one of my co-workers see me in there. My foot tapped nervously. The phone rang a third time.

"Yo, who dis?" the voice on the other line asked.

"G," I calmly replied.

"Shoot," the voice on the other line responded.

"Bennigan's, Neptune Plaza, tonight, maroon Maxima, rollin' on dubs and loaded up."

"Look at them rims, aahhh," the voice indicated his pleasant surprise. Stealing rims and the system on the same vehicle was like killing two birds with one stone. Neptune Plaza did not have great visibility to the highway in front of it.

Fish in a fucking barrel.

"We cool?" I asked keeping my eyes on Tony's office window.

"Yeah, we cool," the voice answered. "Cash tonight after the pickup, say midnight."

"Ah'ight, bet," I smiled and hung up the phone. I placed the Dorito bag on top of the phone and made a quick exit. I shut the door to the office behind me and smiled as I walked away.

I guess I should have felt guilty. I didn't. If I didn't arrange to have that shit stolen, it was about a one in three chance that Tony would have his crew do it. Fred would be robbed by my crew within hours. The insurance would reimburse double for the equipment he had just paid half price for. He had paid half because the equipment was either stolen or scammed to a lower price to begin with. Everybody wins, except Tony, I guess.

Fuck Tony.

******

Gonzo, 7:15 p.m.

I was a born hustler. It's why I left the Navy. I could never pass up the prospect of quick cash, no matter how dirty it was.

I finally wrapped up my afternoon shift. I unlocked my car door catching my reflection in the window. I was wearing a red golf shirt with "Tony's" silk screened in small letters across the upper left.

And I thought wearing a blue shirt and dungarees was depressing.

I had an entire collection of retail-oriented golf shirts in my closet. I regularly took out of town retail jobs to front my thievery. I made sure people didn't know or remember me at the places I worked. Eventually I'd "soil an area" as people got suspicious and I'd pack up shop and do the same damn shit at another place across town. I was running out of unsoiled territory. Unfortunately, collecting bookies didn't give a shit about my long-term career prospects.

I thought about the two hundred bucks I'd get tonight. It was about quadruple what I would get paid for working this afternoon at Tony's. I needed the money and I needed to find a more regular place to stay at night. I'd been crashing from couch to couch for the past six months.

Hustling, that's what landed me here in the first place. Back in my enlisted Navy days I was making a few benjis a month hustling contraband underway. Smokes, alcohol, nudie magazines, uppers, downers, there was no naval vessel on planet earth that had enough supply to fit the demand. It was the easiest money I ever made.

A good multi-month deployment was like winning on the "Price is Right." I bought a car after my first deployment and installed every fucking toy Tony would sell me after my second. Still, the magnitude was never enough. I didn't just want to dabble as a hustler. I wanted to be a professional. I was already in way over my head. I could have left town long ago. I didn't. I needed a better game plan.

I jumped into my car and fired up the ignition. It wasn't the same car I had in my Navy days. It was a used Honda Civic with a rusted-out floor. I could see the pavement beneath me as I drove out of Tony's parking lot.

I sold my nicer car about a year ago, along with my television and about everything else I owned of monetary value. I had gotten kicked out of my house and needed cash quick. My ex and I were putting the finishing touches on our divorce. All because North Carolina State couldn't cover a five-point spread at home on Thursday night football. They took a knee on the ten-yard line as time expired to win 24 to 21. They won the game. I lost another thirty-five grand. It was a double down to chase the seventeen grand I went in the hole for two weeks earlier.

I was stopped at a red light a few miles down from Tony's when I saw a twenty-something dude sitting on the cement island separating the opposing lanes of traffic at the intersection. Half conscious, he was barely holding a coffee can upright, collecting money from anyone who might spare a few coins. He was loaded and I could see a few obvious Navy tats peeking out from underneath his shirt sleeves. We may have very well served on the same ship four years earlier. For a millisecond I felt bad for him. Then I looked up and saw the Bennigan's in Neptune Plaza. Like him, I thought things would have worked out differently for me. Like him, they didn't.

Two years earlier I was a plebe at the Naval Academy. I was too fucking stupid to be satisfied with that. Instead I ended up getting involved in a drug hustle. We pulled that shit off. I duped my Naval Academy roommate into driving a bunch of drugs across half the country with his cousin. I ran some front-end logistics with minimal exposure. I made fifty fucking grand off that shit. I took that money and hustled my way out of the Navy.

Within six months I started betting seriously with a local sports bookie. Six months after that I was up a hundred grand. Six months after that I was selling my stepmother's pearl earrings to a pawn shop to pay off the daily interest on the sixty grand I was in the hole for.

I've been running side hustles like this car stereo gig on top of minimum wage shit jobs to keep the collectors from breaking my fingers. This one goon in particular, Trey, he was no motherfucking joke. I'd personally seen him rip a debtor's thumb off with his bare hands. I needed longer-term plans at twenty-three. I didn't have them.

I pulled in front of my ex's house. It was a decent place, much better than our digs when I was still enlisted. I remember putting down the seven-hundred-dollar security deposit in cash. I had just made ten grand off Monday Night Football. She would be getting evicted next month. I felt bad for the daughter I had with Jennie. As for Jennie, she could go fuck herself.

I stepped up to the front door. All of the street lights were off, as were all of the interior lights. I approached the door and was preparing to knock when it suddenly swung open. My backpack was tossed through the opening before the door slammed shut again.

"That's the rest of everything you own. Get the fuck out of here, NOW!" said a voice from behind the door.

"Can't I come in to see my daughter?" I asked through the door. I knew Jennie was still there looking through the peephole.

Twenty seconds passed silently.

"Don't you think she'd like to see her dad?" I asked one last time.

The door cracked open but the chain lock remained intact.

"Listen to me, you son of a bitch. When I close this door, I am dialing Freddie and Trey!"

"Okay, I get it." I took the threat seriously. "I'll come back another time."

The door remained cracked. Jennie had to get the last fucking word in, exactly like when we were together.

"Don't come around here any time soon. We can let the judge take care of things," she continued yapping behind the safety of a locked door and a direct phone line to people wanting to break my bones.

I debated not walking away right then. I'd love to give her an answer to her last fucking words. I knew for a fact that she was already fucking some bitch ass named Tommy in a place that they expected me to contribute rent towards. Then I thought of Freddie and his asshole gorilla henchman Trey.

"And tell your friend Bird to stop callin' here. He called twice last week. I got enough fucking problems with Freddie and Trey. I wrote Bird's number on your favorite shirt with a sharpie, fucker. When you talk to him tell him not to call me ever again. I don't need any more of your problems chasing me."

My heart skipped a beat. I picked up my backpack off the ground and hustled towards my car. I left the bitch chirping behind me in the dust.

I had found my long-term plan.

Part VI

Spiderwebs

Chapter 17

November Rain
Monday, November 3rd, 1997
Mick, 2130 hrs.

"Decent?" I asked knocking on the door. I thought that even plebes deserved a little privacy after hours.

"Yes, sir," I heard from the other side of the door.

I opened the door and headed inside.

"Speneti, Walker, Johnston. What's up, fellas?"

"Not much, sir," Speneti replied.

"Ah man, it's cool. Behind closed doors you guys can all call me Mick. I'm not much of a yes sir no sir type," I said.

The plebes were supposed to call upperclassmen sir right up until Herndon at the end of the academic year. That wasn't my style. I had gotten to know plebe Mark Speneti fairly well. We spent time together daily. We both had the unfortunate honor of being squad mates with Dickley for the fall semester. That was a badge of honor unto itself. Speneti was also on the football team and had dropped by my room a few times to talk to N.D. I wouldn't say we were quite friends, but this far into the semester, we were at least friendly.

All three of the room's plebes looked much more relaxed compared to how I was used to seeing them. Out in public formations and at meals plebes were routinely getting flamed. My squad mates Speneti and Wilson dealt with daily helpings of Dickley.

"I was coming by to return this," I said.

I pulled out the folded newspaper from beneath my arms. I hadn't read the visible money section of today's USA today. The paper was merely camouflage for what I was really flipping through in the men's room a few minutes before. I threw the November '96 edition of Playboy on Speneti's desk.

Speneti laughed. "Dude, that centerfold in there is so hot."

He grabbed the magazine, walked over to his con-locker, and pulled down a box from the overhead storage. He neatly filed away the magazine in appropriate chronological order. The box contained every Playboy published since 1983.

The collection had been carefully curated by a lucky room of plebes until passing it along to the next year of plebe guardians. It was a tradition ten years in the making. N.D. and I had that honor during our plebe year.

The Playboy box meant less these days given the internet. Our upperclassmen didn't have internet. They handed the box to us like it was the Ark of the Covenant. Despite the declining value of the box, Speneti's room carried the torch this year with appropriate care.

"What can I say, I was in a blonde type of mood tonight," I justified my loan from their library. I knew the whole collection well. We may have had the luxury of internet porn, but I was still old school. Besides, it was easier to wank off in the privacy of a toilet stall. My room-mates may have been willing to pee in our room's shower, but shitting and masturbating were the last bounds of personal privacy.

Given my circumstances of the moment, Miss November was the best I could do. Summer and I had officially broken up last month and jerking off was about all the action I was getting at the time. I went from regularly having sex with the hottest girl on campus to wanking off with the plebe Playboy collection.

Fuck my life.

"Aside from Dickley, everything else cool?" I asked, checking in on our company librarians.

The room of plebes all nodded. I tried to make my way out quickly so they could enjoy the last few minutes of free time before plebe-mandated "lights out" at 2200.

"Thanks for the loan, fellas. Have a nice evening." Feeling relaxed and refreshed, I strode toward the company wardroom for a night of television.

******

Mick, 2155

Ed clumsily opened the company wardroom's middle fridge. It was one of three. He was seeing nine of them. He had done the same to the adjacent fridge. He peeked inside looking like a hungry bear aimlessly sifting through garbage cans. Clearly Captain America's prank had done little to curb his drunken food mooching habits. He settled on a can of chocolate protein shake. He probably noticed it had been in there for more than a day and was likely forgotten.

And harder to tamper with.

Ed was loaded. Second class mids didn't even have liberty that night, but Ed always had a work around. Every Monday evening, he'd head across the yard and grab beers in the Officer's Club. It was one of the yard's best kept secrets, a fully functioning bar that you could visit without ever leaving the academy grounds. It took most mids until firstie year to hear about it, but Ed had been going there since he turned twenty-one his youngster year. At the time he had been knocking boots with a firstie from the company a floor above us. She had lasted two weeks, his relationship with the O Club bar was still going strong.

The crowded room reeked of burnt popcorn and feet. Ed cracked open the can and took three large chugs of his pilfered snack. He saw N.D. and me sitting in the middle row couch. I had parked myself next to N.D. after dropping by Speneti's room.

N.D. was still getting over a painfully close loss to Notre Dame on the road a few days earlier. The Navy football team hadn't beaten Notre Dame since 1963. That previous Saturday they had the winning touchdown pushed out of bounds inside the five as time expired.

Ed let out an enormous belch and made his way over to us. I could smell the chocolate flavored Coors Light stench of his burp.

I was relieved knowing that the open seat next to me would be filled by a friend and not some jackass like Dickley. I was still pissed at that motherfucker for yacking off about Summer.

I had been spending a lot more time in the wardroom these days. Summer and I had been splitsville since our blow up a month earlier. I had gotten over what went down with Hackett once my temper cooled. Unfortunately, getting over Hackett wasn't enough for Summer.

After about three weeks of trying to make things right, I had officially given up. Summer avoided me and the rest of the company in general as much as she could this semester. Soccer and playoff season kept her distracted enough. We hadn't spoken in weeks. I still wanted her back, but trying now was pointless, if not sadistic.

She's so fucking stubborn.

The wardroom was the only place any midshipman could watch television in Bancroft Hall. Televisions were not permitted in individual rooms. As a shitty alternative, each company was assigned a single wardroom. That wardroom typically included seven to eight mice infested couches, at least two working refrigerators, a collection of VHS tapes, a VCR, and one glorious cable-equipped thirty-inch television set. That single television was all one hundred upperclassmen had to watch on weekdays. It was better than being a plebe. They only had wardroom fridge privileges. Television was off limits to them for the year.

Channel and show preference were a mixed bag. Some nights show selections were unanimous. Thursday night 9 p.m. was almost always standing room only for Seinfeld. A year earlier a made for television drama about a Naval Academy plebe involved in a murderous love triangle had everyone in the brigade wanting to watch the same thing. That was an extreme example.

On a majority of nights, channel selection wasn't nearly as agreeable. Monday nights were often a point of conflict. They would pit professional wrestling fans against whoever's hometown NFL team was playing football that night.

There were fights a plenty when it came to arguing what ultimately graced the screen on any given evening. I'd like to say that things were settled democratically or even remotely fair. They usually weren't.

Typically, the most dominant personalities of the company, a handful of firsties or second-class dudes, bullied everyone else into whatever they wanted watch. Most girls didn't even bother coming in the wardroom unless they knew ahead of time that a particular show or movie would be on.

That Monday night the Steelers were playing the Chiefs. There weren't any mids from Kansas City in our company. The two Steelers fans were watching the game down the hall in another company's wardroom. That Monday night the 6th company wardroom was all about WCW Monday Nitro.

Ed plopped between N.D. and me in one of the four open couch seats remaining. "S'up, Micky, s'up, N.D.," he said as he settled into his seat.

"S'up, Eddie," I said in return.

"Whaddup, Ed," N.D. replied in his usual relaxed tone. He had his head buried in chemistry homework. He had barely looked up since I walked in a few minutes earlier. Not only was N.D. a football star, he was also majoring in chemistry. Chemistry was one of the academy's toughest majors. It was also the required major for any midshipmen competing for a handful of Navy doctor slots. Most division one football stars were fantasizing about the NFL draft. N.D. was dreaming of becoming an orthopedic surgeon.

Ed adjusted his position, letting the remainder of his open protein shake spill between the couch cushions. It didn't matter. The couch was already gross. I moved slightly so that I didn't get wet and returned my focus to the television set.

Tonight's WCW Monday Nitro featured your standard fare of white trash soap opera. With no one flipping channels back and forth between wrestling and football, extended conversation was dedicated to debates over Hogan leg drops and Ric Flair chest slaps.

"Diamond Dallas Page is such a pussy!" Ed drunkenly chimed into the conversation. "DDP looks like a fat roadie from the '87 White Snake tour. No way can that guy hang with the likes of Macho Man Randy Savage. Nothing is stopping the NWO this year."

Then Ed and a firstie were having an in-depth conversation about the romantic plot between the Macho Man and Miss Elizabeth. That was the first time I had ever heard him talk about anything related to romance. He wasn't the romantic type. The night before, I was awoken by Ed and his horse cock getting a blowjob sitting bare-assed on our sink at 3 a.m.

The notion reminded me to nag one more time. I leaned in towards Ed and lowered my voice. "Yo, you still need to scrub down that sink, man. I had to brush my teeth in the men's room sink this morning."

"Dawg, I'm sorry about last night. I forgot all about that. Consider it done. I'll Scrubbing Bubble that shit tonight," Ed replied.

Most of the wardroom was hardly paying attention to the wrestling. The majority of us were more entertained by the people in the wardroom watching wrestling. N.D. was still immersed in his chemistry lab report.

"Dude, just get rid of the pubes," I said half-jokingly. "Yours AND hers."

"No problem, man," Ed assured me. "Everything else with you cool?"

"Yeah, I guess," I said. "Typical late fall blues type of stuff."

"What do you mean?" he asked.

"You know, Naval Academy shit. Commissioning Week everybody is so happy to be promoted to the next rank. Then after a few months of having those new privileges you realize it still sucks to be at the Naval Academy."

Ed nodded in understanding. It was all bullshit. We both knew why I was feeling down. We sat quietly through the remainder of the televised match. Wrestling coverage eventually broke for commercials.

"Oh shit!" Ed blurted out as he slapped my shoulder trying to cheer me up. "Check it out, Mick, there's your girl!"

There she was on the TV screen. The girl I had hooked up with in Tijuana. She hadn't been talking shit at the bar. She really had filmed an AIDS television commercial.

N.D. looked up from his homework and backhanded Ed lightly on the chest with a facial expression that said, "Not too loud, man!"

Loose lips sink ships.

I appreciated N.D.'s cover. My roommates and my

Vandegrift compadres from summer cruise were the only people in the company that knew about my Tijuana escapades. Summer and I may have been presently broken up, but I still didn't want her hearing about it. It would ruin any remote chance left for us getting back together.

Lucky for me, no one heard Ed's drunken babble. Before the first commercial was halfway through, the wardroom's lights started flickering on and off. Tribal chants began and loud rhythmic clapping ensued.

"Here we go again," N.D. said flustered. He gathered up his books and papers and made his way to the door. "Yo, I'll see y'all up in the room. You two can hang around for this crazy white people shit. I got homework to do."

The clapping and light flickering intensified as N.D. exited the room. All eyes and heads pivoted toward the third row couch. There sat the targeted prey. Midshipman 3/C Mark Povotski and his roommate Vin Gabbernino were sitting ducks.

My company classmates endured their initiation into male wardroom membership a year earlier. This meant nearly all male sophomore midshipmen in our company would receive a beat down before they were formally initiated into our sadistic country club.

Last year, the tradition was particularly strong. The class of '97 company mates were passionate about passing along the "come uppance" to us. '99 took our beating with a chin up. It was part of the hazing process. Luckily our room was exempted. My roomies and I usually went to the wardroom as a group. No one was stupid enough to tangle with N.D.

The class of '98 firsties weren't as into the beat downs

as were their class of '97 predecessors. Lucky for the sake of tradition, dumbass former class of '97 Midshipman Tony Castiglio flunked micro-economics class for the second time last spring semester. The class was in his major. The academy made him wait until the end of the '97 fall semester to graduate. He was graduating a full six months after the rest of his classmates graduated. He was now officially in the class of '97.5. He had a half a year extended prison sentence as a midshipman living in Bancroft Hall. He was lucky. They didn't let too many mids graduate in longer than four years.

If being in the class of '97.5 bothered Castiglio, he never showed it. He picked up this fall semester right where he left off last year. He was the godfather of organizing, tracking, and executing all beat downs in the wardroom. He was also the jackass that flipped the light switch on and off and led the tribal chants for now three years running.

A year ago, I remember seeing Castiglio pinned to the floor of the same wardroom for yet another company tradition of hazing people on their twenty-first birthday. He was screaming in agony with his pants pulled down as his classmates edge-dressed his balls. It was mere payback for all of the awful abuse he had handed out to them in similar situations. Despite his mental scars, Castiglio still loved that type of shit.

Castiglio flickered the lights two more times and the wardroom went black. The lions converged on the unsuspecting wildebeests.

By the time WCW Monday Nitro returned from the commercials, Gabbernino exited the wardroom wearing half of a shirt and the elastic waistband of his underwear pulled around his neck.

Chapter 18

Tyler
Friday, November 7th, 1997
Summer, 2350 hrs.

"Come on, girl, you know you want to suck on this," Jaimie said holding a lit cigarette up to my face.

"No, no way," I said pushing the flaming stick away.

"Come on, bitch, I know your season is over. Have a fucking smoke!" she insisted as she chased me around the sidewalk.

Jaimie knew my season ended over a week ago with the Patriot League playoffs not going our way. Jaimie, on the other hand, had just started her Navy Women's basketball season. For her, social drunken binge smoking knew no off season.

"Get that thing away from me!" I said laughing. I nearly face planted trying to push Jaimie's hand more forcefully away. The half-smoked cigarette bounced to the ground.

"Ugh, you BITCH!" Jaimie scolded.

My group was trying to blow time. We were about seven people deep into a line that hadn't moved in ten minutes. It was cold outside. The evening wind coming off the Chesapeake moved up Main Street like a wind tunnel. The line of people behind us continued to grow.

We were all waiting to get in to Acme Bar and Grill. It was the last major nightclub scene at the top of the brick paved Main Street in downtown Annapolis, commonly referred to as DTA. Post-11 p.m., Acme was the center of Annapolis nightlife. The meat market was in full effect. Steam from too much body heat inside the bar fogged the restaurant's windows facing the street. The red and blue dance lighting moved around the window pane which rattled with the bass of the music coming from within.

I was out with an eclectic group of USNA woobs. Two of them, Josie and Michele, were my soccer teammates. Well, I guess Josie was actually the only current teammate. Michele played soccer with us for two years but quit after last season. We were still friends. Jaimie was her basketball-playing roommate.

Katie and Jen made up the remainder of our gang. Neither of them played sports. They were firsties. Jen and Jaimie had graduated high school together in New York. Jaimie spent a year at prep school before entering the academy, which is why she was still junior and not a firstie. Katie was Jen's roommate as well as the Brigade Executive Officer, the second highest ranking midshipman in the academy.

The line remained at a dead standstill. Josie and Michele were being entertained by two '97 grads who were currently Marine Corps 2nd Lieutenants grinding through "The Basic School" officer training ninety minutes down the road in Quantico. The girls had been flirting with them since they bought us three free rounds of beers back at Griffins. We had been bar-hopping for three hours so far and I had only paid for one drink.

The longer we sat outside the more we had to entertain random guys gawking and hitting on us. We were collectively about the closest thing to celebrities in DTA.

The DTA nightlife was fun, but it was also a small, centralized place. Well over half of the bar patrons were legally of age midshipmen. One hundred percent of those male midshipmen knew exactly who every single attractive female midshipman was. Other than one or two cute girls working at the mid-store, we were about the only thing they had to look at Monday through Friday.

While that sort of attention might sound good, it definitely wasn't. Most of the attention was unwanted. Even when the physical attraction was mutual, it almost always came with strings attached. Was he in my company? Is he friends with someone in my company? Has he hooked up with my friends or teammates? Will she be mad if I talk to him? Is he just a player? If those questions weren't asked with each new introduction, a girl like me could learn to regret it.

"Summer, Chad Tyler. Chad, Summer Harris," Jaimie pulled me into a group of three male classmates of ours.

"Hey, Chad Tyler," I said with a smile. I tried to be friendly enough. Like all midshipmen man-children, I had to handle early conversations delicately. Male midshipmen tried to act tough, but in reality most of them were incredibly insecure. If I shut Chad down at introduction, his friends would bust his balls all night long. The next morning the only thing anyone would remember was that their hot classmate Summer Harris was an icy bitch.

"I know Summer," Chad bragged to Jaimie. "We were in Naval History class together plebe year."

He looked familiar, but admittedly I didn't have the same level of personal recollection. That wasn't always a bad thing. He was good looking enough that I was willing to listen.

Chad drunkenly chattered on for the next five minutes about himself. He told me stories about his high school sports prowess, how much he drank that night, and how much he loved the movie "Swingers." All three topics bored me to tears. He became less desirable with each word that tumbled out of his mouth. By the time the line started moving again, I was hoping club entrance would break up the conversation without me having to actively blow Chad off.

Another large group of people exited the club. We were comfortably close to entrance, so I prepared to scoot in and ditch good old Chad.

Oh thank god!

I flipped my license to the large rectangular-shaped bouncer. It was still a relatively new experience for me. I was on the older side of my classmates and had turned twenty-one a month earlier. Save a wild birthday celebration that left me puking in a garbage can beside the USNA cobbler shop, soccer season kept me out of the DTA bar scene. It was still a thrill to get carded and approved entrance. No sane midshipman would be dumb enough to pull a fake ID out in downtown Annapolis. That type of risk carried an all but certain chance of getting caught. I was heading into once forbidden land. It was exciting.

The bouncer shined a hand-held pocket flashlight

feigning to check the birthdate on my license. He was a bad actor. I could feel his stare on my breasts.

"Eyes up here, sport." Jaimie slapped the bouncer before a drop of drool fell from his bottom lip. "Need to get this sweater puppet show on the dance floor."

We're going to get kicked out before we even get in.

"Have fun," the bouncer said. His blush indicated his embarrassment over being called out. It was flattering and disturbing all at once. He snapped back into his stoic gatekeeper mode.

Chad and his friends followed behind our group and the bouncer dropped his hand in front of them.

"Sorry, bud, at capacity," the bouncer blockaded Chad's entrance. "Need to wait for a few more people to exit."

I wasn't sure if capacity was a genuine reason for not letting Chad's group in. Deep down the male bouncers loved playing cock-block to their male midshipmen patrons. Even though I was still new to the bar scene, I could tell the bouncers got off on it.

"Ah, what the fuck, man. Seven people just left!" I heard Chad protesting behind me. The bouncer didn't seem open to debate. I smiled to myself, relieved I wouldn't have to make any great effort to ditch my new friend.

"Follow me, I'm gonna see if I can score us a round of free Kamikaze shots," hollered Jaimie over the deafening rap music. I followed her and the rest of the ladies towards the bar. The smelly combination of sweat, booze, and cigarette smoke smacked me in the face.

Acme was packed. It was a midshipmen sausage fest. Everyone in the club was dressed in civies, save a handful of prior enlisted sophomore youngsters. The civies were poor camouflage. The male midshipmen with their short haircuts and general jackassery stuck out like sore thumbs.

Before even reaching the bar, Jaimie was walking towards our group with a six-pack of beer cans.

"Bros, hoes, and Natty Bo's!" Jaimie narrated loudly above the music. She was mocking the scene around us. Acme was well-known among mids for their good price on Natural Bohemian sixers at the bar. Mids drank it as a source of pride and an economical way to keep their beer buzzes going.

I cracked my first Nattie Bo and settled back into my group. I took a sip. It tasted like shit. We stood at the entrance of the dance floor at the front of the bar. Jaimie lit and puffed her fourth cigarette of the past hour. I continued nursing my Natty Bo, if only as a rite of passage.

"SUMMER!" screamed a voice from the crowded dance floor. It was Jack, a nice enough firstie from my company. "God damn, girl! You look smokin' hot in civies."

Maybe that's why they call this place "Smack Me."

I chalked off Jack's over-the-top comment to too many beers. He was normally a sweet guy up in Bancroft. It still annoyed me.

"Summer, SUMMER!" I heard my name called from another direction. It was Katie, the Brigade XO. It sounded like she was arguing with a super-drunk Jaimie.

"What's up?" I replied. I was happy to be engaged in conversation with someone not actively trying to get in my pants.

"That guy over there," she pointed to the front window. "The guy in the black sweater standing next to the tall guy in the red."

My eyes scanned the dance floor following her narration of visual cues.

Ah FUCK!

She was pointing to Mick. I kept my poker face.

"Isn't he that hot new Air Force Captain that started teaching in the poli-sci department?" she asked.

"Ehhhhhhhhhh, WRONG!" Jaimie replied. "I know that shady yet tasty morsel of a Zoomie officer, and NO, that is NOT him."

When all of the guys were in civies it was much harder to differentiate the older mids from the younger officers. Most of them were young, fit, and sporting a short haircut.

Jaimie's memory was correct, even as drunk as she was. Thankfully she didn't know about my history with Mick. Only a few of my soccer teammates knew about my relationship with him. Most everyone else was in the dark. When Mick and I were dating we had to keep it a secret because we were in the same company. Even after Dickley ran off at the mouth a month ago, very few people knew of our relationship.

"So, do you know him?" Katie excitedly continued. "He's cute."

"CUTE? He's fucking HOT!" Jaimie chimed in. "I think I want to lick him!" she continued as she struggled to keep her balance.

Might be time to cut Jaimie off.

"That's Mick," my soccer teammate Josie inserted herself into the conversation in time to save me. "He's '99," she said, intentionally withholding several details on my behalf.

"Do you know him?" Katie asked.

Name, rank, serial number.

"Yeah, he's in my," I began explaining.

"Come on, girl, let's bounce," Josie grabbed my arm mid-sentence.

I took her lead. Before I had time to protest or suggest alternatives I was feeling the sting of cold air out on Main Street.

******

Summer, 0045

"You know, you didn't have to do that back there at Acme," I explained across the table to Josie. I took another long swig of my chocolate milkshake from my seat in the booth.

"I know," she replied.

She was being a good friend. I didn't trust myself either and a part of me was happy she pulled me out of Acme. We spent an hour drunkenly walking amongst quaint brick townhomes a block off downtown's Main Street. Josie listened intently to my venting about boy problems. She had heard the same version of the story about ten times over already. Eventually I smoked my only cigarette of the night, then we decided to treat ourselves to dessert.

My straw slurped as I sucked down the last few drops of my milkshake. Chick & Ruth's milkshakes were a staple of my midshipman experience. The diner was one of the few places an underage midshipman could hang out in downtown Annapolis. Their milkshakes were to die for. I had been pounding them since I was a plebe.

Chick & Ruth's was a five-minute walk to the main gate of the Naval Academy. It had a prime location right in the middle of Main Street. It was a hub, close to all of the most popular bars, reasonably priced, and providing every staple that any good diner should have.

Originally started by its namesake, Chick and Ruth Levin, the married couple ran the downtown restaurant for decades. It was already a landmark. The place had since been taken over by their son Teddy Levin. Teddy was a natural heir to the restaurant, sharing the same passion his parents used to make the place great. During a typical weekend day you could find Teddy socializing with tourist guests and performing magic tricks for their kids.

Chick & Ruth's was so much more than a tourist stop or a popular mid hang out. The entirety of the restaurant's interior was a seventies era orange and yellow throwback. The kitchen shared the first-floor space with the tightly packed dining space. It felt more like a ship's galley than a diner.

The wall behind the kitchen was filled with about a hundred plaques dedicating names of sandwiches to local celebrities and politicians. The rest of the walls were covered with hundreds of pictures of friends, family, and visitors. There were naval pictures from across the globe, autographed pictures of visiting celebrities, and an entire wall dedicated to people that had gotten engaged in the diner.

Post-midnight Chick & Ruth's was a different animal. Teddy and his magic tricks had long since disappeared for the evening. The African American little person working the grill had no less than five meals cooking up at once. His kitchen utensils clanged in an impressive flurry of hustle and execution. A waitress carried a heavy serving tray in each hand. They carefully wobbled above her shoulders as she deftly wove through packed tables and drunken patrons. She did all of this while wearing a black eye patch like a pirate. The place had character, loads of it.

When Josie and I arrived fifteen minutes earlier the place was relatively dead. There was no Friday night liberty for plebes and youngsters. Most of the firsties and my classmates were still sapping the last few minutes of bar time before the flipped lights of closing time prodded them elsewhere. Once the clock ticked past 1 a.m. the bar's burly bouncers kicked everyone on the street. Very few people wanted to head homeward at that time and Chick & Ruth's was the only place within walking distance to the academy that remained open. Besides, nothing quite complemented a ten-drink buzz like pancakes and french fries.

The booths around Josie and I filled in a hurry. The bells hanging from the entry door clanged like an avant-garde jazz tune. Drunken idiots, most of them my fellow midshipmen, flooded the diner until it was standing room only. I watched people climb over each other to make it to their seat. The line to the broom closet sized bathroom was already five people deep and someone had puked by the donut case by the register up front. Josie and I resolved we'd let the puke cleanup and influx of humanity from the bar rush die down a few more minutes before we braved our walk to the cash register to check out. The door bells clanged loudly as another pack of mids made their way in.

Oh shit.

At the center of the shenanigans was Jaimie and the rest of our original crew, plus a few new male friends. Jaimie was hurling vulgarities from her place between two of my taller women's basketball playing classmates. She hung on their shoulders as they drug her in. Mick came strolling in right behind them, chatting it up with his new friend Katie, the Brigade XO.

"Hey, there you are!" I heard a male voice from behind me. Knowing that it was anyone but Mick made it a welcome interruption.

I spun around, happy to oblige my distraction. "Oh, hey." I did my best to hide my immense disappointment. It was Chad Tyler, the guy talking my ear off at Acme that I ditched earlier in the night. He was the one person in Annapolis I wanted to run into less than Mick.

"Thanks for fucking ditching me back there," he immediately ripped into me as he stood next to my chair. His friends had a table a few feet away and I hadn't noticed them walking in.

"I was just," I began rifling my slightly buzzed brain to garner a feasible excuse.

"You know what, spare me the excuse, sweetheart," he talked over my feeble explanation. He leaned closer towards my personal space. I could smell his boozy breath. "You woobs thinks you're the hottest shit around here," he arrogantly scolded, "but let me tell you, at any normal school, like the kind where you aren't outnumbered nine to one, nobody would give you the time of day."

"Oh, okay, thanks for that. I hadn't heard it explained that way before," I sarcastically replied, fighting an urge to punch this guy in the face. I grabbed the check and made my way over to the register. Josie instinctively followed along.

Fuck the puke cleanup, we'll step over it.

"Wait, I'm not finished," Chad said. He grabbed my arm to hold me in place.

"Get your fucking hands off me!" I said. The bar went silent for a split second as everyone's heads turned toward the yelling. I could feel my adrenaline pumping.

This scene caused two small mobs to converge on each other. Chad, who was suddenly dealing with several male mids ready to teach him some class, let go of my arm. Chad's table of friends urgently got up from their table to join the conversation.

"Rip his fucking head off!" Jaimie screamed right beside the fray, colorfully barking orders like a grizzled gunny. Pushing and shoving ensued. We were about five seconds from Chick & Ruth's turning into a mosh pit.

I felt another arm grab me from behind and I swung a punch around without looking at its landing spot. I had no more patience for bullshit.

"Come on, follow me," Mick pulled me away from the confrontation. He didn't seem bothered that I had un-intentionally punched him in the face. Josie was already beside him. He cleared a path to the entrance door. He violently pushed anyone trying to impede our progress out of the way. I did not look back but could hear the ruckus escalating. By the time we made it on to the street and down one block I could hear the police cars making their way to the diner.

"Just another night in Crabtown," Mick broke the silence as we continue to walk toward the yard.

"What was your crew up to tonight before all that?" Josie said trying to prod along any assemblage of conversation.

"You know, the usual," Mick replied. "A couple of Bud Bombers at Riorden's, a few Long Island Iced Teas at O'Brien's, and then shut down Smack Me. "How about you guys?"

"Same, a little DTA bar hopping," Josie explained.

Translation: avoiding you.

I had only been of legal age a little more than a month, but I was rapidly learning how small a place DTA was. It would be virtually impossible for Mick and me to be downtown without seeing each other.

"Sorry for hitting you," I apologized to Mick. "I thought you were one of that dickhead's friends."

"Yeah, no worries, I figured as much," Mick accepted the apology as he rubbed the welt on the right side of his cheek. "Though I feel bad for anyone that has to spar with you in boxing class next semester."

Another block of awkward silence and we had hit Gate 1. I grabbed my military ID, relieved I made it onto the yard safely.

"Well, I better head back and see if I need to bail out any of my friends," Mick made an excuse to exit without having to awkwardly walk into company area together.

"Literally," Josie added. We all had a good laugh secretly hoping that none of our friends were actually arrested. Mick laughed a little more nervously than we did. He left our trio and headed towards Main Street.

Once inside the security gate, I looked Mick's way one last time. His silhouette was indeed heading towards his friends.

Hopefully not towards Katie.

Chapter 19

Damn, I Wish I Was Your Lover
Saturday, November 8th, 1997
Mick, 1645 hrs.

"Is homie done primping his hair yet?" I asked. I stared down at my watch.

Another gust of wind stung my face. I gathered with several of my company mates at our post-football game festivities. Ed and I were in the perfect spot for our 6th company tailgate, midway between the tapped keg and the food table. We already had a burger and a beer in our hands. We mocked the long line of sober plebes now waiting twenty deep for a burnt hot dog. The same hot dog they essentially paid quadruple price for in annual wardroom fees used to subsidize tailgate beer they couldn't drink and a wardroom movie collection they couldn't watch.

Welcome to the Navy, motherfuckers!

Our company's tailgater was settled in the grassy portion of Navy Marine Corps Stadium's parking lot. We had all watched a three-hour dismantling of the Temple Owls football team. The keg of beer provided by our 6th company wardroom fees was enough to keep me out there freezing my balls off for at least another hour or two. If I drank too long in DTA, my bar tab would be my month's pay.

"You know our man, Ndbuze," I continued my roommate bitching, "he's gotta have his hair perfectly brushed before meeting his fans."

"Or he might be taking a post-game interview from the sports writers," Ed provided an alternate theory for the tardiness of my roommate. He sipped his fourth beer and smiled.

"Or he might be primping his hair for his post-game interview," I countered. We both chuckled.

I took another deep chug of draft beer from a red disposable cup. I had left my pewter 2 for 7 beer mug back in Bancroft Hall. The surface of my beer rippled from my shivering. I tried to drink myself warm.

I had forgotten my winter jacket when I stuffed my civies in Ed's illegally parked Jeep stashed a few blocks away in a nearby residential neighborhood. Ed was mastering the art of stashing his Jeep around town without paying for parking or towing services. Second class midshipmen were not permitted to park their cars on the yard. It was typical evil academy shit. Let the juniors drive and have cars, but don't let them park on base.

"Ah man, that's fucking BULLSHIT, you can only goal tend AFTER it hits the fucking cup, dude!" I heard an alcohol-fueled argument over the rules of beer pong escalate. Ed and I turned our attention towards the heated competition.

"Hey fellas, what's goin' down?" I heard a familiar voice approaching from the side. A firm hand slap on my back followed.

"Damn dude, I thought you were planning to sleep in the locker room," I joked to N.D.

"Yo man, what did you expect?" he replied. "We won by four touchdowns. You know coach gotta be praying with the team for at least a half hour after a win like that!"

"Your hair looks good though," Ed added.

He was right, N.D.'s hair was perfectly faded and wavy.

"MaaaaAAAAAaaaan, fuck you," N.D. said with a smile. "You know I gotta stay looking sharp."

It's not that N.D.'s vanity was overly bothersome to us. He was such a well-rounded person otherwise. It was about the only thing we could bust his balls over.

"Oh, man. I forgot to mention," N.D. moved to another topic. "Change of plans for the evening, fellas."

"Dude, you're killing me, man," Ed verbalized his disappointment. We had all been looking forward to an off-campus house party slated for later that evening. A few of N.D.'s teammates rented a place down the road. Anticipating a good time, N.D. had asked us to join him.

All of this was highly illegal by midshipmen standards. Off campus rentals were not only prohibited, but also likely punishable by restriction, and that's just for being at one of these parties. Getting caught renting could get a mid in serious trouble, even expelled. These middie "stash houses" were typically shithole dumps in bad neighborhoods. Most importantly, they almost always had the best parties.

"Nah, nah man, it's good. It's a GOOD thing," N.D. pleaded our optimism. "Party at the football house has been postponed, not cancelled," he continued.

"Man, that sucks," I replied in a frustrated exhale, wondering how this would turn into a good thing.

I spent most of the previous night trying to avoid the pain of seeing Summer out socially in DTA. I still ended up seeing her at half of the places I went to. By the end of the night, I was almost involved in a fist fight on her behalf.

Summer had made it clear over the past month that she didn't want to get back with me after our big blowout. I tried more than a few times to make things right. I realized I had overreacted about Dickley's claims. I tried to apologize. After the fifth rejected attempt, I gave up hope for any near-term reconciliation.

Our breakup was never about the fight in the first place. That was simply the straw that broke the camel's back. I was too dense to realize our mounting problems in time. I was mature enough to accept that now, but not mature enough to gracefully be reminded of it in public.

Seeing other guys hit on Summer out in public was a recipe for disaster. Being around her at this point made me feel desperate. I had been looking forward to a night away from the downtown scene. The cancelled party was a real bummer.

"Trust me on this," N.D. hyped his explanation. "The Temple Owl dance team, you know, those ladies workin' it on the field today," he clarified, eyebrows up. "Five of their finest will be meeting with us at O'Brien's this evening for cocktails."

"The girls on the field today?" Ed asked for clarification. He was salivating already.

"Indeed," N.D. replied. "My boy Chris on the team, he went to high school with one of the girls on the Owl's dance team. Five of them are spending the weekend in

Annapolis. Five of them, three of us right here, plus EZ
and Chris makes five for five."

"Man UP, dawg!" EZ hollered from ten yards away,
finally making his post-game appearance from the locker
room. He must have already been scrubbed into the plans.

"Did you see that fourth quarter booty bouncing to
Missy Elliott?" EZ continued selling the goodness of this
change of plans. He and N.D. had plenty of time today to
watch the dance team in the fourth quarter. The coach
pulled most of Navy's starters out by the end of the third.

"MMM!" N.D. vocalized the enjoyment of his visual
recollection with a smile. "Sun always shines on the midshipmen homies!"

Evening plans were solidifying. It looked like we were
going to stay at the tailgate for at least a few more hours.
N.D. was starting to get tied up with fans asking him endless questions about the game. He obliged with his typical
poise and charm. He could turn it on with the flip of a
switch. Ed looked to be successfully scoring with one of
our prettier classmates on the women's swim team. Both
of my roomies were in their element. EZ and I hung by
the keg. Seeing him bundled up in his fur rimmed goose
down winter jacket made me feel cold.

I looked around in search of a spare jacket, but it was
fruitless. Another cold gust of wind tore through my
t-shirt thin Old Navy sweater. I resolved to chug a little
faster, trying harder to drink myself warm. I made my
way towards the keg line.

I chugged two beers then waited for ten minutes in
the Porta-Potty line before ditching it. Instead, I pissed
behind a parked car when no one was looking. I made my

way towards EZ, N.D., and Ed. The crowd was thinning, but getting much rowdier. I had witnessed two fist fights in the last hour.

Darkness fell and the temperature dropped another ten degrees. I was drunk, but had hardly drunk myself warm. I was going to find my roomies and see where they wanted to meet before our Temple dance crew rendez-vous. I needed an hour or two to sober up and thaw out. I had long since given up hope on finding a jacket.

"MICKEEEEEY! Good to see you, buddy, how ya makin' it?" I heard a voice approach me from behind.

I turned my head. It was my summer cruise buddy Anthony. I don't think I had seen him since our last day aboard the Vandegrift back in San Diego last summer.

"Hey man, long time no see," I replied to be polite. Truthfully, I was hoping it'd be a short conversation.

"Yeah man, feels like it was yesterday that you were killing it in TJ," Anthony continued. "I can't BELIEVE you hooked up with that chick on TV!"

"What's that?" I said playing naïve.

"That chick on TV, you know, the hot chick from the AIDS commercial," he clarified the retelling of a story I had wished forgotten.

"Oh man, I don't think I hooked up with that chick."

"Fuck yeah you did, I was there," he verified his tale's authenticity, as if I needed it authenticated. "You guys were all over each other that night!"

"Man, I was so drunk that night. I don't remember much," I tried to play it off. I looked around to check for witnesses. The last thing I needed was some passerby from my company to hear this conversation. If I had any hope of getting back with Summer, that TJ hook up could never come to light.

Yes, I know that is incredibly hypocritical, imagine what Summer would think.

"That's a shame. That girl was hot. I give you props every time that shit comes up in the wardroom," Anthony replied.

That's the last fucking thing I need.

"Alright man, I gotta bolt. I'm supposed to meet up with my roommates downtown in a bit," I gave my conversation exit alibi.

"Cool man, where you guys hitting up?" he asked.

"McGarvey's at 9:30 I think," I replied.

That was a lie. I was doing what I had to do. The last thing I needed was Anthony bragging about my TJ exploits all night.

I renewed my search for my roommates. It didn't take much longer to find them. Fortunately, N.D. was a large enough man to suck at hide and seek. I saw him talking to a pack of girls by the tenth company tailgate.

"Ah hey man, speaking of the devil," N.D. turned with a happily surprised smile.

Ah SHIT!

There she was, standing in the middle of the group. Summer. I acknowledged her with a brief wave. Summer gave a nonchalant smile and then engaged in another conversation. She must have thought I was stalking her by now.

Fuck me.

With an angled nod I silently asked N.D. to temporarily step outside the social circle.

"Damn dawg, you're a popular man these days," N.D. said once we pulled from the broader group.

"I'm bolting, man. I wanted to see where you and Ed wanted to meet up for dinner and the Temple girls."

"Dawg, another change of plans."

"Damn dude, again?"

"Shiiiiiiit, like you should be complaining," N.D. criticized.

"What the fuck does that mean?" I asked. My pulse was still running high with the anxiety from being around Summer. I wanted to get out of the tailgate and find a different scene for the evening.

"I heard you made quite the impression on the Brigade XO last night," N.D. explained.

"Who, Katie? How do you know about that?" I asked. I looked around to ensure no one else was eavesdropping on our conversation.

Could everyone please shut the fuck up about my romantic life?

"She told me about twenty minutes ago when her and her friends were hanging around here."

"Once she heard I was your roommate, I felt like I had another post-game press conference," N.D. said with a chuckle. "You just missed her."

I had spent about thirty minutes in Chick & Ruth's hanging with Katie. This was after the dust settled from Summer's encounter with her drunken asshole suitor. Perhaps my chivalry caught her attention. Katie and I had a nice conversation over a 3 a.m. crab omelet and I was on my way. I thought she was nice and cute, but she wasn't

Summer.

Maybe I hadn't given up yet.

"Brigade, SEATS," N.D. mocked me, standing at attention as though he was the XO giving orders in King Hall.

"Funny," I said.

"You know it is, dawg."

"So what, you think I should dump the Temple Owl dance team and go chase the Brigade XO?"

"Tempting," N.D. replied, "but nah."

"Who then, might I ask, are you suggesting I hunt down?"

"Here," N.D. said. He reached in his pocket and pulled out a folded piece of paper.

"What's this?" I asked.

"An invitation I suppose. It's not my message to read. I'm merely delivering."

"An invitation to what?"

"An invitation to go up to our room, shower up, sober up, and get your shit together."

"And then what?"

N.D. looked me in the eye. "Read the note, dawg," he said as he extended the folded piece of paper towards me.

I grabbed it from his hand.

"And this time, please don't fuck it up. Ed and I are tired of seeing your ass mope around the room."

My heart skipped a beat. I looked towards the group I had pulled N.D. from moments earlier. Most of the people were still there. Summer wasn't.

"Whatever or however this happened-" I said to N.D.

"Dawg, say thanks and get your lucky ass back to Bancroft," he interrupted.

I still hadn't opened the letter, but I got the gist. I gave N.D. a big, joyful hug.

I headed out to Bancroft and desperately searched for the nearest street light so I could read the note. Even before reading the note I knew who it was from. Summer carried a mini-notebook everywhere. Before I was in her doghouse, I would bust her chops on its sheer nerdery.

I picked up the pace and gripped the note extra tight. I wasn't even a little bit cold anymore.

Chapter 20

It Was a Good Day
Wednesday, December 3rd, 1997
Summer, 1220 hrs.

"MIDSHIPMAN SECOND CLASS GREEN!" bellowed Midshipman Fourth Class Turlington from two tables ahead of me. "YOU HAVE BEEN ASSASSINATED!"

With that announcement, Turlington took off on a dead sprint toward the King Hall exit. Plebe cheers and upper-class jeers coaxed him onward.

Before I had the chance to turn my head and find out exactly where my fellow 6th company classmate was sitting in our company meal area, I heard a chair tumble and a fork fall to the floor. A body zipped by me in a blur. I assumed it was 2/C D.J. Green in hot pursuit of Turlington.

Turlington had about a twenty-yard lead. That might not be enough to outrun Green up four flights of stairs back to company area. If it wasn't, Turlington would surely get a beat down. If he did make it to his room, he could successfully lock his door and avoid immediate retribution.

I looked under the table behind me where the chair lay on its side. There was the evidence of the crime scene.

An empty Hershey syrup bottle and its chocolaty contents widely puddled on the floor. Moments ago Turlington was secretly dousing D.J.'s meticulously spit shined shoes with a full container of chocolate syrup. This under-the-table business was known as "assassination."

Assassinations were surprisingly not that uncommon this time of year. We were in the middle of Army Navy week, smart people kept their head on a swivel. During the week preceding the annual football game against our arch rival, it was accepted tradition that plebes retaliate against their upperclassmen antagonists. It was a small window of amnesty to get payback on the people that made their lives miserable for the past half year. It meant that the three or four biggest dickheads in the company would get tortured by the plebes for a week while everyone else grabbed popcorn and enjoyed the show.

"Man, you guys are wasting valuable energy on Green," Mick said from his table seat beside me.

He wasn't talking to me. He was talking to Speneti and Wilson, the two male plebes remaining at his squad lunch table. I was joining the table as a guest.

"You guys need to focus that rage on Dickley," he continued.

Mick was right. Dickley more than had it coming, especially this week. Three days earlier that idiot almost handed the Army Football team the biggest gift of the holiday season. He had brought a tray of ex-lax brownies to the company watch desk outside of the wardroom after evening meal. N.D. came up from dinner and ate about half the plate. Six hours later he was at hospital point fighting extreme dehydration. He missed two days of practice and lost about ten pounds. Considering he was one of the school's best football players, he was the last guy we needed injured for a game we'd lost five times in a row.

Goddamn, boys are immature.

"He hasn't had the balls to show up at tables all week, sir," Speneti replied.

Speneti was right. Dickley had entirely avoided meals since Sunday night. He knew that he'd have a giant bull's eye on his head all week, and that was before the brownie incident.

"Not to worry, sir," Speneti said after a brief pause. "We'll get some justice for Mr. Okafor."

"Fucking A right you will," Mick replied. "Wilson, you still gotta earn your penance."

Dickley wasn't the only culprit of N.D.'s woes. Wilson was the baker of the ex-lax brownies. They hadn't been intended for N.D., but for Dickley. Wilson had snuck a plate of the brownies into Dickley's room Sunday afternoon following Thanksgiving break.

Dickley had been a victim of Army Navy pranks enough times last year to not naively eat random food left on his desk the first night of Army Navy week. As soon as he saw the brownies, he brought them out for company distribution. I'm sure he had assumed somebody like Mick or Ed, two of the biggest food moochers in the company, would gobble them right up.

No such luck.

"How's N.D. doing today by the way?" I asked Mick, interrupting this rare moment of plebe harassment.

"Good to go, thankfully," he said. "He was fully cleared by Doc this morning. He's out practicing again with the team today. He is still down a few pounds of water weight though."

Mick and I were not only back on speaking terms, we were back together. I tried hard to hold my ground for a month against his advances. When I sensed that he was giving up hope, it only made me want him more. After spending a weekend indirectly watching him get hit on by someone other than me, I caved.

"So digame," Mick resumed his chat with Wilson. "What's the game plan?"

"Game plan, sir?" he asked for clarification.

"Fuck man, the game plan for payback," he answered. "You're lucky to be standing here. If Dawson and I hadn't restrained Okafor Sunday night, you'd surely be a dead man. You owe us. You owe N.D."

He wasn't wrong about that. Initially, Mick's room had only heard about Wilson baking the ex-lax brownies. It took a few hours before all the details came to light and they were able to pin the preponderance of blame on Dickley. N.D., normally mild-mannered off the football field, had wanted to crush Wilson's skull with his bare hands.

"So come on, man, what do you guys have on tap? Army Navy week is halfway over and that douche is sitting upstairs completely unfucked with. That's beyond un-fucking sat."

Mick was tapping into his influence. Up in company area he hardly engaged with the plebes. He generally avoided messing with them altogether. When Mick wanted to lead however, he could turn on the charisma easily.

It wasn't the only thing getting turned on.

Mick waited through another minute of silence. It

was all deliberate theatrics. I knew how he operated. All Wilson and his plebe squad mates could do was stare silently at the carnage of Z Burgers and onion rings leftover from lunch. Sweat beaded on their faces. They were feeling uncomfortable.

"Nothing, Wilson?" I finally chimed it.

"Ma'am," he replied, then stopped.

"Well spit it out, Speneti," Mick insisted.

"Sir, I don't want to discuss our plans in front of a lady," Wilson finally explained his silence.

"Oh no, no, no," I responded. "Speneti, you may not know me very well, but one thing you should know is that I don't get offended easily. I'm a big girl. I wouldn't be here otherwise. Spit it out."

"Ma'am," he said, and hesitated again. "We're planning a Barbershop Treatment for Mr. Bickley's room."

"Barbershop Treatment?" Mick asked. "It's not the Baltimore Aquarium I was expecting, but you have me intrigued. Tell me about this Barbershop Treatment."

"Well, basically we're going to shaving-cream bomb his room," Wilson began unveiling the plan. "Then we're dumping a bag of hair all over the shaving cream."

"Okay, now we're getting somewhere," Mick expressed his approval. "So where are you getting the hair, and how much of it are we talking about?"

"A pillow case full, sir," Speneti expanded upon his roommate's plan.

It wasn't the craziest Army Navy week prank I had heard, but it was decent and would be a pain in the ass to clean up.

"Let's talk pragmatic details," Mick continued. "First

off, hang the shaving cream bottles from the ceiling with a string, that way they splatter from above. If you throw them on the floor, you won't do nearly the damage."

Both plebes nodded in approval.

"Next, make sure when you stick the pin in the side of the bottle, that you heat the bottle with a lighter before you pull the pin out. That generates more pressure in what sprays out."

Another round of nods proceeded.

"Do you have the hair from the barbershop yet?"

"No," Speneti answered.

"Do you at least have the bag of hair lined up from the barbershop?"

"Not exactly, sir."

"Well fuck man, you're not doing very much to cover your tracks," Mick scolded. "Do you know how many upperclassmen get haircuts in the barbershop during the week? Someone might spot you."

"Sir, we're not getting the hair from the barbershop."

"Okay?" Mick replied confused.

Another minute of silence followed.

"Well FUCK, do I need to ask? Where are you getting the hair?" Mick pressed.

"Sir?"

He rolled his eyes, visually conveying his frustration, something he rarely did with plebes.

"Sir, didn't want to be inappropriate in front of…"

"Oh for fuck's sake, Wilson! You heard her, she's unoffendable. Spill the fucking beans, man!" Mick jumped in before I had the chance to.

"We've been collecting shavings throughout the year."

"Shavings? You'd have to be shaving your entire time at the academy to get enough stubble off these fresh faces. Half of you look like you don't even need to shave," I replied.

"No, ma'am," Wilson replied. "Not face shavings."

Mick and I erupted laughing. He even started applauding before he toned it down. We didn't want to give the idea too much attention and inadvertently let the cat out of the bag.

"Ma'am," Wilson continued, "we even got the girls to participate."

"Aaaaaand, that's my cue," I said.

"Unoffendable?" Mick teased as he sarcastically pointed his finger at me.

I left my chair and leaned in closely to Mick to whisper a message intended for only his ears, "Come up to my room in ten minutes and let me show you what I just shaved."

Mick forgot all about the barbershop prank.

"So, what's the Baltimore Aquarium prank?" I heard Speneti ask in the distance as I walked back towards the King Hall exit.

I hoped Mick wouldn't spend too much more time chatting with the plebes. I had an itch that needed to be scratched.

Chapter 21

Lakini's Juice
Wednesday, December 10th, 1997
Mick, 1255 hrs.

The euphoria of finally beating Army in football a few days earlier had yet to wear off. Before Saturday's victory, Army had won the prior five in a row. That meant a half a decade of football misery. The two classes before us had lost all four of their years at the academy. Most of those losses came in heartbreaking fashion. Last weekend's trip to the Meadowlands changed all of that. Bancroft Hall was still buzzing.

Nobody was happier to see N.D. ring the Japanese Bell, a team tradition post-Army victory, than Dickley and Wilson. Thankfully the ex-lax brownies were not a factor last Saturday. N.D. played a spectacular game.

There was plenty to cheer about all around. Not only had we beaten Army for the first time since I had arrived, but we also got to enjoy a week of Army/Navy pranks on the biggest upper-class tools in our company. These were indeed happy times.

We had spent this week wrapping up our last fall semester classes and prepping for finals. After a week of finals we would have nearly three joyous weeks of leave.

Like the end of every semester, the mids had been given two "study days" ahead of the start of finals. As usual, our room wasted those two days stranded in Bancroft napping and playing video games.

My room, along with the rest of the company, had been woken out of our pre-holiday hibernation for our company's version of a Christmas party. The unofficial company get together was an annual tradition since I was a plebe.

The festivities started with a brief talent show. A group of youngsters performed an original rap and choreographed dance to the tune of Digital Underground's "The Humpty Dance." The alternate lyrics had largely been written by me and Ed earlier that day as a way to roast our company-mate firstie Darnell "Dr. Doom" Woodson. The performance slayed. It provided a proper audience warm up to Secret Santa, the night's main event.

"Dear Santa," Tony Castiglio read aloud to a captivated audience of most everyone in 6th company. "All I want for Christmas is to not be suffocated by my sweater of body hair. From Second Class Greer."

The crowd responded with a modest laugh. It was a tame joke considering the event. Castiglio fidgeted in his chair placed in the middle of the company's main hallway. Most everyone in the company sat around him on the floor like a group of raucous kindergartners ready for story time.

"Man, that's WEAK!" a disappointed Castiglio exclaimed. He crumbled the small piece of paper and threw it towards the wall. The mostly seated crowd applauded in approval.

Tonight was one of 6th company's favorite annual traditions. Secret Santa was our company's chance for extreme ball-busting and public humiliation. Participants in the annual ceremony were encouraged to write down theoretical gift requests to Santa in an effort to humiliate other fellow company mates. The notes to Santa were anonymous so the repercussions were few, which made it that much easier to be harsh. I had written a pile of notes over the course of the past 48 hours.

Matt Hackett, the second reader, reached into the box between Castiglio's chair and his. This was his first Secret Santa reading duty. It was an honor given to the two firsties with the least amount of discretion.

Hackett unfolded the paper and read the note silently. He laughed out loud before handing the note to Castiglio.

"This one should go to you, buddy," Hackett justified his exchange to the crowd and slapped Castiglio on the back.

Hackett wasn't quite as uncensored as Castiglio. He was smart. A week earlier the entirety of 19th company lost their Army/Navy liberty over some company shenanigans. Even an Army/Navy win six years in the making couldn't get those poor bastards off the hook. The "Free 19" movement, complete with an Army/Navy game Hawaiian shirt protest, had proven futile. Testing the limits of academy discipline these days was as risky as ever.

"Dear Santa," Castiglio read with embellished theatrics. He paused, then smirked. He really didn't give a fuck about discipline at the moment. He'd read anything written. He shared my level of love for this event.

"All I want for Christmas is some new woobs in this company. Half of them have already blown me!" Castiglio read excitedly before pausing. "From," he resumed, "Second Class ED DAWSON!"

The crowd erupted in laughter. Castiglio stood up for the cheers a acknowledging the curtain call.

This note was a homerun. Ed might not have actually gotten a blow job from half of the girls in the company, but I knew of at least two. Regardless of the actual stats, his WUBA slaying exploits were the stuff of legend.

Ed remained seated next to me against the wall a few feet from where Hackett and Castiglio were sitting. Ed waved his hand to the rest of the crowd with a smile.

Ed was already standing out from the crowd. He showed up to the event wearing a fluorescent yellow and green golf get up. His pancake hat had a large white pom-pom on top. It perfectly complemented his argyle socks and fluorescent green knickers. Ed had finally earned his entry into the company's annual skylarking tournament.

Skylarking was a sport of sorts, a putt-putt golf course designed throughout the entirety of Bancroft. A foam Army/Navy mini-football was smacked around with lacrosse sticks in a competitive by-invitation-only tournament. It had been invented two years earlier when a group of water polo players were fucking off and got scolded by a company officer on duty. He accused them of "skylarking" and the name forever stuck.

After a year of indoctrination as a caddy, Ed had earned the right to play. I refused to caddy a year earlier, so I would again be a lowly spectator. The tournament teed off twenty minutes after Secret Santa.

The laughter eventually died down. Hackett reached in the box to resume the festivities. Summer sat beside me trying not to appear completely annoyed by the event.

This year was the first time Summer had attended our Secret Santa show. Most of the time she wrote it off as "silly boys behaving badly." She wasn't wrong. She knew I loved it though, so this year she braved it out and bit her tongue. Next year, it would likely be Ed and me up there reading.

Summer and I were finally back to some level of normal. The journey to normal had been fun.

My dick was pleasantly chafed. Summer and I had two solid weeks of makeup sex under our belts. The hottest of which happened in the afternoon behind a locked door and a running shower.

Sex in the Hall was distinctly forbidden by academy rules, with threats of immediate expulsion if caught. Summer and I pre-scheduled the times we had off and her roommate was out. Even though Summer wasn't permitted to lock her door, nobody other than her roommate would question her for doing it. It felt so good to be so wrong. Life was good.

Even in issued shorts and a t-shirt, Summer looked hot. I wanted to put my arm around her. I wanted to hold her hand. I couldn't.

I never really cared if anyone knew about us as long as we didn't get busted for it. Summer felt differently. People paid more attention to her than me. The girls around here lived under harsher scrutiny and judgement than we did. I tried my best to be understanding and continued to play along with the secret relationship stuff. Resisting the temptation to affectionately touch her in the moment made me want her even more.

For the last two weeks, Summer and I had been having fun making up for lost time. She finally accepted my apology for overreacting about Hackett. We hadn't re-opened any of our other prior issues and I knew that day would eventually come. I was trying to appreciate the moment we were in.

I glanced down at her taut upper thigh. My gaze lingered over every inch of her leg down to her red toenail polish. I was hungry to have those legs wrapped around me. I diverted my attention back to the Secret Santa show as a distraction.

"Dear Santa!" Hackett exclaimed loudly. Based on previous experience, I knew the loud announcement meant Hackett had picked a winner.

"Thanks for dumping all of the pubes in my room last week," he read with a smile plastered on his face. "It really made a few dicks like us feel right at home."

Hackett maintained his composure, barely. All eyes shot to Dickley. He was sitting around a few of the more tool-ish youngsters. Even they thought they were too cool to hang with him. He looked like a sad child.

Dickley's arms were folded across his chest. He was waiting for the whole thing to be over with. In reverence to the etiquette of Secret Santa, the crowd withheld its reaction until the name was finally read.

"From," Hackett resumed, "Second classes Dickley and Captain America!"

"OOOOOOOOOOOOOHHHHHHHHH!" the crowd erupted in laughter and yelling. The joke of the night had

- 219 -

been read. I had written it.

Hackett stood from his chair in the midst of the cheering and took a hearty bow.

Hackett and I had never really spoken about his role in my breakup with Summer. He had been a drunk asshole. I had done the same thing in Tijuana. I wasn't happy about either. Rocking that boat would not have helped resolve my fight with Summer. For the sake of getting Summer back, we coexisted.

Fucking prick.

It had been a bad week for Dickley. The plebes pulled off the best Army/Navy prank I had witnessed to date. As promised, "The Barbershop" prank was delivered flawlessly. A week after the prank I could still hear him and Captain America loudly complaining about finding random pubes in their room. In the ongoing prank war between our rooms, we had struck a critical blow.

Karma's a bitch.

I found it odd that Dickley was out for this event in the first place. He skipped it entirely as a youngster knowing that even then the plebes hated him enough to make him half of the night's punchlines. I wasn't sure why he would want to hear twenty plus jokes about pubes being in his room.

Captain America had wisely played hooky. Two days before the Army/Navy game the plebes duct taped him into a rolled-up bed mattress and threw him down four flights of stairs. Between that and the pube prank, he was done pressing his luck.

Why wasn't Dickley?

I thought about the mystery of Dickley's attendance over the course of the next ten Santa wishes. Five more of them were about him. Three were about him and his fellow bible thumping girlfriend he had been bonking since she was a plebe.

Something was strange. He kept sitting through it all, without an ounce of reaction. I couldn't figure out the reason for his stoicism, especially given what an absolute fucking spaz he was otherwise.

Then it dawned on me. He wasn't suffering. He was waiting.

The jokes continued. Four more about Dickely, two more about his roommate Captain America, then a string of jokes busting Castiglio's balls for not graduating on time. Dickley continued sitting without the slightest hint of a reaction.

Castiglio peeled open one of the last remaining notes from the Secret Santa box. He was eager to get the embarrassing topic of his delayed graduation out of the minds of everyone else. He read the note and then smiled. He looked my way.

"Dear Santa, thanks for hooking me up with a Hollywood actress this summer in Tijuana," Castiglio read in his dramatic cadence.

My heart paused.

"Maybe you can land her something bigger than an AIDs commercial sometime soon."

Castiglio's showmanship was killing me. His pause felt like an eternity. I already knew the punchline.

"Second class MICKY MCGEE!" Castiglio directed his exclamation my way. He relished the drama. "Way to go, stud," he added in a compliment.

I shrunk three inches. I glanced towards Summer. She stared forward, stewing. She had enough poise to not make a scene. She waited for the crowd to calm down and focus on the next joke before she made her exit. She hid her anger well, but I could see it in the rigidity of her spine as she walked away. This was what Dickley had been waiting for.

Counter strike!

I shot an angry glance his way. He hadn't left the event yet. He was waiting for me to look his way. He was smiling like a Cheshire cat.

I didn't know how Dickley knew about my TJ hookup, but I knew he wrote that note. He knew I had egged on the plebes to execute the Barbershop. I certainly hadn't been shy in my coaxing of them. This was his payback.

Ed looked over and put his hand across my chest. He knew instinctively that I was ready to fight. All I could do was sit there, wanting to scream and cry simultaneously, and glare at Dickley. He was loving every fucking minute of it.

I thought through every explanation I could give to Summer. No matter what my brain came up with, I knew it wouldn't help. She would never forgive me for this, especially after the huge deal I made about her NOT hooking up with Hackett.

Summer and I were over for sure this time. I was wrecked.

Part VII

Harvester of Sorrow

Chapter 22

Heart Shaped Box
Wednesday, February 25th, 1998
Mick, 1255 hrs.

I heard a plate and utensils drop three tables away from my own. I looked over instinctively to find the culprit. Some plebe, obscured from my full view, was already getting his ass chewed for it. I could hear the snarky lecture from Captain America.

I was sitting outside of the company area for lunch. N.D. had invited me to join him at battalion "fat tables" with his football teammates so I could stuff my face with extra portions of lunch. I had spent the past thirty minutes listening to N.D.'s buddies bust his balls about breaking his sparring partner's nose in his boxing "jab class."

I caught Summer in my peripheral. I wasn't trying to. I wished I hadn't. She was seated with her back towards me in 6th company area. Hackett was parked out on a chair right next to her. They had been making a recent habit of doing that.

Summer had been completely ignoring me since the Secret Santa blow up two months earlier. After our fight at the beginning of the school year she had tried to avoid me, but wasn't all that successful. After our last fight, she was much more successful in doing so. There had been no more randomly running into each other at the bars or late nights at Chick & Ruth's. We'd said less than ten words to each other in the past ten weeks.

I looked at Summer tip her head skyward and laugh at something Hackett said. She put her hand on his shoulder and leaned in to whisper something into his ear before leaving the table. I convinced myself I was seeing things. I scanned the company area for a distraction.

I shot a glance two tables over to Dickley with murderous rage. He didn't notice my glare. He was too busy yelling at plebes for some bullshit. If that douche hadn't spilled the beans about my Tijuana exploits, I'd likely be the one sitting next to Summer. The plebe pube hair stint seemed like small potatoes compared to what he'd done to me. In our year-long series of prank battles, Dickley was clearly winning the war.

I hated that motherfucker.

Back in my room, I ran through a depressingly standard routine. I checked my desk, chair, and under my bed pillow for notes. Then I sat at my computer and triple checked my day's inbox. I had excruciatingly verified another morning of Summer's complete radio silence. Countless emails, love letters, and mixtapes had done nothing but find their way in her trash can.

I scrambled to find a clean white works uniform for my afternoon of classes. There was a large peanut butter stain from last Wednesday's lunch on the lone set of white works sitting in my con-locker. EZ connected two good head shots at boxing last week and I forgot all about them needing a wash afterwards.

My macroeconomics class started in twenty minutes. It was at least a ten-minute walk to the classroom. Boxing class was after econ. I needed to throw something over my PT gear. I wouldn't have time between boxing and macro to get changed in my room. I had to act quickly to find a suitable set of white works.

I didn't even bother to look into N.D.'s con-locker. He was a full three sizes bigger than me. There was no way I could walk around the yard without getting shit on by a Marine for looking that slovenly. I couldn't find anything in Ed's closet either. My room was out of options.

Then I remembered where my second pair was hiding. I'd left a pair in Summer's room at the end of last semester. We had snuck in a nooner after swim class.

I put on the white works pants over my gym shorts. At least that part of my soiled uniform set was clean. I threw on my sneakers and tucked in my shirt. I grabbed my book bag and cover. I still needed to find a clean white works blouse close enough to my size.

I tried twice, unsuccessfully, to talk myself into searching in another room. Many of the male mids were around my size. The white works blouse didn't have any rank insignias. I could have just asked a room full of plebes. Before I tried talking myself into borrowing a third time, I was at her door. It was closed.

I knocked and received no answer.

I knocked a second time, this time a little harder. That's when I noticed the door was locked. I listened a little more closely. The shower was running. I took off in fear of hearing anything else going on behind that door.

I spotted classmate D.J. Green five doors down the hallway. He was about my size.

"D.J.," I called out once I made it about ten paces away from Summer's door. "Can I ask you a quick favor?"

"Sure Mick, what's up?"

"You mind if I borrow a clean white works top?"

"Sure man, no problem. Come on in my room, I have a spare set."

I ducked into D.J.'s room. My mind was racing. Was I imagining the worst-case scenario on the other side of her door? Maybe she wanted a private shower without some creep mid barging into her room.

I'd been torturing myself like this since Summer and I split before Christmas. It was slowly driving me crazy. I wasn't over her. She sure seemed over me. The worst part was how easily she seemed to get over me. Then it hit me. That feeling of nausea, anger, and heartbreak all in a single pang.

"Here ya go, man," D.J. said as he handed a perfectly clean white works shirt to me.

"Thanks, man," I said in a daze, temporarily forgetting why I was in D.J.'s room in the first place.

D.J.'s roommate, a genius mathematician we all called Bobo, was doing his physics homework on his perfectly clean desk. The entire room glistened, without a speck of dust. He looked up and gave me a salute before burying himself back into his work.

"Drop them by whenever you're finished. No rush."

I threw the clean white works top over my head. It was a perfect fit. I grabbed my bag and cover from the floor.

"Thanks man, I owe you," I said as I bolted out of the door and into the hall.

That's when I almost bumped into Hackett. He was coming from the other end of the hall. He was in PT gear and flip flops. His face was flush. His hair was wet. He looked like he had just taken a hot shower.

"Hey Mick, how's it goin', man?" Hackett asked as he passed me by. He couldn't wipe the smile off his face. There was a time when I knew that same feeling.

I returned the salutation with a civil head nod. My blood boiled.

Chapter 23

Highway to Hell
Wednesday, February 18th, 1998
Ed, 2145 hrs.

I stared intently at Jimmy Jarvis as I awaited his verdict.

"Ball two," Jarvis replied sixty feet in front of me. He was standing in the middle of the hallway directly in front of the door connecting the fifth and seventh wings of Bancroft Hall.

I pulled my head back with a grimace. "Ball two? You gotta be fucking kidding me, man!"

"What can I say? It was outside, dude."

"Whatever."

"Two and two."

I shook it off, that should have been called strike three. Those were the breaks in impromptu hall ball. We could rarely find willing umpires to call balls and strikes for our athletic showdowns. All subjectively assigned balls and strikes were on the honor system, or whatever paltry interpretation Jarvis adhered to while down two strikes. Per our agreed upon ground rules, the batter owned the final discretion on called strikes.

It sure looked like strike three to me.

Jarvis could sense my continuous silent doubt. He called out to a random company plebe walking, as prescribed post-8 p.m., down the middle of the hallway. "Yo, Pilson, I know you saw that shit. That shit was outside, right?"

The plebe looked over to both of us, smiled, and shrugged his shoulder. He silently squared his corner and headed through the bathroom door without saying a word. Pilson was a smart plebe.

"He stayed quiet because he knew that shit was a BALL!" Jarvis continued his argument.

I turned my back to the plate and paced away from the mound shaking my head, as though this would somehow be featured on Sports Center tonight. I bit my lip and tried my best to gather myself.

The great irony in all of this was that neither of us even played baseball. I hadn't pitched in a formal baseball game since little league. Jarvis, Navy's returning net minder for the varsity Navy Lacrosse team, had never even played the sport in an organized fashion. Somehow, all of that didn't seem to matter.

A week into the academic year, Mick and I were playing PlayStation with Jarvis into the wee hours of the night. When that lost its buzz, we transitioned to more directly physical confrontations. There had been one-on-one foot races, darts, nerf basketball games, and even the occasional slap boxing match. Jarvis was the best goalie Navy had seen in decades for a reason. His athleticism usually found a way to win in virtually anything we competed in.

Baseball was the exception. My arm was more than Jarvis could handle. In the past month, I had struck him out three of the last five showdowns. When he didn't strike out, he was hardly hitting the ball very well. All of this drove Jarvis nuts. He kept on asking to play, thinking eventually he'd get the win over me. He was a good enough athlete that he'd eventually start beating me with practice. In the meantime, I loved beating him.

He tapped his newspaper stuffed whiffle ball bat on the folder that was currently acting as a makeshift home plate. He squinted slightly and stared me down.

"Come on, man, quit moving the fucking plate," I complained. He hadn't moved it. He stepped out of the box, pissed that I had intentionally delayed my pitch. He was already torqued up that I had delayed my second pitch of the at-bat by selling a classmate chewing tobacco out of my hidden room stash. Jarvis almost always pressed too hard with two strikes. I was trying to rattle him a bit.

"Man, I didn't move the GOD DAMN plate. You're inventing shit to get mad at now."

I took a deep breath, my nerves calmed, and I mentally zoned into the game. I wiped the sweat from my brow and placed my foot on the piece of masking tape we had measured and stuck to the hallway floor, establishing appropriate plate-to-mound measurements. I stepped forward with my right foot and leaned over it. I held the tennis ball in my right hand behind my back glancing over my left shoulder at an imaginary base runner that wasn't even there.

"Mr. Dawson."

I ignored the summoning from behind me.

"Mr. Dawson! Mr. Okafor is calling from the main office with an important message," said Midshipman Fourth

Class Simpkons. Simpkons was unfortunately assigned the nightly Company Mate of the Deck watch. N.D. was manning the watch a few floors down in the Bancroft Hall main office. Just like everyone else currently standing watch, he'd be stuck there till midnight.

I stepped off the mound as if this were an official baseball game. "Fuck, Simpkons! Can't you see that this shit is important?" I scolded. "Tell him I'll give him a call in five minutes."

Simpkons slinked back to his post at the company watch desk outside of the wardroom. I stepped back on the mound. Jarvis dug into the imaginary batter's box. I renewed my pitching posture.

"Sir!" I heard Simpkons yell from the mate's desk.

WHAT?!" I yelled with increased frustration.

"Mr. Okafor told me to tell you, and I quote, 'to get your ass on the phone.'"

I slammed the tennis ball down in frustration. "This isn't over," I said pointing to Jarvis.

"Three-minute rule, man," he reminded me hands up, shaking his head in non-verbal disagreement. "You give me more than a three-minute delay and the count starts over. You're on the clock!"

I resisted the extreme temptation to argue Jarvis and his attempt to weasel his way out of the two-strike count. Instead I made my way towards Simpkons and the mate desk.

"This better be fucking good," I told Simpkons as I snatched the company phone out of his hand.

"N.D., what's up?"

"It's Mick, man, he needs our help."

"What's up?"

"He called me at main office, loaded out of his mind. Said he needed a ride."

"So get a fucking cab, man, what's the deal?" I was still venting from getting pulled away from striking out Jarvis.

"I don't know, man. He sounded barely coherent. He mentioned something about a car accident, cops, and serious shit," N.D. explained. "I don't know if he was drunk babbling, but he was at least sober enough to remember that I was on main office watch."

Unfortunately, this Mick shit show was becoming a common occurrence. Sure, Mick liked to drink since I'd known him, but the past two months were different. I caught him drinking from a bottle of Jack Daniels stashed in his desk drawer before morning classes last week, and that was during the week of restriction he had earned boozing on duty. Mick had been lucky, N.D.'s football teammate Kenny Bryans had been given a Black N for virtually the exact same "drinking over duty weekend" offense last fall. Mick just earned a suspended one, meaning if he got fried the rest of the year, instant Black N. N.D. and I were doing our best to look out for him.

"Where is he?" I asked.

"Denny's, the one up on Route 2, I think."

"Whose car did he wreck?"

"Fuck if I know man, I don't want to talk too much about it. I got a quarter of the company down here standing main office watch with me. Let me know if you can help him. You got two hours to get him in ahead of bed checks."

I took a deep breath. "I need a few minutes to find a

car parked on the yard."

"Bet, thanks, dawg. Call me when you get in. I'm down here till midnight."

I slammed down the phone and yelled from behind the mate's desk over to Jarvis, "You're a lucky man."

He smiled and responded, "New count, Eddie."

I replied with a defeated middle finger.

It was hard being around Mick in his current state. I felt bad for him. Since he and Summer broke up, something inside him snapped. He'd been a train wreck since we got back from the holidays.

I made my way to Hackett's room. I knew he had a car on the yard, but more importantly he wouldn't ask any questions. He wouldn't rat me out for sneaking off the yard either.

I had to hustle. Assuming Hackett was around, and willing and able to lend me his car, I only had two hours to get Mick in ahead of bed checks.

I swung open Hackett's door without knocking. He was sitting behind his desk spitting tobacco in an empty soda bottle.

"Ed, what's going on, big guy?" he responded positively to my impromptu visit.

"Hacksaw, my man, quick favor to ask."

"S'up?"

"You mind if I borrow your car? Only need it for an hour or so."

Most every other firstie in the company would have at least asked what I was up to, or where I was going. Instead Hackett immediately reached into his desk to grab the car keys.

He looked for five seconds in his open drawer, shifting some contents around. Then he checked the drawer beneath it. Then he stood up and checked his con-locker.

"Damn," he said. "Someone either already borrowed my car or I lost my keys."

I felt the door open behind me and a firm tap on the shoulder. "What's going on, Eddie?" said Hackett's roommate Chris Mackadoo.

"Whaddup, Mac?" I returned the greeting and a hand smack. I returned my attention to Hackett.

"Mac, you know if anyone borrowed the car?" he asked his roommate.

"Nah, didn't see nothing like that. Why?"

"I can't find my keys. Ed needed a car."

Mac headed directly to his desk. He opened his con-locker and tossed me his keys. Navy's starting quarterback's toss was right on the money.

"Take mine," he said. "You scratch it, I'll fuck your shit up," he said with a smile.

"Thanks man, I'll take good care of her."

Now I just need to find Mick.

******

Ed, 2230 hrs.

Traffic on Route 2 was much heavier than expected post-10 p.m. on a weeknight. I drew closer to the Denny's that I hoped Mick was still sitting in. Within a hundred yards of the restaurant, I noticed the flashing police lights. Then I solved the mystery of where Hackett's car was. The wrecked black Mustang GT was left perpendicular to the lanes and blocking the northbound section of the highway. A tow truck was in the middle of hauling it out of the way. A policeman directed traffic onto the shoulder and around the wreckage. Suddenly I was hoping Mick wasn't anywhere in sight. Thankfully I didn't notice him sitting in either of the two police cruisers parked nearby.

I passed the accident and made my way into the Denny's parking lot. It was a slow weeknight at Denny's. I pulled into a spot near the main entrance of the restaurant. That's exactly where I saw Mick. He was leaning on the newspaper vending machine smoking a cigarette.

"Eddie! Thanks for coming out, man!" Mick exclaimed in slurred speech. If the newspaper machine wasn't holding him up he'd surely be laying in the mulch next to the restaurant's entrance.

"Fuck man, you gotta get outta here," I ordered. "Did the cops see you or talk to you?"

"Those guys? They're clueless," Mick said with a hiccup. "I've been eating a grand slam breakfast for the past hour, watching those assholes try to figure out which idiot wrecked their car and parked it in the middle of the highway."

"Yeah, I noticed the park job," I commented shaking my head in disbelief. "Does Hackett know about this?" I asked, trying to get Mick to explain what was going on.

Mick was about to respond when he paused, putting his index finger over his lips as if to hold in whatever was bubbling up. He swayed like a groggy boxer in the tenth round. Then he let out a large belch. It reeked of booze and pancake syrup. I was impressed he didn't puke.

"That Hackett," Mick began his explanation. "He's an

asshole. He thought he could steal my girlfriend, so I figured I could steal his car."

Shit, he found out.

I had only known about Hackett and Summer for
about a week. They'd been hooking up for the past month.
It seemed to be more than a fling. N.D. told me about it
a week ago. He had heard it from a few of his football
buddies.

We debated breaking the awful news to Mick. N.D.
convinced me not to do it. He said that as fucked up as
Mick had been since Christmas, news like that wouldn't
help things.

I liked Hackett, and he hadn't done anything wrong
this time. I knew that he had pulled some shit with Summer at the end of Plebe detail. When I tallied it all up, I
just liked Mick better.

"Come on, man, let's load up the whip and get you the
fuck outta here. We still have time to get in before bed
check. You sure nobody saw you get out of that car from
the highway?"

"Totally sure," he replied in a slur. "The waitress crew
in there spend ninety percent of their time smoking cigarettes in parking lot out back. They didn't see shit."

Convinced there were no direct eyewitnesses, I cau-
tiously brainstormed what other incriminating evidence
he might have left. There were certainly prints in the car,
but Mick could explain that away from previous trips.
He'd been in the car several times in the past year. The
cops would lose interest in a case this small in a matter
of hours. I shifted my focus on getting Mick to Bancroft.

"We gotta roll, dawg, let's go," I coaxed Mick into the

car. In no time we were back on the road home riding in style in Macadoo's new Jeep Grand Cherokee. Even better, the SUV had military stickers to accompany those plush leather seats.

I hoped the guard at the gate eight entrance would assume I was a firstie and wave us in without hassle.

"Dude, whatever you do, tell me if you have to puke and I'll pull over. Mac told me he'd kill me if I returned his ride fucked up."

******

Ed, 0045 hrs.

I sat on the couch beside a vocal Mick in the wardroom. Thankfully forty-five minutes after final bed check most everyone was asleep and the wardroom was empty. Miraculously, we made it back to the yard in time for bed check and Mick wasn't in a police car. We were very lucky. I had pulled off some crazy shit in my days at the academy, but Mick took the cake tonight.

Five minutes earlier I had put *Goodfellas* in the VCR hoping that watching it for the seventy-third time might distract Mick enough to pass out on a wardroom couch. I avoided our room since N.D. was currently sleeping after spending four hours stuck on main office watch duty. Mick was loaded, but he held his shit together enough to not get busted for acting disorderly.

I had never seen Mick cry before tonight. He had been depressed since he and Summer broke up a few months earlier. Today his worst suspicions with Summer and Hackett were confirmed. This was new territory in the post-Summer order. He spent the whole car ride home explaining how dumb he was to lose her. Then he'd sprinkle in a mention about what a dick Hackett was. He was a real downer tonight, but he was still my friend.

The door swung open. It was Hackett's roommate Mac rolling in to search the wardroom fridge for a late-night snack. He always had two to three boxes of Chinese food stashed there at any given time.

"What's up, Mac," I said as he entered the room. "Did Hackett give you those keys I dropped off a little while ago?"

"Yeah man, we're good."

"Thanks for letting me borrow the Jeep by the way. I left it in show room condition."

"Yeah, whatever man," Mac responded with a smirk. "Yo, speaking of cars, did y'all hear what happened to Hackett's ride tonight?"

"Dance Spider! That fucking Spider is gonna fucking dance!" Mick drunkenly yelled at the movie playing on the screen. He was oblivious to anything happening around him.

I ignored Mac's mention of the car. I figured if I didn't respond he might not mention anything more about it. This was not the case.

Mac continued, "Dawg, the cops show up at main office an hour ago lookin' for Hackett. He goes down there, they ask him a bunch of questions. Someone stole his car and wrecked it up Route 2 tonight. Shut the whole road down and shit."

"Damn," I said with as little emotional reaction as possible.

"What was that?" Mick's attention was distracted from the movie.

I slapped his chest with Ric Flair like force. I was hoping it would wake him up enough to not say anything that would reveal he was in fact the idiot that stole and crashed Hackett's car.

Mac continued his story. "Damn police made me come down for an interview and shit. Just to validate that Hackett wasn't the cat that stole and crashed his own car. Man, who the fuck would steal and crash they own damn car? Unheard of man. Unheard of."

Mick leaned forward about to chime in. "Maybe it was those asshole '96ers from 9th company," he jokingly referenced the firsties that had been arrested two years earlier for operating an illegal car theft ring.

I grabbed Mick and aggressively drug him to the hallway. I caught him by surprise and was able to get him out of the wardroom without much struggle.

"Damn Mac, Mick's about to hurl!" I yelled back towards Mac, hoping he would buy the excuse for our quick exit.

Once we hit the hallway, Mick regained his balance. He began to struggle and put up a fight. I wrestled him down the hall and through the bathroom doors. Eventually I pinned him against the bathroom stall. If he had been sober it would have been a much harder fight. The angrier he got, the harder he fought. He began to yell and I smacked his face. We were both huffing and puffing.

"YO! Shut. The. Fuck. UP!" I said trying to talk sense in him. "That was Hackett's roommate in there. Next to Hackett, THE last guy you want to be chatting about the evening with."

Mick came to his senses enough to stop struggling. "Alright, I get it," he said catching his breath.

"Come on man, N.D.'s asleep by now. Let me get ya a shot of Nyquil and a barf bucket and we'll be waking your hungover ass up for morning quarters formation before you know it."

Mick smiled, "Thanks, man."

We made our way back to the room. I stood close to ensure he didn't face plant, or try to escape. Right before our room, he stopped short. He turned.

"That motherfucker! That motherfucker Dickley. If it weren't for that motherfucker none of this shit would have happened," he angrily pointed at Dickley and Captain America's door.

I silently let him vent. I was confident most everyone on the floor was asleep this late on a weeknight.

"Here's what I got for those motherfuckers!" he exclaimed before pulling his penis from beneath his shorts and urinating in their trash bucket left outside in the hall for morning pickup. It was an impressive show of accuracy, stream power, and quantity.

I heard a rustling behind the closed door. Somebody was actually awake in there. I grabbed Mick and yanked him toward our room as the door opened. A trail of urine followed us. I was fairly confident we made it into the room before anyone saw us. I hoped the pee trail didn't give us away.

Chapter 24

Let It Loose
Wednesday, February 25th, 1998
Summer, 2135 hrs.

"Decent?" followed three light knocks on my door, an academy-mandated courtesy of any male entering my room.

"Yeah, come on in," I responded from my desk.

A silhouette as big as the door frame entered my room.

"How's it going, big fella?" I greeted N.D.

"Aww'ight, I guess," he replied. "Is Sarah around?" he asked before taking my roommate's chair for a seat.

"No, you're good. Sarah is finishing a lab project with her partner from another company," I answered. "Knowing her, she'll be gone until bed check.

"Cool, cool, cool," he said, pulling out the chair and grabbing a seat. He took a deep breath and hesitated speaking next.

"Congrats on making captain by the way," I complimented N.D. He had just recently been elected senior defensive captain of the varsity football team. It was the first time I had the opportunity to congratulate him since finding out about it a week ago.

"Thanks," he replied with a forced half-smile. I could tell he wasn't here for small talk.

I hadn't seen much of N.D. the past few months. My breakup with Mick had me avoiding their room entirely since Christmas break. It sucked because I liked N.D. and still considered him a friend. Whatever beef I had with Mick had nothing to do with him.

Another minute of awkward silence ensued.

"Look," he finally broke into his planned agenda. "We gotta talk."

"About what?" I replied already suspecting the answer.

He gave me a look that verified my hunch without words.

"FUCK Mick," I said angrily shaking my head.

"It's not like that," he assured me.

"Does Mick now need your help in his romantic pursuits?"

N.D. took another moment of silence.

"Well?" I asked perturbed.

"He knows."

"Knows what?"

"About you and Matt."

"GOOD!" I said. "Explain to me how that's anybody's business or remotely my problem?"

I was happily dating Matt Hackett. I didn't care how Mick felt about it. Frankly, if Matt hadn't so vehemently denied our boat hook up when the rumor mill was spinning, Mick and I would have never gotten back together again in the first place.

"It's not your problem," N.D. tried to pacify my building anger. "Mick though, I'm really worried about him.

You heard what happened last week?"

"What, the Dickley pee can incident?" I replied. "It doesn't take Sherlock Holmes to figure out Ed was covering for his drunken asshole roommate. I guess even Teflon Man bleeds every now and then."

N.D. let out a chuckle. "I guess restriction karma did finally catch up with Ed. That's some Al Capone tax evasion type shit right there."

Captain America had been waiting outside the Company Officer's office at 0630 the next morning to rat Mick and Ed out for pissing in his garbage can. Ed took the blame for Mick, or so I not so astutely surmised. Ed was restriction-bound before he took his morning's first bite of blueberry flapstick.

"Look, Summer, I'm not worried about what you got goin' on with Hackett. It's none of my business. I like both of you, so we all good there. It's Mick, man. He's been a drunken disaster this entire semester. I caught him swigging on some bum liquor bottle before class the other day."

"Yeah, that sucks, but not my problem," I said coldly. "Lucky for Mick, he's got friends like you that care about him," I continued. I wasn't about to let Mick's immaturity and irresponsibility drag me any further down than it already had.

"Look, Summer, I'm not here to ask you to take care of Mick. I'm just sayin', now that he knows, can you try to be a little more discrete between you and Matt? At least for the next few weeks? I'm seriously worried about Mick. I'm afraid he might end up hurting himself."

"Mick's an adult. Maybe he should finally put on his "big boy" pants and grow up, or maybe he should get some help."

I wasn't completely callous. I knew that buried deep down inside of me there was a place that felt sorry for Mick. I didn't have the time to find it, nor the desire to see what else those feelings might open back up. I wasn't having any of it. I still had my own shit to deal with.

We both remained silent for a few more minutes. N.D. looked disappointed, but he kept his mouth shut. He'd delivered the message. I'd received it. The only other place this could possibly escalate to was talk of "hate chitting" out of the company.

N.D. got up and left. He didn't have the balls to go there with me.

Chapter 25

Dazed and Confused
Wednesday, February 25th, 1998
Mick, 1845 hrs.

"Sir, you now have twelve hours and fifteen minutes till morning quarters formation, and fifteen minutes till midshipman health lecture!" four male plebes screamed from the other side of my room's closed door. They were beginning a modified version of a regular chow call. It was loud enough to be heard over top of the Method Man rhymes blaring on our room's stereo system.

Regular chow calls were an unfortunate reality of plebedom. One day a week each plebe was assigned one of six stations in the middle of the hallway to announce two iterative time warnings until formations. These human alarm clocks usually happened twice a formation for two formations. It was chum in the water.

"Twelve hours and fifteen minutes till formation? Fifteen minutes till health lecture?" I queried in criticism to my room while shaking my head in disgust. "That's not even a real fucking chow call."

The script of a chow call was standard stuff. The plebe chow caller would announce time, location, uniform, and meal menu. A chow call was to be fast, it was to be loud, and it was to be perfect. If it wasn't all of those things, one of the company dicks would assign "all calls" for the entirety of the week. A tool like Captain America would invent his own plebe chow calls as an additional opportunity to harass plebes.

Imperfect chow call execution isn't exactly what landed Mason, Chung, Gillie, and Jimmereson on "all calls." The four plebe roomies had fallen victim to the company's two biggest tools under different circumstances. Captain America caught Gillie, the room's smallest occupant, sneaking in an unauthorized daytime nap under the sink cabinet he was small enough to fit in.

Captain had a standard playbook for plebe torture, all calls were usually a part of it. The plebes would do their all-week mandated chow calls right outside our door at the end of the hall. Dickley and Captain loved torturing plebes conveniently located so close to their room. They also knew it annoyed the shit out of our room.

I could already hear Captain giving the plebes shit. They hadn't even made it halfway through the chow call before he was dressing them down.

"OOOH how nice of you gents to actually make it on time," I heard him sarcastically compliment the doomed foursome on the other side of the door. "Guess you guys didn't get caught up rolling around in your room together, like before lunch formation, huh?" he continued.

Captain was constantly dropping these sorts of inappropriate innuendos. I could never tell if he was trying to be funny, mean, or resentful.

"Good ol' Captain America," Ed said as he walked

through the door shaking his head in disgust and patting specks of dust off his service dress blues uniform with a piece of tape wrapped around his palm. His patting was incessant.

The opened door allowed the volume of Captain's scolding session to increase for a moment. It gave me a headache.

"Why are you all dressed up?" I asked looking for a conversation to distract me as the door behind him finally closed. "I thought the uniform for the briefing tonight was blue and gold jogging suits? I swore I heard the plebes yell it out a minute ago before gayblade out there started laying into them."

"Dickhead Duty Officer tonight," Ed explained. "All restrictees have to wear SDBs today because in the morning's first restriction muster three people pinned their uniform ribbons a half centimeter too high over their jacket pocket. He said all restrictees lost Blue and Gold privileges for the briefing. He's even visually inspecting us when we sign out of Bancroft to head over."

Ed's predicament was all my fault. He saved my ass from the Denny's parking lot and kept my car theft story secret. Then I had to be a drunk asshole and piss in our neighbor's garbage can.

Captain America was up that night. He should have been asleep by then but he was pulling an all-night study like the nerd that he was. He heard us horsing around outside the room.

Without hesitation, Ed took the blame for me. He knew that I had a prior Black N, and one more hanging over my head in probation for drinking on watch. He jumped on the grenade. I didn't want him to do it, but he confessed to the crime he didn't commit anyway. A contradiction to his story would have landed both of us an honor offense. I kept my mouth shut.

The police caught up with Hackett and his trashed car but they never did figure out that I was the drunk asshole who lifted it and parked it wrecked in the middle of Route 2. The insurance, which I doubt he paid himself, covered the repair expenses. I hardly felt bad for him and that was before I remembered he was fucking Summer.

"Ah the lovely world of restriction," N.D. chimed in, distracted from a heated game of Madden with EZ on the PlayStation.

"Wait, it gets better," Ed continued. "At lunch that douche assigned everyone on restriction an extra seven fucking days!"

It was a harsh reality of restriction. Being on restriction you could much more easily be assigned extra days of restriction. There was no due process to it, some Duty Officers handed extra days out like candy. Ed had been on restriction for almost a month. He had barely chipped more than ten days off of his sixty-day sentence because of all the days iteratively added to his punishment while on restriction.

"Fucking Marine Captain," Ed continued complaining. "Fucker shows up to 6 a.m. restriction muster with a ruler and spends the next forty minutes measuring everyone's ribbon placement."

N.D. and I knew the stories all too well. We had both stood our fair share of restriction musters. Each of us had earned the notorious Black N, the academy's version of a scarlet letter, our plebe year. N.D. earned his at a public comedy performance that culminated with him drunk-puking on an Air Force Colonel. I incinerated my car in the middle of T-court during Army Navy week. We collected our hundred demerits, marched hours of tours, and did well north of sixty days of restriction a piece.

"Nah, ah hell nah, we're not pausing and walking away from this game now!" N.D. screamed at EZ. EZ was already putting on his Blue and Gold jogging suit top after pausing the Madden game on our illegally hidden PlayStation and TV. They had both been playing since they had returned from remedial swim class earlier in the afternoon.

"Man, it's time to go, dawg. My company officer's been riding my ass all month over timeliness to these things. He's personally taking attendance and everything, dawg," EZ rationalized his exit strategy. "I already got busted by Satan for showing up two minutes late for lifting stretches yesterday, had my ass on Jacobs Ladder for fifteen minutes. Almost puked after ten."

Satan was the nickname of the varsity football strength coach. He routinely assigned tardiness punishment on Jacobs Ladder, a hellish inverted ladder treadmill contraption. I think half of what made EZ so damn hard to box this semester was because he was so well conditioned from all of his collective Jacobs Ladder punishments.

"Come on, dawg, we got a minute thirty left in the game. You're down two scores, no timeouts, and it's fourth and twenty-six from your own thirty yard line," N.D. complained loudly. "Punt the damn ball, turn it over on downs, or hand me some trash interception. I'm getting the ball back, takin' a knee, and TAKIN' your damn title!"

It was widely known that EZ was the reigning champ at Madden. I hadn't heard about anyone beating him in at least two months and I had personally seen him beat N.D. four times this week. N.D. dominated almost everything and anything in life that he put his mind to. The fact that he couldn't beat EZ on a regular basis only made him want it more badly.

"EZ, take it with grace, my friend," Ed said on his way out the door. "This game is over. Punt him the ball, and let him bring in the victory formation."

The door remained open as EZ contemplated staying. I once again had to listen to Captain dressing down the plebes right outside of our door.

EZ sat back down in front of my con-locker, which held our contraband electronics. He unpaused the game and dialed up the punt team. N.D. put in his "punt safe" return team. The ball snapped and EZ ran a fake punt, scored a touchdown, and pulled within four points.

"Bring out your damn HANDS, TEAM DAWG!" EZ was standing on his chair in excitement. EZ was a good football player in real life, just not nearly as good as N.D. was. EZ loved being able to hold this PlayStation victory over him.

The door popped open. It was Captain America.

"Hey, N.D., you taking attendance tonight?" he asked as he poked his head through the door.

N.D. had assumed platoon sergeant duties this semester from Summer.

N.D. instinctively slammed the con-locker door shut as EZ was executing his onside kick on Madden. The controllers both fell on the floor and N.D. scrambled to hide the gear in my con-locker.

"Yeah man," N.D. answered, "we're good."

After three years together as company-mates, we all knew that Captain America always skipped out on the annual pre-spring break STD briefing. He justified missing it for religious reasons. It was always the same argument. He would never even consider sex outside the sacred bonds of marriage, much less seek it out from some disease-riddled hussy down in Cancun. He therefore didn't need to listen to corpsman preach on about it for an hour in Alumni Hall.

As if he could even get laid if he wanted to.

I wish N.D. was a big enough dick to make Captain go to the briefing against his will, for spite's sake, but he didn't think that was a battle worth fighting. I wasn't so sure.

Two weeks after the pissing incident and I couldn't even look at, much less speak to that douchebag Captain America without wanting to pound the brains out of his skull. It was for the better. I was in so much hot water with all of my disciplinary issues that anything short of being an angel would have me packing for home with a sixty-five grand dinner tab. I sat in silence staring blankly at my desk's computer screen. Captain ducked out to the hall without harassment.

EZ stood up miffed. "Dawg, that's some buuuuuuuullshit. I win, you forfeit. I'm still the damn champion 'round here." He raised his fist and headed out the door. He wasn't mad. He just didn't want to walk a half mile to Alumni Hall and listen to N.D. bitch and moan about how he was going to eventually win the game.

"Come on, Mick, let's bounce," N.D. nodded his head in my direction.

I zipped my jogging suit jacket and intentionally waited to be the last out of the room. I snatched the flask hidden underneath my neatly folded t-shirts. In momentary isolation, I took a deep swig and tucked the booze into its hiding place. I hurried out to the hallway so no one would notice my lagging behind them.

"You know EZ was getting that onside kick," I said as I caught up with my pack.

"Unheard of man," N.D. said.

******

Mick, 2025 hrs.

"And this last picture is one example we saw after a West Pac back in ninety-two," the Navy Corpsman narrated from the stage set up atop the basketball court of Alumni Hall stadium.

In unison, the audience let out a cringy groan. Before them in twelve foot-big screen television glory was a picture of a genital wart the size of Jabba the Hut.

I tried to look at anything other than the giant television screen. I caught the visual of Summer and Hackett sitting together for the lecture. Now that I knew about Hackett, I was able to realize how little Summer cared about hiding it from me. I could feel my heart eating away before forcing my attention back on the giant genital warts. My buzz was starting to wear off.

"So if you find yourself in a sexually oriented situation next week," the presenting corpsman continued his lecture, "please remember this stuff."

"You taking notes, Micky?" Ed elbowed me from the seat next to me.

I let out an awkward laugh. The weight of my guilt made all of my interactions with Ed awkward. Those feelings piled on top of what I was going on with Summer had me horribly depressed.

God, I need a drink.

The lecture continued for five more minutes with detailed descriptions of where free condoms would be accessible throughout Bancroft before spring break departures. It capped off over an hour of staring at hundreds of disturbing STD pictures. Part of the lecture was educational, part of it was to scare the shit out of us.

Mission accomplished.

The brigade was dismissed from Alumni Hall and we were slowly filing out of the stadium seats and returning to Bancroft. The delayed trudge gave everyone excited for spring break ample time to brag and pontificate about their plans for debauchery. It only made my stomach sink more.

"Hey man, did you cash my check yet for the deposit?" I asked while making my way down Stribling Walk.

"Nah man," Ed answered.

"Come on, dude, it's the least I can do."

"Forget about it, Mick," Ed said calmly as he kept walking. "Dude, did EZ pull off that Madden comeback?" he said, trying to change the subject. He knew damn well that N.D. lost. If he had won, N.D. would have been mouthing off about it to his football teammates for the past hour.

"Come on, man, I'm serious," I said as I grabbed Ed by the elbow. "Seven hundred bucks is the least I owe you," I didn't give up on the topic. "If it weren't for my drunk ass, you'd be boarding a plane to Cancun in less than twenty-four hours."

Ed stopped and shrugged his shoulders. "Okay," he finally gave in. "I'll take it."

Ed knew that I didn't come from much money. He did. He also knew that I deserved to pay every penny of what I had made him lose. He was just too good of a guy to make the poor kid pay. In time he realized it was about more than the money to me.

It was the first thing that evening that made me feel remotely okay. I had been trying to pay Ed for the down payment deposit he lost on his trip since the moment he got fried covering for my sorry ass.

Every member of the class of '99 had received their second class loan a few weeks earlier. It was a low interest financial advance of seventeen grand that we didn't start making payments on until after graduation. Half of my classmates had already planned to blow theirs on the usual suspects of cars, excessive bar tabs left on credit cards, and spring break. I guess I was following the trend. It just wasn't my spring break that I was paying for.

"So, are you still down for my photography mission over spring break?" I asked Ed.

"Yeah, for sure," he replied. "And dude, I'm not taking your money for that either."

"Come on, man," I pleaded. I had previously asked Ed to take some pictures inside Bancroft Hall while he was stuck on restriction over spring break.

"You know I'm down for doing that shit for free," he replied. "I've already played six hundred games of free cell on the computer. At least this task will give me something to break up the boredom."

"The money ensures that you do an extra good job," I pleaded. "Plus, it would make me feel better."

"Fuck man, okay, OKAY, I'll take the extra grand for the pictures too," Ed agreed. I think he was accepting my penance offerings to get our friendship back to normal.

"Awesome. I picked up the digital camera in the mid store this morning."

"At this pace, I'll have my second class loan paid off before I even graduate," Ed said to lighten the mood.

Our walk down Stribling ended in Tecumseh Court. I walked atop the discolored white bricks that replaced the original bricks burned by the car I blew up on that very spot a little over two years earlier.

Even the best plans can go up in flames.

"Alright man, I gotta check in with my dipshit CDO," Ed said as we parted ways. "Does my uniform look all right?"

I nodded my head, "Lookin' sharp as always."

"Cool, see you up in the wardroom to watch Dazed and Confused after hours?" he asked. Ed was forbidden to use the wardroom on restriction, but he was willing to press his luck in the wee hours of night before spring break.

I nodded. Even under bad circumstances, I never missed the traditional showing of the movie Dazed and Confused the night before any extended vacation period.

I made my way to the left towards the first wing of

Bancroft. Ed headed up the main entry stairs of Bancroft back towards main office check in.

I entered first wing and intentionally walked by the phone booths. The late-night lecture meant the line was still short. In another thirty minutes it would be packed with people calling home to square away various spring break plans. I looked down at my watch. It was almost 9 p.m.

He'll be off work and home by now.

I made my way into the phone room and jumped in the first empty booth. I closed the door, locking the smell of sweat and body odor inside the booth. It felt like a wooden and glass coffin. I pulled out my calling card and quickly dialed my codes into the pay phone. Soon the phone was ringing.

Come on, man, pick up.

The phone rang a third time.

"Yo Waddup," said the voice on the other line.

"Farm, hey, it's Mick."

"Hey Mick."

"How's Seacrets in February?" I asked. I was simply making awkward small talk. My heart was racing.

"Quiet, man. Once winter hits it's just me and my brother making alcoholic slushies for the local drunks," he humored me.

"Any word from my cousin?" I cut straight to the chase.

"Yeah, I finally heard from him. He said he'd be in town by next week."

I exhaled deeply in relief.

Part VIII

Swallowed

Chapter 26

Friend of the Devil
Tuesday, March 3rd, 1998
Bird, 10 a.m.

The road ahead curved gently to the left. The horizon opened to a magnificent view of Assateague Island with the shimmering Sinepuxent Bay in front of it. My eyes fixated ahead on the Verrazano Bridge. All of this was a sight for sore eyes. After over two years in hiding, this morning was the first time I had been back to the Delmar-va shoreline.

The fifteen-minute drive down Route 611 had hyp-notized me with familiar statues of cowboys, sharks, and chickens along the way. The brown vegetation of a typical mid-Atlantic winter was strangely majestic.

I manually rolled down the window of my pickup truck. It wasn't even fifty degrees outside. I could instant-ly smell the saltwater of the approaching bay in the cool wind entering the cab.

The Verrazano Bridge was the only drivable access point to Assateague Island, the home of the National Sea Shore. The island stretched for roughly twenty miles. Only about a third of the island was accessible via paved roads. The island's lone access point was about ten miles south of the southern-most tip of the Ocean City inlet.

The National Seashore was a treasure of untouched natural beauty. At one time, every inch of the Delmarva shoreline was like this. Assateague was the last shoreline in Maryland without a condo or a Dough Rollers Pizza shop in sight.

The island was a fully functional national park, with rangers and all. There were campgrounds, bike trails, and several public beach spots on the ocean and bayside. There were even a handful of bath houses and showers for people to hose down under after a day in the surf.

I snapped out of my daze. I didn't want the warmth of familiarity to divert my focus. I was making this trip for a reason.

In summer months, this trek would have been far more crowded. Locals, day trippers, renters, fishermen, campers, and the rest of the "fats and tats" poured in daily onto Assateague Island via Verrazano.

The two-lane road twisted through the island. After three minutes of driving the snail's pace speed limit, I still hadn't seen a living soul. The most famous Assateague residents, the ponies, had been living between the coastal islands of Chincoteague and Assateague since documented history. No one ever really figured out how the ponies got there in the first place. No pony mysteries today. Without tourist trash to sift through this time of year I guess they were elsewhere on the island hunting for food.

I finally approached two single-manned guard shacks blocking the entrance to the remainder of the drivable roads on the park. The ranger occupying the only operating shack was the first sign of humanity I had seen since crossing the bridge. The ranger wasn't anyone I knew. I let out an exhale in relief. If my mom got word that I came here before visiting her, she'd lose it. I hadn't seen her or my cousin Mick in over two years. I paid cash, appreciated my preserved anonymity, and drove on.

Save park rangers on duty and the occasional hippie chicks hunting for seashells, only a crazy person had reason to visit the island between January and Easter. I guess that's why Mick picked it as a rendezvous point.

This wasn't part of my original plan. My goal was to stay away until after Mick graduated. I had never wanted my stupid missteps to hurt his chances at the Naval Academy. He was the one who stuck his neck out to save me. Staying away long enough to not fuck things up was the least I could do. Then Gonzo inserted himself back into things and plans changed.

I had no idea what Mick knew about our current Gonzo problem. Farm told me that Mick called him around twenty times two weeks ago trying to find me. He didn't tell Farm much about anything other than needing to see me. That wasn't something Mick would normally do. It was the reason my plans had changed. It was the reason Farm spent a week trying to find me.

Did Gonzo get ahold of Mick? If he did, what did he tell him? What did he show him? These were all questions I needed to ask in person. I had asked them myself no less than a hundred times over the past couple of weeks.

I turned my car left into the first public beach lot past the guard shack. It was empty save one other truck parked there. It had to be Mick's. I parked directly next to it. The cab was empty.

I wiped the sweat from my forehead and noticed my heart racing.

Chapter 27

What It Takes
Tuesday, March 3rd, 1998
Mick, 1045 hrs.

My face was on fire in the icy cold ocean water. It had been that way since I jumped in five minutes earlier. Replacing the burning was the feeling of a ten-pound weight between my eyes, in the middle of the forehead. Next would be numbness. My polar wetsuit would only keep the water temperature bearable for another twenty minutes.

Spending spring break on a beach was nothing novel, though most beach-bound spring breakers picked a warmer place to admire the sand. I was home at the Delmarva shore for the full week of my spring break.

This surf session was impromptu. I was on Assateague Island for a business meeting but things were running late. I was tired of waiting so I decided to assuage my anxiety with the surfboard from the bed of my pickup.

March was typically the doldrums of surf. There wasn't a soul in sight. Cold water be damned, I wasn't in Annapolis. Anywhere but there was exactly where I wanted to be.

Where did I need to be? I asked myself that question often the past few weeks. I was thinking more and more that the answer to that question was "not in Annapolis."

A few weeks earlier I was informed that my San Diego aviation summer cruise was being replaced by a submarine cruise in 'rotten Groton,' Connecticut. At a time when I should have been worried about service selection and what I wanted to do in the Navy after graduation, I was instead feeling dejected and sorry for myself.

I had found myself in a vicious cycle. Thoughts of regret and remorse over Summer led me to the bottle. The bottle only led to more trouble in the Hall.

The Summer situation was all my fault, not Dickley's, not Hackett's, and certainly not Summer's. No matter how hard I rationalized against it, I had nobody to blame but myself. I drank to forget.

Sick of being stuck in this cycle, I longed for a change. When things were particularly dark, I briefly thought about ending it all. Thankfully that notion hadn't stuck. I needed better options before it did.

I sat atop my board for another ten minutes. There were no rideable waves in sight, but the cold water had quieted my mind. I paddled my board back to the shore. That's when I saw who I was waiting for.

I hadn't seen Bird since a fateful Sunday afternoon in November over two years earlier. We had just survived a non-stop cross-country ride, half of which was spent smuggling a felony-load of drugs. It was an emotional goodbye. We had been through some shit. He needed to run and then hide for some time.

I did all of this because I was duped. I had been

tricked into believing that accompanying my degenerate asshole of a cousin was the right thing to do. That somehow being along for the ride was going to save him from a certain arrest as well as save my roommate at the time from getting run out of the academy. When I found out that was all a sham, everyone disappeared.

My roommate, Gonzo, left immediately following our disciplinary hearing. We had blown up my car in Tecumseh Court. I thought we were burning our drug load to hide evidence. I found out later that was bullshit. It was all bullshit. It didn't matter, Gonzo got what he wanted, the ticket price for getting out of Annapolis. I was looking for that exact same thing.

I approached the only person I knew that could make that happen.

"Hey Bunkie, long time no see," Bird offered his salutations.

"You're late," I said coldly.

I walked right past him without looking at him and headed back towards the footbridge over the dunes.

"I'm sorry, Mick. There was an overturned tractor trailer off 97," Bird did his best to explain his tardiness.

I wasn't particularly interested in hearing his excuses. He was supposed to be here almost an hour ago. Three more minutes of silent walking and we were in the near-empty parking lot.

"Only a crazy person would be in the water today," he said still in chase. "Farm told me you called twenty times looking for me, now you won't even talk to me. What the fuck is going on with you?"

I lowered my board onto the parking lot asphalt and

turned with anger in my eyes. "You don't have the fucking right to ask that question. You sit there patiently and wait for what the FUCK I have to say. Got it?"

I composed my nerves as best I could. I wanted to slug Bird in the face. Who the fuck was he to think that he could simply write me an apology letter six months after nearly getting me arrested and all would be forgiven?

Fuck that!

I reminded myself that I was the person asking for the favor here.

"What did Gonzo tell you?" he asked.

"Gonzo? I haven't seen or heard from that asshole in over two years. I hope I never see that fuckface for the rest of my life."

Bird looked confused.

"I need a favor," I resumed the conversation.

"Name it," he replied.

"I need your help scoring me some quick money. I'm willing to mule again. You're the only person I know that can make that happen."

"Man, talk to me straight. What the fuck did Gonzo tell you?" he asked again.

"Fuck man, I told you, I haven't seen Gonzo since we helped with your dirty work."

"Your brain must be frozen from that water. Look Bunkie, if you need money, I'll get you some."

"You got sixty-five grand lying around?" I asked. I already knew the answer.

I picked my board up off the pavement and headed towards my truck. Sitting next to Bird's turd of a truck, it still looked shitty. That was quite an accomplishment.

"You don't need sixty-grand to buy a new truck," he commented.

"I don't want a new truck," I snapped.

Most of my classmates were already blowing their low interest seventeen thousand dollar differed payment second class loan on Mustangs, Jeeps, and SUVs. I avoided the temptation and avoided the big-ticket purchases. Instead I stuck with the beater truck I had bought the previous summer.

"I'm leaving Annapolis, and I need to pay the tab," I said as I dropped my board in the rusted out pickup bed.

Bird stood speechless.

"Mick," he started what I assumed to be an attempt to talk me out of it.

"Spare me the lecture, Bird," I interrupted. "You sure as shit weren't a father figure two years ago when I bailed your ass out. Don't try to be one now."

"Mick, look, you know I'm sorry for that. I've lived with that guilt for two years, but I never asked to be your father figure."

"That's reassuring, because you would have been a terrible one."

I knew that statement hurt him. That's exactly why I said it. Bird looked down at the pavement. I wanted him to punch me. I wanted him to give me a reason to beat the living shit out of him.

"Look, you were the one who asked to see me. You wanted me to drive out of hiding to berate me, fine. So say what you gotta say."

"I said what I had to say. I need you to find me a quick cash deal."

"Look, Bunkie, leaving the academy may not be the end of your world. I get that. But you get caught on the wrong end of a deal, you could be in jail for the next decade. I still haven't forgiven myself for putting you in that position the first time. Why would I do it again?" Bird asked.

I grabbed him by the coat and slammed him violently against the truck.

"Because you fucking owe me."

Chapter 28

If My Homie Calls
Tuesday, March 3rd, 1998
Nellie, noonish

"My darlin Micky, how ya doin', kiddo?" I greeted my favorite nephew as he slowly climbed up the old wooden stairs on the side of my bay-facing pier house. The creak that came with each step was a constant reminder that it was a decade beyond needing replaced.

"Hey Aunt Nellie," he said with a kind smile as he made his way towards me on the deck. I knew him too well. It felt forced.

"FOUND IT!" I exclaimed upon finally finding the TV remote I had been looking for all morning. It was right where I had left it, outside on top of the barbeque grill beside my cordless telephone.

Mick snatched a beach towel hanging off the deck.

"I'm gonna grab a shower," he announced.

"Were you in the ocean today?"

He turned and made his way down the stairs.

"You know only lulu birds go surfing this time of year!" I shouted down the steps.

"So I've been told," he replied from the outdoor shower

stall beside the house. I could hear the water pipes squeal as the hot water made it down to the outdoor shower head.

I lit a cigarette and took in the bay views. Something about menthol and salt water went together so well. I grabbed the phone from the grill. It reminded me of the message I took for Mick earlier. I resolved to puff my cig and remind Mick when he finished his shower. If I went back inside, I would forget. It's how I was wired.

Micky had been staying at my place since Friday. He needed a place to stay during his spring break from Annapolis. I could sense something was off about him from the moment he walked in the door.

Micky had plenty of changes in his life these days. He spent all of Christmas break boozed up or hungover in my house. We heard all about what happened with him and Summer. His mother and I bombarded him with questions the moment we didn't see her with him when he came home for Christmas break.

Poor kid.

Then there was Barb, Mick's mother, my little sister. She was the reason Mick was staying with me in the first place.

Barb found something she hadn't in years, a relationship. She wasn't quite sure it was love. She was certainly happy to have a male roommate to romp around with. His name was Todd. He was still in his thirties and a bit of a bullshitter. At least he treated Barb really nice.

Mick didn't particularly like Todd, but he liked seeing his mom clean and happy, so he stayed with me for the time being. He really was a good kid. He had heart of gold.

Mick made his way silently back up the stairs, still dripping wet with shower water. The steam coming off his skin in the cold air made him look like a barbeque coal.

"Micky, I meant to tell you, your HOMIE Ed called about twenty minutes ago," I said using finger quotes with the word "Homie."

"Did he say anything?" he asked.

"Not much. Just said that if you came in within the next hour to give you this number to call." I picked up the Chinese food menu with the number scribbled on it. "Here ya go."

"Thanks Aunt Nellie," he said. He grabbed the menu from my hands.

"Is it cool if I dial an Annapolis number from the up-stairs phone?" he asked politely.

"Sure thing, kiddo."

He scrambled behind the closed door where I as-sumed he dropped his swim trunks, dried his legs, and hustled naked up the stairs to call his "homie" Ed.

I waited another few minutes on the deck, enjoying the last few puffs of my cigarette before I flicked it off the deck. I missed my own son, but I was enjoying Mick's company while it lasted.

I knew what Bird was doing for Mick, staying away to keep Mick out of trouble. All in an effort to keep my scumbag of an ex-husband out of my life.

I knew about the coast to coast drug smuggle. I learned all about it well before Mick walked in the door three days ago. Bird left me a novel of a note explaining everything shortly after he went into hiding.

My attention shifted to Mick inside. There was something wrong with his smile. His normal shit-eating grin with a sparkle of devil seemed off as far back as December. Today, it was entirely gone. The smile he wore these days was a fake smile. I hadn't seen it on him before.

I looked down at the wireless phone in my hand. I pulled a wad of tissues out of my pocket to cover the phone's mouth piece and clicked on the house's single phone line. Mick hadn't lived with a snoopy mom so he never seemed to notice my eavesdropping. I'd done it a few times listening to arguments between he and Summer. I hadn't earned the name Nosey Nellie for my schnoz. Oh, the scolding I'd get from Bird if he only knew.

I put my ear to the phone.

"So you got the picture and the file backup?" I heard Mick ask what I assumed to be his homie Ed.

"Yeah man, exactly like you said. Waited till I heard the bumping on the wall, dropped the ski mask, flicked the lights, snapped the picture. Actually I snapped about three."

"Are you sure? Did they develop okay?" Mick asked.

"Totally sure," Ed assured Mick. "They literally sat under the covers screaming "Not decent" for the thirty seconds until I flipped the light switch off. By the time he put his underwear back on, I was gone without a trace."

"Holy shit, that's awesome news," Mick replied with the first hint of happiness I had heard in him all week.

Whatever Mick was up to, it wasn't good. That hurt me, but as much as it did, I decided to let it go. Mick was an adult.

Mick had worked very hard to get where he was in life. Even though my jackass son almost ruined everything, he was only one year away from graduating Annapolis. He had found his way in there on his own, I trusted him enough to find his own way out. He'd earned that trust.

Still, I worried.

Part IX

Closing Time

Chapter 29

Got Me Wrong
Sunday, May 24th, 1998
Mick, 1000 hrs.

> *Smitty's mom gives great head.*

I read the immortalized phrase etched in the side of the wooden portion of the closed phone booth door. It had caught my eye when I slid in the empty booth and closed the door.

The carved message had been carefully crafted. Each letter was long and skinny. The sentence ran the full height of the booth door, floor to ceiling. If you didn't know to look for it, you'd never know it was there, which is probably why it lasted.

The epitaph was subtly accentuated in black ink. Not enough ink to make it too conspicuous, but enough to make it jump out to anyone stuck staring at the door long enough.

I remember when my plebe roommate Gonzo had boasted about this handiwork back in October of '95. It was the Tuesday evening after our asshole squad leader trashed our room and assigned us a weekend class alpha inspection for a pillow left on the floor. It was my pillow that was left on the floor. Gonzo had told me that evening to go check out the booth. I remember how brightly he smiled over his achievement. It made me smile back then too. Now it was like everything else, a reminder of a past I wish I could forget.

I hadn't intentionally chosen this booth. It happened to be the first available booth that I noticed on this quiet Sunday morning. Most of my classmates were still nursing their Ring Dance hangovers in fancy hotels. The rest of the brigade was enjoying the remaining weekend liberty ahead of Commissioning Week. I was doing neither. Instead, I was trying to close out some very important details in my life. This morning was just the start.

The booth was hot and smelled sweaty. I took my eyes away from the door and snatched the phone with my hand. My fingers punched the numbers, inclusive of my calling card code for my long-distance minutes. I could have borrowed one of my more affluent friend's parent-paid cell phones, but I wanted this call to be private.

Twenty seconds of digit punching and finally a voice on the other line.

"Yo."

It was my cousin Bird. If it had been my Aunt Nellie, I would have hung up and called in an hour.

"Yo," I replied with equal brevity.

"What's up, Bunkie?" he interrupted the ten seconds of silence.

"You tell me, what's the word on what we've been talking about? You know those odd jobs down at the shore. Any prospects?"

I had asked him this same question every two weeks

since seeing him in person over spring break.

"Nothing yet, but I'm working on it. I promise. The type of deal you're looking for, they don't just grow on trees. It has to be the right opportunity. Risk reward type shit. You have to be smart on these things," he explained.

On one hand, I believed him. He'd been to prison. He knew all too well how things looked when they went south.

On the other hand, I didn't believe him. Maybe he was being honest. Maybe he was trying to stall me long enough to get cold feet and change my mind. It was hard to tell.

"Yeah," I acknowledged, "I need you to keep working on it."

"I am Micky, I am. I promise," Bird replied.

"Look, I'm calling to tell you that I'm coming home in a few weeks."

"Awesome man, the water is finally warming up a little and there are a few fronts off the coast that may actually make a few good days of June surf. You should see how the 46th Street break is going off since last fall's storms," Bird rambled about the surf.

Bird had ended his hiding period the moment the two of us connected in March. Nellie really let him have it for the first few weeks he was home, at least that's what she told me. Three months after the fact, she was floating on cloud nine having him home.

"So you have vacation over June? Where are they shipping you to after that?" he asked. Nellie must have been educating him on my typical summer cruise schedule.

"It's not a vacation," I answered. "I finished up my spring semester weeks ago. Three years of college in the books. A 3.14 GPA at the Naval Academy can certainly get me transferred into Salisbury or College Park when I'm ready for school again. This time I'm coming back for good. We do the gig you're going to find me to pay my dinner tab here. I make a few bucks mowing lawns for cash under the table. I surf every day I can. I'll be a college graduate in two years, and I'll never need to set foot in this fucking place again."

I had talked myself out of staying at the academy at least a thousand times using this same damn narrative. Given my misery with Summer and my continuing problem with academy rules and discipline, it was a hard narrative to argue against.

"What? No, come on, Mick. Let's think this through," Bird began his opposing plea. Like he was even remotely qualified to give sensible life advice.

"I submit my resignation letter this week, I should be processed out by end of month," I interjected.

"Yeah but, where ya gonna stay, bunkie? You know how up in your shit my mom and your mom are going to be when you come home after dropping this bomb on them? Not a great atmosphere to be plotting and planning high paying odd jobs, don't you think? You must be out of your fucking mind," Bird initiated his well-honed guilt trip skills.

"Our moms won't know shit. I'll hang with you and your mom at your place for a few weeks. Everyone will think I'm on vacation from the academy. You wouldn't be any the wiser if I hadn't just told you differently. After that

I've got an entire summer's worth of high school buddies' couches I can sleep on clear through Halloween. No one will know a damn thing. Meantime, you need to find me sixty-five grand. Get your shit together."

I didn't need Bird's permission. I wanted him to feel my sense of urgency. I wanted to get out of this place, get this deal done. I wanted to move on with my life. He needed to get on board with that plan.

"What about this fucking deal? You think we can keep that plotting, and planning, and prepping secret with both of us down in Ocean City? Good ol' Aunt Nellie knows half the people in this town and talks to about every one of them on a weekly basis. Yet she'll still have time to eavesdrop on every other call from you to me in this house. She'll know your next move before you do," Bird's narrative sped up.

I interrupted him mid-sentence, "I'll be home in a week or two. We'll connect when I get in town. You keep looking. I need that gig."

I heard Bird continue his argument from the other end of the receiver right up until I slammed it into the holster. I calmly stood and exited the booth. The phone rang behind me as I left the vacant phone room. I made my way back up the stairs. I could faintly hear the continued rings behind me.

I had a busy day ahead.

******

Mick, 1335 hrs.

After my phone call with Bird I went down to King

Hall and ate a hearty breakfast. I carefully inventoried my supplies for the remainder of the day up in my room. I had more than enough saran wrap and duct tape.

Bancroft Hall remained a ghost town at lunchtime. N.D. was still out of town, attending the overnight Ring Dance afterhours boat trip into Baltimore. There was a whole crew of varsity athletes that paid for a multiple day Ring Dance experience starting and ending in the Baltimore Harbor.

Our entire room had been invited to the Baltimore weekend. N.D. was the only member that made it to the party. Ed was stuck on the yard serving day number eighty-nine of his extended original sixty-day restriction sentence. As for me, I had zero desire to be in the same zip code, much less the same building or boat, as Summer, Hackett, and that much alcohol. Besides, Ring Dance meant much less to me than it did to N.D. and Ed given my near-term exit strategy.

Ed was outdoors on the yard happily cleaning up the post-Ring Dance tables, chairs, and trash from the night before. After spending almost three months under the confines of Bancroft Hall restriction, any chance to get outdoors was welcome. Later in the night would be Ed's last restriction muster. It was the end of a long journey. He couldn't keep his excitement indoors.

Ed and I went to Ring Dance together, but not as each other's dates. We each individually brought giant German glass beer mugs as our dates. Ed had borrowed them from his sponsor family. With a frothy pour of a pilsner and a corsage on the handle we each had a good looking blonde on our arm. We even got our pictures taken with our "dates" under the giant ring prop, guarding the dipping pool of the seven seas, to prove it.

The door to our room slammed open with a booming kick. N.D. entered lugging three giant suitcases in through the door.

"Micky McGee, what's happenin', dawg?" he greeted me with a warm hand-slap and a hug.

"I'm good, man, how was the weekend? I didn't get to see you last night," I agreeably lamented.

"Yeah, dinner out in town ran late, then the limo guy disappeared for twenty minutes. By the time we got to the yard we had to turn around and load up on the booze cruise out in Ego Alley. I think I spent five minutes on the yard. I didn't even get to dip my ring, dawg."

"Damn, that sucks. Don't worry, you didn't miss a whole lot. I can't imagine you and your boys were too heartbroken to miss the swing dancing band they booked."

"Nah dawg, you're right. Swing dancing really isn't my thing. I feel like that's more of a white dude thing," he said jokingly.

"Seriously, you had a good weekend?" I asked.

"Yeah, yeah man, definitely. The pimps and hoes party Friday night was crazy. You should have seen some of the outfits up in that place. Some of those girls' costumes are BURNED in my memory, dawg," his face lit up as he rolled into his narrative. He stopped once he remembered that I didn't attend the event.

I could only imagine how hot Summer looked at that party. That was exactly why I didn't want to go. I put my mind on other things.

"How'd the date work out? You show that Temple Owl

dancer any of your division-one moves?"

"Only on the dancefloor, dawg. A gentleman never tells beyond that. But yeah, it was a great time with a fine young lady."

"How was the booze cruise last night?"

"It was ah'ight. First two hours were fun. Last four were a beer-fueled shit show. Six hours stuck together on a boat, none of us getting laid all the while. Felt too much like being in the Navy."

"Sounds about right," I said with a chuckle.

"Goes without saying you were missed, dawg," N.D. looked up from his unpacking with a smile, "but I understand what you got going on."

"Thanks, man," I replied.

"How did you and Ed make out last night?" N.D. returned the line of questioning.

"Ha, not so bad. Take a look at the blondes we both landed." I handed him a Polaroid of me holding my beer date below the giant class ring prop.

"Unheard of, dawg. This is outstanding!"

I smiled with pride. "Ed got one too. Neither of us scored though. We ended the night in the wardroom drunkenly trying to find the taped version of those two mids that faked their way onto this past MTV Spring Break Jerry Springer show."

Ed was stuck in the Hall all weekend finishing his restriction sentence, but they still let him attend the dance. He wasn't even supposed to use the wardroom, but he took his chances when the hour was late enough. It was actually cool getting a chance to hang exclusively with Ed most of the night. Between him and N.D., I was really going to miss those guys.

N.D. continued his unpacking. Mr. GQ must have packed seven different outfits for the party weekend. These garbs were accompanied by six pairs of shoes. He pulled his toiletry bag from his luggage, along with four separate hair brushes which he neatly placed back into his con-locker.

"Gotta sort this shit and then get everything packed for first block aviation cruise this summer," N.D. said as he began organizing various stacks of clothes as part of his packing pre-planning. "I fly out to San Dawg a week from this morning."

Moments like these were when N.D.'s OCD tendencies shined the brightest. He'd spend the entire week packing for San Diego, squaring away every last pre-planned detail. OCD wasn't a bad trait to have in a Naval Academy roommate. It was small fraction of what made N.D. a great roommate.

I needed to share my exit plans with N.D. but I struggled to find the words. Five minutes of uncomfortable silence later and I finally forced myself to do it.

"N.D., I have some news, man."

"What's up, dawg?" he replied. He likely thought my quiet brooding was about Summer.

I again searched for the right words. I decided to tell him as plainly as I could. "I'm done, man. I gotta go."

"Done, done what? Gotta go where?" N.D. asked. His smile faded as he tried to understand.

"Done here, done with the Naval Academy. I'm getting out of here and going back home this summer. I actually drop my papers in a few days when LT rolls in from vacation mid-week."

"WHAT!?" N.D. uncharacteristically raised his voice. "Dawg, you can't be serious. Are you sure you thought this through?"

"I've been thinking about it for some time now."

"Then why didn't you come talk to me about it? I thought we were tight like that."

"N.D., man, we are tight. That's why I kept this stuff to myself. I wanted to make the decision myself. I knew if I talked to you about it that you'd try to talk me into staying. It's nothing personal."

"Come on, dawg, I know this decision has nothing to do with me or anybody else round here but one person. You and I both know who this is about."

"Like I said, I've been thinking about this for some time."

"Yeah, for like what? Like six months?" he called me on my bullshit.

"It's not about her," I lied again.

I stood up and walked out of the door. The conversation was thirty seconds in and it had already exceeded my comfort level. I walked into the bathroom, continuing the charade that I left the room to take a piss.

I made my way directly to the sink of the public bathroom. I looked around to ensure it was empty and splashed some cold water in my face. I looked up at the mirror, directly meeting the eyes of my reflection.

Come on, don't be a pussy, stick to your guns.

I grabbed a paper towel and wiped my dripping face. I needed to face N.D. He was my friend and I wanted to preserve that.

When I got back to the room N.D. was sitting in the same spot. I cut right to the chase.

"N.D.," I began.

He raised his hand to silence me. "Look Mick, you gotta listen to me. If we're so tight, then you need to give me a chance to talk to you about this."

I nodded in approval. I at least owed him the chance to have his say.

"Plebe year, Air Force weekend," N.D. initiated his plea. "You remember that weekend?"

I nodded. I'd never forget that plebe year weekend. N.D.'s high school sweetheart dumped him with a note right before the big Air Force home football game. He played horribly that day and we lost the game. He then proceeded to get trashed and in a fit of blind rage, he destroyed our room along with his brand-new computer monitor. In the grand finale to an all-time shit show, he puked on a full-bird Air Force Colonel attending an on-campus comedy show in Alumni Hall. He was extremely lucky to not have gotten kicked out.

"Yeah, I remember. That's how you earned your Black N," I answered in summary.

"That's right. About two months before you earned yours blowing up cars with Gonzo," he continued. "I wanted to quit this place so fucking bad after that game. That entire time on restriction, I wanted to quit. I didn't. I couldn't let my football teammates down mid-season."

"Then by the time you rolled off of restriction, I was right there to catch the baton. Like somehow our room had to stand restriction watch all fucking year," I said, smiling at a memory that I never thought would make me smile. It was the bond of shared experience that humored me, not the restriction.

"That winter after football season, I was ready to quit. I enjoyed the holidays that break and gave myself plenty of good reasons to return to civilian life. Had plenty of time to plan my escape. I came back to the Hall in January with shit all plotted out. I'd head home mid-semester, take the spring off, and transfer to another school on a football scholarship that fall. Sure, I'd have to redshirt a year, but I already had three schools lined up with offers after the season I had as a plebe here at Navy. Thought I might even get a shot at the pros if shit worked out right."

"Then why did you stay?" I asked.

"Because of you," he replied. "Gonzo bolted before winter leave. Then it was the two of us for the rest of plebe year. Seeing you get through your own restriction hell with your Black N, I felt the same way about you as I did my teammates in the fall. If I left that spring, I knew it would only be a matter of time before you did. I couldn't let you down like that.

All those times you helped me out when I was on restriction. All those stories you spun on about accountability, hard work, grit, and even some crazy shit about your grandpa's toolbox. Back then, I thought that all of it was some stupid motivational speech mumbo jumbo, but I guess that shit rubbed off on me. By the time you got off restriction, I had a change of heart. Here I am."

I didn't know what to say. I had never heard that story before.

The following silence lasted long enough to deem the conversation over.

"Been a while since I saw that toolbox, dawg," he said before standing up and resuming the unpacking of his weekend bags.

My grandfather's green toolbox was a collectible memory of a man I respected a great deal. It wasn't in our room at the moment. It had been with us every day as roommates until I took it home over spring break a few months earlier. Aunt Nellie had asked me to tighten up some leaky pipes to the outdoor shower.

"N.D., I appreciate that you want me to stay. I'm really sorry, man. It was not an easy decision, but I've made up my mind on this one."

It was all I could say for the moment. N.D. nodded understandingly.

Like the toolbox, my heart wasn't in the Naval Academy anymore. I resolved to remain steadfast to my original plan. I was genuinely depressed being at the academy. I needed to get out. I stood up and grabbed my wallet on the way out of the room.

"I'm going out to grab some lunch at Dahlgren. You want anything?"

"I'm good," he replied dejectedly returning to his unpacking.

******

Mick, 1930 hrs.

I peeked my head out from behind my room's wooden door. There were a few youngsters goofing off on the other side of the hall. I went back into my room. I made sure no one from company area had seen my return to my room. I didn't want anyone knowing that I was in Bancroft. It was all part of my plan.

My room had been empty since I had returned an hour earlier. I don't know where N.D. went after our earlier conversation. I imagined he was either hanging with EZ and the rest of his football buddies out at the bars or laying low at his sponsor's house. I was glad he wasn't in the room. That's why I stayed out for so long. After our conversation earlier, I spent the next four hours blowing time at the Annapolis Mall.

N.D. and I would have other opportunities during Commissioning Week to talk about me leaving. I'm sure he was still a little shocked by my news. When things digested I hoped he would see my side more clearly.

I snuck another look outside. The coast was clear. It was time. I darted out of my door and into my neighbor's empty room without anyone seeing me. I had a garbage bag full of supplies slung over my shoulder. I locked the closed door behind me so no one could come in to catch my wrongdoings red-handed. I learned that trick from Summer.

The class of '99 members of the brigade had liberty until midnight as an extra benefit of the last day of our Ring Dance weekend. Every class in the company other than mine had a Sunday evening formation about an hour earlier and people were generally relaxing and unwinding in their rooms. I had different plans for the evening.

I knew I had at least thirty minutes in the room until Captain America and Dickley returned from dropping Captain's date off at BWI airport. I only knew about the 8 p.m. arrival because Captain made a point to go on and on about him and Dickley having to drop his date at the airport at squad tables. It was like he wanted the whole world to know he had a date.

Even with thirty minutes remaining I knew I didn't have a ton of time and timing was everything with this prank. I focused on the final push.

I neatly placed a sealed enveloped on Dickley's keyboard. Inside the envelope was a special present and message for Dickley from yours truly. It was a parting gift considering my near-term exit plans.

The envelope had the letter "D" written in a bubbly capitalized letter. I had drawn the letter graphic myself, having copied a birthday envelope from his girlfriend I had stolen from Dickley's trash can a month earlier. I wanted the envelope to grab his attention, enough to open it right away. I also didn't want Captain to open it. If he thought it was from Dickley's girl, he'd respect his privacy.

Next, I emptied my garbage bag of supplies on the tiled floor by the sink beside the shower stall. The supply contents included two full unboxed rolls of Saran Wrap, a pocket knife, and two red bricks. I went to work.

First, I removed the shower curtain. That would only get in the way of my scheme. I tossed that on the floor towards Dickley's bunk. I ripped three six-inch pieces of duct tape and used them to completely cover the shower drain. Then I placed the two bricks over my tape job to more thoroughly secure my temporary drain blockage. Once the bricks were submerged in water, they'd hold the drain blockage firm for at least two hours.

I pulled my pants down, squatting my naked ass in the shower stall. I proceeded to drop an enormous shit

I had been pinching off all day. I had been eating a high fiber diet in preparation. Within seconds I had a beautiful Jimmy Dean Sausage lying on the floor of the shower stall. The smell was horrible and immediate. It was a beauty. I was incentivized to work quickly.

Now all we need is an ocean for this shark to swim in.

I grabbed the Saran wrap and started ripping pieces of it from the roll one piece at a time. I started at the bottom and worked my way up, trying to overlap each piece by about half. Eventually my growing wrap wall reached about knee height. I ripped a few pieces of duct tape off and secured both ends to keep my clear plastic wall in place. I temporarily forgot to breathe through my mouth, caught a whiff of my own shit, and nearly gagged.

Once my wall was appropriately taped to chest height I was ready to begin filling the tank. I had calculated the fill rate of my own room's shower head several times in past weeks. I knew exactly how the water valve should be turned to fill a stall in a half an hour. If I filled it too soon, people would see the flood in the hall before Captain and Dickley had a chance to. If I filled it too slowly, the lack of water would make the prank not nearly as extreme.

I reached into the shower and turned on the cold water at precisely the right angle for a low temp and appropriate fill rate. In addition to timing considerations, I didn't want the water to be hot enough to melt down my masterpiece. Once the shower was on I waited for the water to fill the first ten inches of the aquarium and I could see my brown shark happily floating inside.

When I was confident my makeshift aquarium was secure I bagged up the remaining wrap and tape. I picked up the knife, closed it and put it in my pocket. I did a quick room sweep to ensure I had everything set the way I intended.

Satisfied, I darted to the door. I unlocked it and listened with my ear on the wood. It sounded quiet outside. I took a cautious peek in the hall. The coast was clear. I darted into to my room with the remainder of my supplies. Once inside the solitude and safety of my own room, I let out a deep breath. Then I began laughing hysterically.

"Holy shit," I said to no one. "Baltimore fucking Aquarium."

I sat down at my desk with barely contained excitement I hadn't felt in months. My heart raced. Eight o'clock couldn't come fast enough. Ed said that he'd make his way over to our room by a quarter of eight. He'd been down in Jarvis' room playing Twisted Metal on PlayStation between restriction musters for the last eight consecutive hours. He assured me he wouldn't miss a front row seat for the shit show.

The door swung open and Ed loudly exclaimed, "DAWGS, DAWGS, DAWGS, almost show time, motherfucker!"

Ed's smile was so big that it looked pasted on. Not only was he going to see the most legendary prank executed to perfection on our dickhead neighbors, but tonight was also Ed's last restriction muster. After serving eighty-nine consecutive days, which included his originally assigned sixty days and another twenty-nine days added as punitive damages during restriction, he'd take his last restriction muster at 10 p.m. and be a free man. Shortly thereafter Ed would take his long-awaited restriction slide, a head first, fully uniformed baseball slide across a Pledge-slicked tile hallway floor with all brigade fans and friends cheering him on. All of this was happening at the start of Commissioning Week. It was a great day to be Ed.

"You sure you got the pictures in the envelope and shit?" he asked.

"You know me, I triple checked that shit, man. We're good. Dickley's going to see that we have those pictures of him and his lady boning. It's sealed in an envelope that looks like his girlfriend left it for him on his keyboard. Your recon mission over spring break watch bought you this moment my friend. ENJOY THIS!"

We slapped hands and laughed hysterically.

Life was finally good again for Ed. That made me feel better. I looked back up at the clock. Five minutes to go. We were going to get one hell of a good show tonight.

Everything was still going exactly to plan.

Chapter 30

Brick
Sunday, May 24th, 1998
Captain America, 2145 hrs.

Another blanketing of Comet covered the still wet floor. I was beginning to feel woozy from inhaling toxic levels of cleaning solution. My wet hands were already worn raw. I continued aggressively scrubbing the floor. My roommate Dallas had been suspiciously absent for the past thirty minutes.

Everything went down when we got in from the airport at twenty hundred hours. Dallas had helped me take my Ring Dance date to the BWI airport.

When we arrived back to the room the first thing I noticed was the shower curtain on our floor. Then I heard the shower water running and saw the Saran Wrap wall. I didn't see the floating fecal matter until after I reached in to turn off the shower. It didn't matter. The wall and I were overtaken by a wave full of dirty poo water as soon as my hand reached over the plastic wall,

Dallas and I spent the next hour disposing of the poo and drying the floor. There were two full garbage bags of various soiled towels and shit rags sitting outside our room. I had vomited twice during the fecal disposal process. I had already sprayed three bottles of Scrubbing Bubbles on the shower walls. I could feel the bacteria and fungus growing around us. Rage swelled within the deepest trenches of my heart. I dug harder on my steel wool scrub.

Whatever little shit plebe decided to pull this off, they'll pay dearly.

Once we had the flood waters cleaned up, Dallas read the note left on his desk from his girlfriend. He took one quick read and off he went.

"I'll be right back," he said. I hadn't seen him since. That was just like him, a total lap dog, when I needed him the most.

Another wave of dizziness hit me. I stood up from the floor and stepped into the hallway to get a breath of fresh air. I was covered in sweat and wet filth. That's when I heard the chanting from the other side of company area.

"The brick!" the posse of male plebes chanted, "The brick!" They continued marching up the hall. "Who's got the ugliest chick?" they all asked in unison.

Then the mob advanced down the hallway and repeated the cadence in unison. The noise of the impromptu parade had already drawn at least twenty people into the hall. As the group drew ten yards closer, I could see one of the plebes holding a red construction brick above his head triumphantly.

"The brick! The brick! Who's got the ugliest chick?" They continued making their way towards my side of the hallway but turned right to parade down a wing. They maintained the tradition of doing a full loop around company area before granting the award to a usually unsuspecting recipient. I said usually unsuspecting recipient because about half of the time the plebes gave me the award.

The brick was a tradition of granting any male midshipman seen in public with an unattractive female a red brick trophy. The tradition was childish, inappropriate, and insulting. Each of the three times the gang of plebes handed me the trophy, they seemed the think it was the cleverest thing in the world.

With the day I was already having, I wasn't in the mood for my fourth brick. The chants grew louder as the mob turned the corner and fire bloomed in my chest. They were marching my way. At least twenty upperclassmen were gathered in the hall to watch.

If it's a show they want, it's a show they'll get.

Fourth Class Speneti was about three deep into the mob and was still carrying the brick above his head. I'd be damned if I'd be letting that twit put it in my room tonight. Before the mob came within two doors of my room, I charged the crowd in a fit of rage.

I caught the plebes off guard and several of us tumbled to the ground like bowling pins. The brick tumbled to the floor.

"Fuck that! Get him!" I heard Speneti scream.

Suddenly I was lifted from the ground along with the brick. I thrashed aggressively. I wriggled an arm out twice and a leg once. Ultimately, it was useless. The crowd had me overpowered. My door was kicked open and I was aggressively drug in. The crowd around was hooting and hollering.

Once we crossed the threshold I used my own room to my advantage. Knowing the floor was wet from my previous cleanup efforts, I moved my limbs with renewed force. The group slipped on the wet surface and again we tumbled to the floor. I made my way to my desk to grab my chair. It was the nearest significant weapon I could find.

"Get away from me, you ANIMALS!"

They tackled me onto the bed and finished the tradition by shoving the brick into my possession. I immediately shoved it back at them, knocking the entirety of my luggage to the floor in the process. The contents spilled across the floor.

"What the FUCK is that?" I heard Fourth Class Wilson scream in surprise reaction to what was on the floor.

"Dude, is that your fucking Alpha Code on the elastic band?" I heard another yell.

"Yo, he has a collection of our tighty-whities!" another exclaimed.

Oh shit.

"Get the FUCK out of my room!" I yelled. "You can only imagine what's in this bucket!" I smartly threatened a bucket full of poop cleaning water. Word had already spread across company area about the poop in the shower earlier. The threat hustled everyone out of the room before more people had time to piece together what had been exposed on the floor. I was able to eventually clear out my room, but the damage had been done.

I locked the door behind them and sat on the floor with my back against the wooden door. I cried hysterically.

What was I going to do now?

Chapter 31

Insane in the Brain
Sunday, May 24th, 1998
Mick, 10:21 p.m.

A round of rhythmic clapping echoed off the walls of the hallway. A crowd of adoring midshipmen lined the walls of the P-way. The night's final restriction muster had completed and the guest of honor was about to arrive from the Rotunda.

"Fuck yeah, Ed!" I heard a random voice yell out from the crowd.

When Ed finally arrived, his adoring fans egged him on even more. Per tradition, he had turned over his giant ball of tape and restriction log to the next head restrictee. The clapping sped up and intensified. Hoots and hollers came in every direction from the rowdy crowd of mids.

"FREEEEEEEEEEEEDOOOOOOOOOM!" I heard another yell.

The restriction muster slide was a tradition that had been going on since long before we arrived at this place. Any restrictee serving maximum days of restriction, usually garnered from a Black N offense, had the privilege of getting a celebratory final slide down the Hall for their final muster.

Ed, in full inspection-ready summer whites uniform, assumed a modified sprinter position at the other end of the hall. The middle of the hallway sparkled with Pledge from the middle of the hallway all the way down to the double doors guarding the entrance to Bancroft's first wing. Ed, the perfect showman, raised his hand to summon an anticipatory silence. The crowd obeyed.

Ed paused for dramatic effect, testing the crowd's patience. After about twenty seconds he broke out of his stance into a full sprint. Halfway down the hall he initiated a Charlie Hustle style headfirst baseball slide.

Ed's form took off like a rocket across the slippery floor.

"Coming in hot," I said.

The crowd in front of the doors suddenly feared a bowling pin fate. They smartly moved closer to the walls and out of the way of projectile Ed.

A combination of Ed's sprinting exuberance and an overly Pledged deck kept his momentum beyond the typical slide stopping zone. Ed didn't lose momentum and naturally stop like my own slide and every other one I'd seen. Instead, Ed kept right on going.

A loud bang accentuated Ed's headfirst slam into the doors at the end of the hall. His face absorbed most of the impact. The raucous crowd went suddenly silent. Drips of red blood began pooling on the floor.

Ed, woozy, did not let the pain kill the buzz. He jumped up, bloody forehead and all, and the crowd went nuts. Everyone huddled around him to wish him congratulations. I finally made my way over to him.

"Congrats, man," I said when it was my turn to pay respects to the hero of the moment. "I still owe you for all of this."

"All good, man. You don't owe me shit, dawg," he said. "How does this look?" he asked pointing to his forehead. The blood continued to gush from his newly formed gash. He looked like he just finished a steel cage match with Mick Foley.

"Probably should get over to hospital point, dude," I said. "Need a ride?"

"Nah, rub some dirt on it for me," he replied with a shit-eating grin as he swayed back and forth, clearly concussed.

I saw N.D. and Summer closing in to pay their respects with a few other company mates. Someone handed Ed a towel and he wiped the blood from his face.

"Congrats again, man," I said giving Ed one final hug. "I gotta bounce. But seriously, you should get that cut checked out."

I moved away from the crowd and started making my way back to company area. Everyone else stayed behind to pay their respects. I passed N.D. on the way out. He would be there for a bit. I smiled and patted him on the shoulder to say hello. Neither of us said a word to each other. I headed upstairs.

N.D. had been moping all day since our conversation earlier. He would probably spend the rest of the night watching movies with EZ in his company's air-conditioned wardroom. I didn't take it personally. I understood why he was upset.

Confident that my room was safely empty for at least

another fifteen minutes, I headed to my closet. I pulled out a cigarette triple wrapped with sandwich bags under a few t-shirts in my con-locker. I opened the bag and the dank smell of bud reminded me of Bird. The joint in the bag had been bent in the month of transport and storage. I was saving it for a necessary occasion. Today was an emotionally draining day. I wanted something a little different to take the edge off.

I had originally stolen the joint from my friend Farm's glovebox when I was home for spring break. Farm always kept a few spare Js in his car, and they were always rolled to perfection. I felt compelled to steal one vice ask permission. Farm would have never offered me bud. Bird would have Farm's ass if he ever found out he was supplying me with drugs.

I took one last glance out in the P-way before locking my door and making my way to a seat beside the window. The bay breeze coming in for the evening was a welcome visitor to our room. In daylight hours, without air conditioning, we were typically sweating our balls off this time of year.

It was time to celebrate. I lit the homemade marijuana cigarette and took a deep pull. I really didn't know what I was doing, but I had smoked enough cigarettes to figure it out. I pulled in a deep drag. I couldn't spend too long smoking out of my window or my neighbors upstairs would eventually smell it and look down.

I had only smoked pot once in high school. With no more near-term whiz quizzes to worry about, I was in the mood to try it again. The freedom of academy consequences felt as good as the buzz itself. Whenever a twinge of paranoia or guilt came, it quickly faded.

What are they going to do? Kick me out?

I held the smoke deep in my lungs. I took in the night view of the Chesapeake. The moonlight reflecting on the bay was incredible. It was quite a view for a college dorm. Only in a place like this would it take me until now to appreciate it. Only a place as shitty as this could make you ignore it. The notion emphasized the rightness of my decision to leave. I exhaled.

Tendrils of smoke infiltrated my view. Considering my low weed tolerance, I puffed once more and flicked the remainder of the joint out of my window. I would certainly be baked for the night. I felt the head chill of the fresh high consume my brain as soon as I stepped back from the window.

I sat in my chair and hit play to resume the Snoop Dogg cd already loaded into N.D.'s stereo system. I was mesmerized by Snoop's lyrical flow. I wasn't going to miss the academy, but I was going to miss this place. This room, these friends, they would be impossible to replace.

Thinking of them reminded me to cover my tracks on their behalf. There was no need to get my friends kicked out too. I sprayed a healthy dose of air freshener to cover the smell. I thoroughly washed my hands and face in the sink to erase my own guilty stench before Ed returned. I contemplated which bag of chips I should buy from the Gedunk machine down the hall. I resolved that I'd buy three different bags and perhaps order a pizza if I could find a place that delivered this late on a Sunday night.

I still couldn't believe that I had pulled off the Baltimore Aquarium so perfectly. Ed and I had a front row seat for the whole thing. The cursing, the screaming, and the horror of realizing there was a toilet-sized shit flooding out of the shower. It was all so beautiful. Captain getting the brick an hour later was icing on the cake. I wish I could have staked claim to that special treat, but that was all Captain's own doing. The timing of it just happened to be impeccable. Aside from an awkward conversation with N.D., the day was going better than I could have ever hoped.

Word was already swirling about the underwear collection the plebers uncovered in Captain's room. With all of the chaos of the evening, that was the headline of the weekend, and likely the entire year.

Captain had been holed up in his room ever since. Even Dickley had been locked out. He couldn't talk his way in, though he tried several times. All of us were wondering how Captain would be dealt with the next morning.

I still hoped in the coming days of out-processing I'd have time to get back into N.D.'s good graces. Eventually he'd give up talking me out of leaving. He was simply too tenacious a person to give up after only one day of trying.

I heard a knock at the door. "Be there in a minute!" I yelled out before spraying one more blast of air freshener to be safe.

I opened the door. Standing there was the last person I expected to see tonight.

Summer.

"Hey," she said.

"Hey," I replied in an equally dead tone.

"Did you hear about Ed's slide crash?"

"Yup, I was there," I replied.

"Oh shit, I didn't see you."

I knew that was a lie.

"Yeah, well it was crowded and I didn't stay long," I replied without pushing for conflict. I wasn't really up for small talk.

"Have you been crying?" she asked.

"Nope," I replied before walking right past her and out of my room. I wanted nothing to do with this conversation.

"Then why are your eyes all red?" she asked in slow chase.

"Dunno," I said without turning back. I continued my walk.

Summer followed in chase as inconspicuously as she could.

"Look Mick, we need to talk," she said following behind me. "N.D. caught up with me today when I got in."

"Awesome," was all I could say. I kept walking. I could tell she wanted to grab me. Instead she pretended to look away and give me some space. Once ten paces behind, she resumed her follow. She wasn't about to let me escape. She was waiting for a private spot to come at me again. Feeling this, I took a turn down the staircase to get off the floor and out of company area.

I trotted down the steps and headed to the floor below. I had no destination other than wanting to get away from Summer. I was far too buzzed for a rational conversation.

I heard Summer tell the Company Mate of the Deck and the Duty Officer that she and I would be down in the laundry room to collect laundry we had dropped off earlier, giving us an excuse to miss bed check muster should we need to. In chasing me, she didn't have the time to grab a laundry bag to make her excuse look more legit.

Amateur.

"Mick, WAIT! Will you please let me talk to you?" she said resuming her pursuit down the stairs.

I was tempted to keep walking. I wanted to give her the same damn silent treatment she'd given me for the last five months. All those times I tried to talk to her. All those times I wanted to tell my side of the story, to describe how much my heart hurt since losing her. I lost count of how many apology speeches I had memorized. I was never given a chance to deliver any of them.

"Say what you have to say," I said after turning abruptly. I knew she was going to try to talk me into staying after hearing about my departure from N.D.

"What? Like right here in the staircase?" she asked as my confrontation caught her off guard.

I paused in contemplation.

"Not here," she said, "somewhere private."

I paused again.

Summer grabbed my arm. "Mick, I'm serious. This is serious."

Her touch still had an effect on me.

Without a word, I nodded then blindly followed her lead out of Bancroft. I had no idea where she was going.

After passing the soccer facility, I noticed she was walking along the row of cars where my truck was illegally stashed for the evening. It was where I usually parked my truck when sneaking it onto the yard. She must have spotted it on her way in that evening. She was heading directly for it. I watched her unlock it with the spare keys I had never had the chance to collect after the breakup. She jumped in the driver seat of the pickup.

I made my way to the driver's side window and knocked. She jumped as my presence startled her. I think she was expecting me to join through the passenger side.

"What are you doing with my truck?" I asked through the shut window.

She looked up with teary eyes and held up a folded piece of paper.

"Come on, let me in and scooch over," I said as I opened the door. She slid across my pickup's front bench.

"What's in the note?" I asked after an awkward silence together in the truck.

"You should know," she answered. "You wrote it."

Then I recognized it. It was the feeble attempt at a love note I had slipped her right before Thanksgiving break plebe year.

"Do you remember feeling this way?" she asked.

"Yes. No. I don't know." I responded. My actual feelings beneath those words were far less ambiguous.

"I remember the feeling," she said.

"Then where the FUCK did it go for the past six months?" I fired back before catching myself. I took a deep breath and cut right to the chase. "Look Summer, you liking me isn't going to keep me here."

That was a lie and I knew it. Butterflies of hope fluttered in my stomach.

"That's not why I said it," she replied.

My stomach felt nauseous.

"Then why the fuck did you say it?"

"Because it feels like yesterday, but it wasn't. It was almost three years ago."

"Your point?" I asked as I impatiently eyed up the truck door for a quick departure.

"My point is that if three years can go by that fast, then why not hang here for one more year?" she asked.

I sat silently and thought hard about the answer. What would be the hard-ass thing to say? What would be the vengeful thing to say? I took another deep breath.

"Are you serious? Do you really want me to say it? Alright, fuck it. I'm leaving because I can't stand the thought of being around you and not being with you."

"So don't be around me."

"What the fuck does that mean?" I said, quietly questioning whether the joint I smoked earlier had affected my mental faculties.

"It means I'll do it, I'll hate chit out of the company," she replied. "That's why I wanted to talk with you."

"And this helps me how?" I asked. "Where was this three months ago? Where was this before you started fucking Hackett and rubbing my nose in it? Spare me the charity. I'm all good here, thanks."

Summer picked up the note beside her on the passenger bench. She crumpled it in her hand and threw it on the floor in anger. Then she chucked my car keys at my face. "You're un-fucking-believable, you know that? You can go fuck yourself."

She turned for the door looking to exit the truck. I let her have it as she fiddled with the jammed door handle.

"Oh sure, there you go again. Big bad Summer Harris, perfect mid, all-American girl. Walking around like your shit don't stink. Dumping me as soon as you thought I made you look bad. Caring more about what people think than what you think about me," I angrily taunted her.

The door truck's passenger door finally opened. She wasn't about to exit the car without the last word.

"Is that what you think?" she asked about to exit the car. Is that what you REALLY fucking think?"

"Yeah, I guess so," I said coldly.

She shot me glare that could pierce Teflon.

"You guess so? Let me tell you something, Mick," she said with intensity. "You are so full of shit. You can tell yourself whatever story you want about me, or our break up, but I'm not buying your bullshit and deep down neither are you."

Summer exited the vehicle and angrily paced in front of the car. She made her way to the driver's side entrance with stern look. "Give me those fucking keys and scooch over," she commanded as she re-opened the driver side door. This time I scooched over.

She caught me off guard. I handed the keys over to her without thinking. She put them in the ignition. The engine took a few turns and then fired up. She slammed the gear-shift in reverse and peeled out of the spot. My back cemented in my seat as she shifted into first and took off down the seawall like a bat out of hell. She didn't say a word.

"What are you doing?" I asked. Her speed was concerning.

"I was going to, you know, stop being a stuck-up bitch. That's what you wanted, right?" she countered.

I thought momentarily that she was going to drive

us directly into the Severn. She instead peeled left and the tires screeched through the turn. We fishtailed until she recovered. She popped the clutch and escalated into fourth gear like she was some kind of female version of Steve McQueen. I hurriedly buckled my seatbelt.

"Summer, slow down!" I screamed. "You're going to kill someone driving like this."

"Oh, is that what an all-American mid girl like me should do?" she asked without taking her eyes off the road.

She blew the stop sign by Alumni Hall and headed straight for the parade field. I desperately kept my head on a swivel looking for the blue lights of the Jimmy Leg Police Force guarding the yard.

Instead of continuing towards the row of base housing she took a premature right turn.

She flipped off the headlights of the truck. She hopped the curb. My head would have hit the ceiling had my seatbelt not held me firmly in place.

"Summer, this is a bad idea, I don't like where this is going," I commented with increasing desperation.

She turned and my eyes met her scowl. It only increased her resolve.

Summer down shifted and gunned the gas pedal again. She traversed the grass of Warden Field. Once safely in the middle of it, she began twirling donuts on the Brigade's official parade field.

"What the fuck are you doing?" I yelled flabbergasted.

We continued through three more circles in the grass before coming to a dead stop. In a panic, I looked for blue flashing lights again.

"Was this what you'd prefer, Mick? That I'd be some

jackass like you and your buddies. Want me to go do something fucking stupid without thought of consequence or perception? Well here you go, asshole. Must be nice to live that way all the time. Unfortunately girls don't get that luxury here."

The truck came to a stop in the middle of the muddy mess. Summer had proven her point. Things were different for her.

I searched for words. The combination of shock, fear, and the remaining weed buzz had my head ringing. I was speechless.

"You know what, Mick, you're the one killing yourself!" she continued angrily with tears in her eyes. She punched me on the shoulder. Her boxing skills would surely have me black and blue by morning.

"What, cat got your tongue? You know how hard it's been watching you drink your way into the gutter. Watching you piss your life away in your own self fucking misery. You can go, you can stay, I don't give a fuck. Stop using me as an excuse for beating yourself up. I did not cause this situation. You did. You need to get your shit together wherever you go. Wake the fuck up!"

She punched me again, like she was trying desperately to wake me from a six-month daze.

"The whole reason I gave you that note was to make a point. Freshman year, we were simply a boy and a girl dating. We broke up, then I started dating someone else on my floor. That happens at every fucking college in the country."

"Is that what I am to you? Just another boy to date," I asked, hurt by the trivialization of my broken heart.

"That's not what I meant, Mick. You know I loved you. There's a part of me that still loves you. That's why I'm here. I'm only saying that if this shit were going down at any other college, you'd already be dating someone else by now."

Did she just say she loved me?

"Alright, ALRIGHT. You make a good point," I said. "Now we gotta get off this parade field or we'll both be going to different colleges next year."

Miraculously, our donut job on the parade field went unwitnessed. Summer popped the truck in gear and drove across the grass, over the curb, and onto the road. She turned the headlights back on. Four minutes later we were parked in the spot we had left. Aside from some mud on the tires, we were completely inconspicuous.

I thought hard. Shit had gotten out of hand and I was the person that had made it that way. That's why I was drinking uncontrollably, that's why I had smoked a joint, and that's why I was leaving the academy.

I hardly resolved a change of heart. I was far too high to trust my own judgement. I decided that I'd think things through a little more with a sober brain in the morning. I also decided that I was going to try extra hard to keep that brain sober, regardless of what I did next year.

Summer shut the driver door as she exited the truck and tossed me the keys across the hood of the car.

"Thanks," I said.

"Sure," she replied.

"Not the keys, I meant thanks for taking the time to talk."

"I know," she said with a smile. It had been a long while since I'd seen her do that in my direction.

I missed that smile.

Chapter 32

Photograph
Sunday, May 24th, 1998
Dickley, 2352 hrs.

Dear Dickley,
I hope you enjoyed the present I left you in the shower. I wanted you to know that turd was directly from me to you. As you and your dickhead roommate scrub my stinky, soggy, shit off the floor, I also want you to know that my roommates and I are sitting next door laughing our fucking asses off.

One more thing. If you suddenly get the urge to retaliate or tell on me or any of my roomies like the typical bitch you are, think twice. I hope you had a chance to see the photos I left you. Personally, the thought of you naked with anyone makes me fucking sick, but know that I have multiple copies. I sure as shit won't look at them again, but rest assured I'm keeping them in a very safe, very readily accessible spot. The moment you do anything to me or my room is the moment I distribute the pictures of you raw dawging your mousy girl-friend in the Hall. I'd say that would be about game over for you two.

Enjoy the present,
-Mick
P.S. Go fuck yourself!

I had read that note over twenty-five times already. My mind was swimming in panic. In the privacy of a toilet stall, I sat on my porcelain throne wincing as I read the unfolded note. McGee had left it for me in an envelope disguised to look like it was from my girlfriend hours earlier. All in the midst of a poop prank perpetrated by McGee himself.

As angry as the handwritten note still made me, it was nothing compared to the pictures sitting in my other hand. I folded the note and put it safely back in my pocket. In my other hand I resumed flipping through the pictures that accompanied the note.

It wasn't the first time I was looking at naked pictures of women in the company head. I was as human as any of my male horn-ball company mates. Then my mind raced in its typical loop of panic.

Would the pictures come out? Who had them? Where were they?

Then I thought of my girlfriend Sally.

What would she say? Would she ever find out about this? Would she need to?

We both knew the pictures had been taken over spring break. We suspected someone like my neighbors might be involved but I had no proof. I've spent the past two months waiting for the other shoe to drop. Tonight Mick dropped that shoe. Then he shoved it up my ass.

That motherfucker!

My leg was falling asleep from sitting on the toilet too long. I stood up, pulled up my pants, and made my way to the door. I double checked the pockets of my pants. The letter and the pictures were still in there. Then I looked in and around the stall floor to ensure I didn't leave any evidence behind. Even though Mick had other photos, I didn't accidentally want to give the ones I had away for free by being stupid enough to leave them out in company area. My paranoia was my only protection at this point.

I made my way back to my room. I had been locked out since I opened Mick's letter hours ago. Haden and I were cleaning up Mick's turd shower present when I found the note. When I returned after reading it ten times in private, Haden had just received the brick. He's been locked in there ever since and hasn't said a word to anyone.

I had heard the rumors. They were already spreading across the company like wild fire. Even as Haden's roommate, I had no idea he was harboring a collection of stolen mens' underwear. I hadn't seen them personally, but I believed the story. By morning, the whole brigade would know. I was his roommate. Who knows what rumors would be flying around about me.

Knowing it was going to be fruitless, I knocked three loud bangs on my door with the side of my fist.

"Come on, Haden, open up!" I said knowing he was listening on the other side of the locked door. "It's my room too. We're roommates!"

I gave one more trio of aggressive knocks before giving up.

I heard another knock to my left. It was coming from an easy-looking young lady in ill-fitting blue rim and gym shorts. Likely another one of Dawson's sexual conquests. The door opened and she was corralled inside. She sure as shit wasn't a mid.

My mind rushed to vengeance. I could nail that fucker so hard on this. An unauthorized guest having sex in Bancroft, and on his last day of restriction. It was a slam dunk. Then I felt Mick's note and pictures in my pocket.

Motherfucking Mick.

My anger percolated within. Mick had the ultimate collateral. Not only did he have evidence of wrongdoing that would get me potentially kicked out of the academy, but he had the same on my girlfriend. I was powerless. I knew it and he knew it. It was checkmate.

I darted angrily away from our door, letting Haden stay hunkered down and Dawson fuck whatever slut he had wooed up to his room. Reluctantly, I made my way to the wardroom and the company mate's desk. I still had to find Mick. He was briefly in company area after celebrating his roomie's restriction slide. On my way to the bathroom a few minutes earlier I saw he and Summer heading down the stairs.

That girl will never learn.

I knew that the number one topic of conversation in the wardroom would be my room. The shit shower, the brick, the underwear, my room was the center of everyone's universe.

"Good evening, Mr. Bickley," I heard the plebe company mate of the desk say without the slightest bit of fear or reverence. His ear to ear grin seemed to be saying, "I know all about what happened to your room tonight, and I love it."

I contemplated dressing him down, but it was pointless. Herndon was tomorrow and all of these plebes were basically done with their year.

"Has Second Class McGee come back to company area yet?" I asked the CMOD.

"Nope, not yet. I think I heard someone say he was down in the laundry room with Miss Harris. They left a few minutes ago," he replied.

I peeked my head in the wardroom. My neighbor Okafor and a few friends were watching TV inside. Mick was nowhere in there that I could see.

"DICKLEY!!!!!!!" they all screamed, taunting me with the courage of the weekend's fading beer buzz.

"Hey," I replied. "You guys seen Mick lately?"

I waited a minute. No one answered.

"DICKLEY!!!!!!!!!" they all yelled again. Someone tossed a pillow towards my head for good measure.

"Fuck you guys," I said as I exited the wardroom and passed the CMOD.

I made my way to the steps downstairs before turning back to the CMOD. "Tell the CDO I am heading down to the laundry room to find McGee and Harris."

"Sure thing," he replied with a thumbs up.

Where's the fucking sir with that pleber?

I would have lit his ass up a week earlier for the same level of informality, but right now I had more important things to do. I hustled down the stairs reaching in my pockets one more time. The note and the pictures were still there. I walked faster towards the laundry room.

Suddenly, a familiar yelling voice stopped me dead in my tracks. I ran back up the stairs. There was Haden behind an infinitely entertained CMOD yelling into the company area phone.

"Yes, I'm telling the truth. NO THIS IS NOT A

JOKE!" he screamed into the phone's ear piece without even acknowledging my presence. He was in a fit of rage.

When I reached the top of the stairs, I saw the wardroom door swing open. Okafor peeked his head out.

"What is he yelling about?" he asked the plebe CMOD while hitching his thumb towards Haden.

"Captain is saying there is some party going on in your room, with women and music," the CMOD replied.

"Saying WHAT? To WHO?" he asked.

"Main office," said the CMOD.

Both N.D. and I panicked for very different reasons. The damage was done. The Brigade CDO would almost surely be up in company area in minutes.

"Who's in the room?" N.D. confronted my roommate immediately as he easily wrestled the phone out of his hand. He hung it up without even asking if anyone was still on the line.

"Dawson and McGee," Haden replied.

"Dawg, no way. I'm in the wardroom. Ed's in hospital point getting stitched up from his restriction slide. Mick headed downstairs with Summer and I know they ain't back yet."

"Then who's in your room, Okafor?" Haden asked.

"Fuck if I know, underwear boy," N.D. replied. "Don't you have enough problems to deal with tonight?"

"Seems like your room is about to have a big problem tonight. Personally, I don't care who is in there as long as you all pay the price," Haden replied.

"Where's the company CDO?" I heard a voice from down the hall. It was too far off to recognize the face. I did notice the yellow arm band and lieutenant shoulder boards. The Brigade CDO, the highest-ranking military officer on duty that evening, had responded to Haden's request faster than we thought.

My mind played out the upcoming scenario. Regardless of who was in their room, Okafor, Dawson, and McGee would all be held accountable in some way. My heart jumped in my throat and I rushed down the stairs. I needed to find McGee, immediately. If I didn't catch him before the CDO did, he may very well share those photos he was holding over my head. I couldn't let that happen.

******

Dickley, 0020 hrs.

I was pacing between the pay phones in the 5th wing entryway. In twenty minutes, I had already checked every nook and cranny of the 5th wing laundry room three separate times. Mick and Summer were nowhere to be found. Worse than that, the three people in the laundry room said they hadn't even seen them when I asked them about it.

I heard a door slam open. It was a short distance away by the entry of the now closed cobbler shop. I scrambled in that direction.

"Mick," I said as soon as I recognized he and Summer coming in from wherever they were.

He was mid-conversation with Summer. He looked over, gave me a smile, and flipped me the bird.

"Mick, Mick, wait," I begged for his attention as he and Summer initiated their way up the stairs towards what I assumed was company area.

Boy was he in for a surprise.

I was tempted to let him walk into the ambush, but then my mind wondered to the retaliation tools he had at his disposal. I couldn't compete with that nuclear bomb.

"Mick, I'm serious," I begged in chase up the stairs. "The CDO is in the middle of busting your room."

Mick stopped dead in his tracks midway between the entry floor and the first floor of Bancroft. "What did you say?" he asked.

"I said the CDO is in the," I began repeating my previous statement. Mick didn't wait around to listen. He grabbed me by the shirt and nearly pushed me over the stairway railing.

"You are one stupid motherfucker," he replied. His eyes were red with anger. "Guess I get to release those fucking pictures earlier than I expected."

He increased the force of his shirt grab. I was bent so far over the stair rail that my feet left the ground.

"Mick, no, please wait," I said in desperation. I hadn't even had the chance to tell him about what might be happening in his room. "That's why I'm down here. I didn't turn you in. Haden did before I could stop him. He got all pissed off over the brick and underwear stuff that he retaliated with a call down to the CDO saying there was some big party going on in your room. The CDO is up in your room now. I wanted to catch you before you went up there.

Summer looked at me like I had a horn growing out of my head. I guess Mick hadn't told her about his photo collection.

Mick eased off his grip. He rubbed his hand through

his hair as he tried to process everything. Under different circumstances, it would have been such a satisfying scene. Instead, I was scared shitless. My entire academy fate hung in the balance.

"Look, no time to delay," I said through my heart palpitating stress. "I have a plan. Summer you head upstairs and say Mick is on his way. Mick, you follow my lead. We need to get to the CDO ASAP."

Summer looked reluctantly at Mick. "Go, it will be alright," he said to her. "I can take care of this," he assured her. She immediately headed upstairs.

He buzzed past me. "Talk fast," he said.

I hurried behind him on the stairs. I needed to stay close enough to whisper my suggested instructions before we got back in company area but without broadcasting them to the entire stairway.

"This better be a good fucking plan," he warned me. "I know you want to keep my room out of trouble as badly as I do.

Suddenly we went from being antagonistic enemies all year to seamlessly executing teammates. It was a necessity

Part X

And Justice for All

.

Chapter 33

Don't Stop Believin'
Monday, June 1st, 1998
Mick, 0625 hrs.

"Yo, did you hear about Squeak and the mid store a few nights ago?" my new restriction compadre, and stand-in summer roomie EZ asked.

"Mid store? What, was he caught gaffing some shit from inside the store after hours?" I replied.

"Nah dawg, Squeak wasn't IN the mid store. He was on top of that shit. Drunk dialing on his cell phone after a night of drinking over top the mid store entry roof. He falls off, busts his shit up, crawls his ass up to company area in a trail of blood and mayhem, dawg."

We both erupted in laughter.

"So I guess he'll be joining us soon at muster?" I asked.

"No doubt," EZ said with a smile. He continued taping off his uniform and walked down the hall without the least bit of morning muster stress. I knew the look, it was of total focus. In two more days he'd be taking his own restriction slide. He wasn't about to let his discipline slip this close to the finish line. He could smell the freedom.

EZ was also simply happy to still be in the academy.

The stripper-in-the-Hall fiasco from the week before had him sweating bullets for a night or two. He and his roommate Joe were the two people unlucky enough to get caught mid-show in our room by the CDO.

I had to admit, Dickley's scheme sounded stupid when I first heard it, but it worked. It was brilliant considering how last minute it all was. That night, he and I scrambled up to the CDO and convinced him that the whole incident was Dickley's fault. Dickley said it was an ill-advised prank. I stepped up and said that I had helped plan too. We also maintained a unified front that it was intended as a surprise for Ed's last day of restriction. We said no one else knew about the plan. We explained EZ and Joe were friends of Ed's that had happened to roll into the room when it was all unfolding. Outside of Dickley himself, there were no eyewitnesses that could counter otherwise.

Our company officer would have never bought that line of shit. Fortunately for us, he had been out of country on vacation for his brother's wedding while all of this went down. Every other officer in our disciplinary hearing had no idea that Dickley and I hated each other's guts all year long and then some. They bought Dickley's "balloon-graham girl gone horribly wrong story" hook, line, and sinker.

Dickley and I both got Black Ns and sixty days restriction. My purported role in the incident wasn't nearly as bad as Dickley's, it didn't matter. My disciplinary probation situation that carried over from the spring guaranteed that any wrongdoing would see maximum punishment. I had already stitched my first black star above my previously awarded Black N sweater.

Even though I had convinced myself that I wouldn't let them do it, N.D. and Summer had me thinking twice about leaving the academy. I had yet to submit my resignation papers.

Dickley and I were implicated in a major story fabrication with a company officer on duty following the stripper incident. Even though we were past the discipline hearing, I wasn't about to walk away trusting things were taken care of.

There were too many good people's reputations and futures on the line. Even if I ultimately decided to part ways with the academy before graduation next year, I wanted to hang around for a few more months in case Dickley tried to change his story about the stripper in my absence. I wouldn't put it past that weasel. He knew before the stripper incident that I was prepared to release his compromising pictures. Staying around would help me further emphasize that to him, all while keeping my friends safe.

Who was I kidding? No matter the narrative I told myself as a rationale for withholding my resignation letter, I knew the real reason I was still in Bancroft Hall.

'There's a part of me that still loves you.'

I'd played back Summer's words in my head constantly. I needed to find that part of Summer again. I wasn't about to quit the Naval Academy before I did.

Ed and N.D. remained restriction-free. They were both already in San Diego on aviation cruise with a squadron of Seahawk helicopters.

Summer was on her cruise as well. We didn't really get to hang out enough to discuss the details. She was super pissed after the stripper incident. My made up "involvement" in the stripper fiasco that Dickley and I decided upon potentially put visibility into my evening. That visibility meant all the more likelihood Summer could get busted about lying about bed check muster or turfing the parade field. The next day she changed her mind about the hate chit out of the company.

The hate chit was the last thing we spoke about before she took off after graduation. I wasn't sure if she had changed her mind about it to spite me, or to stay around me. My optimism yearned to believe the latter. We at least needed to continue the dialogue we started last week when she cooled off.

I'd survived restriction before, I could do it again. If anything, it was a chance to sober up. I hadn't had a drink in over a week.

Bird continued to be supportive of me staying away from the shore. He said it would be infinitely easier to plot a drug deal for me without having me around. I hadn't yet abandoned that request either.

Got to have contingencies.

EZ and his roommate Joe, who were the only two people caught in my room with a stripper, escaped the incident unscathed. The whole stripper plan was EZ's idea for a present to Ed on his last day of restriction. Joe had a former high school classmate that was stripping outside Baltimore and was willing to do private shows. It was an ill-advised plan, but they had gotten away with it. It was especially lucky for EZ. If he had actually gotten busted with a stripper while already on restriction, the academy might have instantly booted him.

The Captain America underwear bandit incident took a lot of heat off the stripper stuff. The academy was so worried about handling the underwear situation quietly that they put very little attention on our "boys will be boys" stripper incident. They didn't even have time to investigate the turfed parade field. By lunch Monday, any trace of Captain America had disappeared. There was never a public or even company level communication about it. It's as though he, and our stolen underwear, vanished into thin air and were never heard from again.

EZ and I continued silently making our approach towards Bancroft's main office and Rotunda. Almost everyone else was already on their initial assignments of summer cruise or enjoying the first few days of their brief summer break. The handful of us still there were either on restriction or stuck in summer school.

Between my summer training and my extreme level of punishment, I'd be on restriction until fall semester. Hopefully I could sneak in some surfing over my military training schedule.

"Those shoes are lookin' shoddy, dawg," EZ critiqued on our way.

"I know, man," I replied. "I was gonna shine them last night, but then I remembered that we had Smith on the CDO watch bill so I opted for the extra sleep."

"Yeah, I saw that too," EZ replied with an ornery smirk. "Shame though."

"What shame?" I asked.

"Shame you weren't on restriction last week."

"Why's that?" I said beginning to feel apprehensive.

"'Cause then you would have had a day on restriction

with chill assed Lieutenant James Smith," EZ lamented. "He swapped out duty days two weeks ago."

"Swapped out?" I reacted. "With who?"

"None other than Major Michael Narducci, United States Marine Corps," EZ said with a weak attempt at a Marine Corps motivational bark.

"Fuck!" I said as we hit the Rotunda and started down the large main steps on the last floor prior to King Hall dining facilities.

The roughly fifteen of us stuck on restriction were gathering and scrambling at the last minute to ensure our uniforms were absolutely perfect and ready for inspection. Anything less than perfection from any individual meant we'd all get stuck with a few extra days as punishment. That was especially true with an asshole like Major Narducci serving as CDO for the day. Restriction days with guys like that were counted like dog years. One day could easily feel like seven.

"Alright y'all, line it up," EZ instructed the group. He was currently the head restrictee and acting platoon commander of the restrictees.

Dickley was the last of us to make it down the stairs to muster with two minutes to spare. His uniform looked spotless and perfectly squared away as usual. He silently slipped into the third restriction squad, evening out the sparse proportions of the early summer restriction muster. I still hated his guts. I'm sure the feeling was mutual.

"Muster, AH, ten, HUT!" EZ commanded the platoon after looking at his watch. In a rare moment, some of the brigade's most notorious dirt bags snapped to attention. They were on time, their uniforms were sharp, and they were all as bitter as ever. They were exactly what the academy wanted them to be for the time being. EZ executed a flawless about face and waited at the top of the Platoon for the oncoming CDO and whatever henchman decided to tag along.

All restrictee eyes were affixed to the top two visible stairs of the giant marble staircase leading to our muster on our open floor. It was the first visible point of the CDO's path from main office down to restriction muster.

A brief glimpse of a shoe and a pant leg coupled with sound statistics could tell an astute restrictee everything they need to know about the oncoming CDO.

The fate of every restrictee's day revolved around that CDO. A cool CDO would give a few musters, ensure everyone was on time and actually tried to preserve an inspection ready uniform, and let everyone go their merry way.

An asshole CDO could make a restrictee's day shitty in countless different ways. They could assign surprise musters. They could restrict various forms of room and outdoor access. They could assign physical labor working parties, or cleanup parties, or all of the above. Worst of all, they could assign additional days restriction with virtually zero due process. Some of the most evil handed them out weeks at a time.

Suddenly, a crisp green pant leg and shiny small black shoe broke the pallet of our stare. An astute ear could hear the silent groan from our platoon. Of the eight company officers that were Marines, five were male. Of the five male Marine officers, three were well over six foot, with obviously large feet. Of the two smaller-footed officers, the cooler one had stood watch two days earlier.

Before I could even see his sour, surly face, I definitively knew we had drawn Narducci.

I mentally prepared for Narducci's laser stare. I'd get him early in the inspection as I was the third person in from the first squad. I braced for the forthcoming onslaught of antagonistic obsessive compulsiveness. He was stuck there all day as CDO and I didn't doubt that this was one of his favorite things to do on duty.

I took a deep breath as I took mental inventory of my uniform and the various ways inspectors could attempt to pick it apart. Then I thought about my shoddy shoes and my anxiety jumped through the roof. I adjusted my shoe position into what I thought might produce maximum shine.

I could hear the subtle squeaks between floor and rubber soles of executed military movements. Narducci moved across the face of first squad. He was being his typical self, spending an excruciating amount of time on each restrictee he inspected. It took him five minutes to inspect the first man he encountered in first squad. He had already broken out his ruler to measure ribbons on the second guy.

I took one last deep inhale. Fifty-eight days restriction could become sixty-five in the blink of an eye. I focused on standing as straight, still, and silent as possible. Once again, I could hear the finely executed foot pivot-squeaks against the floor. Then that grim motherfucker was in my grill.

I hate this fucking place.

Chapter 34

My Hero
Sunday, May 31st, 1998
Summer, 2 p.m.

I soaked in the warmth of the California sun. I had missed it immensely. Sweat glistened on my newly tanned skin. I briefly considered a dip in the pool until I heard the cordless phone ring next to me.

"Hello," I answered in a sweet voice. I was away from the academy, it felt good to speak with my guard down.

"Hey, how are you?" I heard a familiar male voice say on the other end of the line.

"You know," I said with a smile as I twirled my hair, "working on those tan lines you like so much."

"Don't tempt me to fly out there today," Matt replied. I loved the fact that I could get him riled up so easily. We had animal attraction.

"Save it, stud," I jokingly replied. "I'm back out east in another day."

"Can't wait to see you," he said.

"Me too," I replied. I genuinely meant it.

I listened to Matt's stories about the weekend after graduation. Family graduation parties, DTA bar trips, plenty of drinking, it was standard stuff. I had stayed in town until Friday after graduation, then caught a Friday night flight out of BWI to San Fran for a brief weekend stay in Half Moon Bay.

My mom and step-mom Lizbeth had finally inherited and moved into my recently passed grandfather's home. It was a mere two blocks from the beach and came equipped with its own kidney shaped cement swimming pool. As a child, it was the one place in life that felt normal. I appreciated the chance to ground myself ahead of the orange mud of Quantico Virginia and "Leatherneck" Marine Corps training.

Luckily the shit-show back in the Hall with Mick had seemingly blown over for the time being. Without that added worry, I finally had a weekend to decompress from it all. My single fin leaned against the side of the house while my wetsuit happily hung over the backyard fence dripping with Pacific Ocean.

"What are you up to the rest of the day?" Matt asked.

"Pretty much this," I said, content in my laziness by the pool. "How about you?" I asked.

"I think dad and I are going out on the boat, maybe grab some food by the water," he explained. It was dinner time back east.

"Oh god," I said rolling my eyes. "Behave yourselves."

That was about all I could say. I hated that fucking boat. If Mick and I had broken up under normal trajectory last fall and Hackett and I started dating like normal people, the last year of shit might have never happened in the first place.

"I will," he assured me. "Another week and I'll be with

who I really want to hang with."

He was sticking around in Annapolis until his October Flight School start date in Pensacola. In the meantime, he had four laid back months of duty teaching Plebe Summer sailing. He already had a nice two-bedroom apartment rented for the summer. We'd have a place to crash and be together all summer long.

"So much fun ahead this summer," I replied happily distracted from thinking more about his dad's boat.

"Cool, well I'm going to get going. Call me when you land tomorrow."

"Will do," I obliged.

"I like you," he ended the call in salutation.

"I like you too," I replied with a smile as I clicked off the phone.

I was glad Matt and I decided to keep things slightly less than serious with this relationship. I had let myself get too serious with Mick. With Matt leaving for Florida in a few months, we both decided that we would focus on having fun this summer and deal with the long distance stuff later, if at all.

I already had my fill of love at the academy, and I was still recovering. I didn't go to the academy to find love. I didn't need a knight in shining armor. With one year left at USNA, all I wanted was to refocus on why I went there in the first place.

"No girls allowed" would never sit right with me. Neither would it sit with any number of women currently fighting their way through the Naval Academy. I sat in the sun and resolved to renew my goal that originally brought me to Annapolis, with vigorous intent. The rest of my life's drama was water under the keel. It had to be.

Whether it was skippering a combatant ship or flying fighter jets in the sky, our sisterhood couldn't wait to show the world what we world class ladies were all about. For all of the men lining up to cheer on our failure, there were plenty more ladies like me itching to prove them wrong.

One more day of rest, tomorrow this badass bitch has a legacy to build.

I was at the Naval Academy to be a hero, not to find one.

N'd

#WeWUBA

The term WUBA being used to describe a female midshipman is hardly a new one. "Woman Used By All", and a few other slightly diverging versions of the same insulting anagram, were common in the midshipmen vernacular circa 1995-99.

By the time I showed up for my I-day in the summer of 95', nineteen full years after the Naval Academy went co-ed, there were still plenty of problems with the way we treated our female classmates. I mention all of this not as a 'holier than thou' reporter of inequity. Instead, in the reflective process that I employ in writing my own novels, I was reminded of just how poorly at times I had treated my own female classmates over the years at the Academy. I used terms like WUBA in jest, and on occasion in more hurtful ways. It's certainly a regret. For those moments, and others like it, I am truly sorry.

My hope with this book is not to glorify bad behavior, nor to harp on the flaws of the time, nor to exonerate my own bad behavior. My grandest of hopes for this book would be to convey one thing to every woman that has ever braved it through a Naval Academy education:

RESPECT.

From the moment female mids first walked on the yard in 1976, they have since fought mightily for acceptance. That acceptance was earned iteratively, through blood, sweat, and tears, over the course of four decades.

While there remains plenty more work to be done, the Naval Academy is a better place because of our women alum's dedication to it.

In hindsight, this fight for acceptance seems so completely ridiculous given the collective track record of women from the U.S. Naval Academy. Whether commanding combatant ships, fighting on the front lines in aircrafts or otherwise, flying space ships, running for Senate, or just generally being their awesome selves, the women graduates of the US Naval Academy are heroes that should have been celebrated into our ranks from day one. You never asked for our respect, you just went out and earned it.

As for WUBA, let me just say that we Were Ultimately Being Assholes, and that's about all WUBA will evermore mean to me.

For over 40 years, you've been the crème de la crème. Thanks ladies, you are total bad asses!

Ricky Conlin

Acknowledgements

I'd like to thank my fans: family, friends, and otherwise. Your love and support of my first book made me want to write this one.

One fan I'd like to particularly thank is Kevin Jeras, a former boss and one of my earliest supporters. Thanks for your early words of encouragement when I was just beginning to think about writing, it was a big catalyst for me.

I'm lucky to have so many great friends willing to spend their time helping my literary aspirations. That sentiment particularly extends to Carolyn Menke, Robb Wirts, Mike Waits, Robin Siddoway, Tanya Keetch and Amy Shafer.

Thanks to fellow USNA 99' classmate and Dream Oak label-mate Sean Patrick Hughes. Seeing your dedication towards writing so many important messages over the past years has kept me motivated to bring forth my very best.

Special thanks to Stacy Conlin, my wife and President of Dream Oak Publishing, this book and trilogy would not be possible without your leadership. We both so badly wanted to do this book the right way. Thank you for assembling a kick-ass, all-women production team to help get us there.

Last, but certainly not least, thanks to the mighty

Ricky Conlin

UNSA class of 99'. We may not always agree on lab goggles, 503c tax exemptions, or tailgate swag, but when it comes to the important stuff, things like "excellence without arrogance" or "navigating with honor", there's nobody better. I'm so lucky to call you all classmates.

Made in the USA
San Bernardino, CA
10 January 2020